"Come, sweetheart . . . "

"You've kept me at arm's length long enough. 'Tis time we had this out between us."

Quintana faced him, her silver eyes flashing. "Indeed? Then why don't you explain to me, sir, precisely what is between us?"

"I've known a lot of women in my lifetime, Quintana, but never has a woman had the effect upon me that you do. You're in my blood . . . and I can no more quench this burning need I feel to make you mine than I could will the moon from the night sky, or curse the stars from the heavens."

He touched her, and she weakened. He brought her soft and yielding self against his lean, hard length, and their hearts thundered in unison.

Quintana's will to resist gave way with the sound of a softly uttered sigh.

Draper thought it was the sweetest, most welcoming sound he'd ever heard.

Embrace The Wild Dawn

SELINA MacPHERSON

AVON BOOKS ◆ NEW YORK

EMBRACE THE WILD DAWN is an original publication of Avon Books. This work has never before appeared in book form. This work is a novel. Any similarity to actual persons or events is purely coincidental.

AVON BOOKS
A division of
The Hearst Corporation
1350 Avenue of the Americas
New York, New York 10019

Copyright © 1994 by Susan McClafferty
Published by arrangement with the author
Library of Congress Catalog Card Number: 93-90818
ISBN: 0-380-77251-5

First Avon Books Printing: May 1994

AVON TRADEMARK REG. U.S. PAT. OFF. AND IN OTHER COUNTRIES, MARCA REGISTRADA, HECHO EN U.S.A.

Printed in the U.S.A.

RA   10   9   8   7   6   5   4   3   2   1

This book is dedicated to my dear friend
Twila Hanna,
for believing in me during my darkest hours . . .
and for listening;
and to Marcy Graham Waldenville,
my almost sister,
who knows all of my demons by name . . .

When your army entered the country of the Six Nations, we called you "Town Destroyer"; and to this day when that name is heard our women look behind them and turn pale, and our children cling close to the necks of their mothers.

—CORNPLANTER TO
  GEORGE WASHINGTON, 1790

Chapter 1

London, England
February 18, 1778

The afternoon was nearly spent, and the fire that blazed so brightly in the great hearth was burning low, its glowing embers the only illumination in the otherwise darkened room.

Quintana Alita Wade, seated close by the hearthside, was keenly aware of the light and warmth that seeped slowly away as the blaze died, the same way Rowena Chamberlain Wade had departed life the previous winter, a gradual, quiet descent into the grave, leaving only her daughter Quintana to mourn her loss.

Rowena's passing had gone unremarked. No friends or acquaintances had come to the grave side for a final farewell; no sympathies were offered.

There had been only Quintana and the four servants remaining out of a staff of twenty in the once thriving household: Tilly Bascombe, Quintana's aging maid; Nigel Bird, the footman and Tilly's nephew; Martha, the cook;

1

and Bridgett Tanderlay, the chambermaid—a
pitifully inadequate end indeed for the woman
once touted as the "Gilded Rose of Dorset"
and lauded for her beauty.

Quintana's gaze fixed upon the orange
glow of the hearth, and she wondered what
would have become of her mother had the
ill-fated Rowena never laid eyes upon Winston
Halcourt Wade.

Yet met him she had, and she had married the handsome rake despite the vehe-
ment objections of Rowena's aging sire, who
believed that Wade was an unscrupulous bastard and would bring the gentle Rowena nothing but heartache. Rowena's father had been all
too right, thought Quintana.

Outside, sleet hissed against the house, striking the leaded panes of the mullioned windows like tiny tapping fingers and grating on
Quintana's nerves.

She gazed into the deepening gloom.

Waiting out the darkness had become an
evening ritual. She'd long ago sacrificed the
fine beeswax tapers Rowena had always
purchased for less expensive tallow dips
that burned with an unpleasant fatty odor.
Then, as her situation gradually worsened,
she'd become so conscious of the need to
conserve even the cheap tallow candles that
she purposely delayed lighting them until full
dark descended.

It was just one example of the many small
concessions she'd been forced to make in order
to cope with her straitened circumstances, yet

as she glanced around the richly furnished drawing room, Quintana knew it wouldn't be the last. If she didn't soon find a way to ease her financial difficulties, she would be forced to sell some of her possessions.

A discreet scratching sounded on the great double doors of the drawing room, breaking into Quintana's musings. She called out for entrance, and Tilly Bascombe, her lady's maid, appeared, an apologetic look upon her thin, angular face.

"Sorry to disturb you, miss," Tilly said. "But there's someone here to see you. He says I'm to tell you he's here on urgent business."

Quintana frowned, and for an instant she pondered the possibilities of what her visitor's "urgent business" might entail.

She hoped he wasn't there to demand money. But the likelihood seemed strong.

She'd striven hard in the year since her mother's death to satisfy her creditors. There just never seemed to be sufficient funds to go around.

The thought of facing yet another dun demanding money that she did not possess was extremely distasteful, yet Quintana knew she had no alternative. If she attempted to turn him off without a hearing, he would only call again.

With a sigh of resignation, she turned to Tilly. "Show him in. I'll light the candles."

As Tilly bobbed her mobcapped head and hurried from the room, Quintana rose from her chair. She took a straw from an ornate tin box on the mantel, touched it first to the peat that smoldered in the grate, then touched it to the candle wicks one by one.

The candles flared brightly, and the encroaching shadows quickly fled before the sudden spill of light. Quintana felt her flagging spirits stir, and even went so far as to place another brick of peat upon the dying fire.

Ragged tongues of golden flame licked greedily at the fuel, sending a small burst of warmth and a delightful accompanying crackle into the chill air of the room, but the sound was not sufficient to mask the ring of boot heels on the parquetry floor of the foyer just outside the drawing room doors.

She turned to face her visitor, but as he stepped into the room, she caught her breath and her manners deserted her completely. She gaped at him. She could not help it, for the most exotic-looking man she'd ever seen was standing in the doorway.

He was tall and spare, with exceptionally broad shoulders and slim hips. Hair the shade of soot fell past his shoulders, sparkling with diamond-bright shards of sleet. That, along with several days' growth of black beard, fringed leather shirt and leggings, a belt and pistols, lent a certain wildness to his appearance that was strangely appealing.

Quintana allowed her gaze to wander briefly down his hardened frame before returning to his lean, hungry face. If indeed he was a dun, then he was without a doubt the most magnificently made dun in all of England.

As she stared at him, a slight smile touched his lips, and his thick black lashes lowered over amber eyes the shade of whiskey. There was something unsettling about those eyes, Quintana decided, and wondering fleetingly if he had somehow read her thoughts, she had the good grace to blush.

"Are you Mistress Quintana Wade?" he asked in a voice both deep and drawling, a voice that was strangely pleasing to the ear.

Quintana slowly emerged from her shock. "I am," she said. "And who, sir, might you be?"

"Captain Draper Catworth Boone, of the Seventh Virginia." He came into the room, glancing around as he did so, and Quintana had the distinct impression that those unsettling clear golden eyes missed no small detail. "So this is England," he said.

It seemed a strange remark, but since he had yet to make unrealistic demands upon her ragged pursestrings, Quintana decided to humor him. "Indeed it is."

"It's everything I had imagined it would be."

"And how is that, Captain?"

His gaze slid back to Quintana's. "Crowded, with no room for a man to move without bumping into someone else. The air is tainted with the smell of smoke and poverty, the prevailin' attitude is one of unfounded superiority and rudeness, and the streets are clogged with filth—"

Quintana tilted her head back and looked down her nose at Draper Catworth Boone.

Strikingly handsome he might be, but his manners were deplorable. "Since I assume you haven't come here specifically to insult my homeland, perhaps you will be so kind as to enlighten me as to what 'urgent business' you and I can possibly have to discuss?"

He stretched his hands toward the warmth of the blaze, and the golden signet ring he wore on the smallest finger of his right hand winked in the firelight. He stared into the fire as if entranced by the leaping tongues of flame, and the golden glow filled the clear depths of his eyes with an otherworldly light. "I am your father's emissary," he said softly. "And I've come to England to escort you home."

Quintana stared at him, openmouthed. "Home? But sir, England is my home," Quintana said.

"Not for long," he replied.

Fingers of cold dread traced their way up Quintana's spine. "You cannot be serious. Why, I haven't heard from my father since he joined those fractious American rebels in their insurrection against the Crown! There is no earthly reason for me to believe that he should wish to see me now!"

"Suffice to say, Colonel Wade has had a change of heart," Draper replied.

"And I am supposed to accept that without question?" Quintana said with a harsh laugh. "To accept you at face value? This is ridiculous! I am not as naive as you seem to think. How do I know you are what you claim to be? You might just as well be some canny-minded fraud thinking to use me in order to extort money from my family."

Draper Boone looked pointedly at his surroundings. "If your family had funds to spare, the plaster molding wouldn't be crumbling, the chair on which you sit would not be threadbare, and you'd be burnin' coal instead of peat."

"Why, you insolent beggar—" Quintana began, stung by his blunt rejoinder, by the truth of his statement.

Draper neatly cut her off. "Perhaps this will convince you." He drew the signet ring off his finger and dropped it onto her velvet lap.

Quintana stared at the intertwined initials . . . *WHW*. A quiver of rage coursed through her, sweeping up from her slippered toes, seeping into her voice. "Get out," she said.

He stared at her, his expression growing darker. "It's your father's ring, and I'm not goin' anywhere."

"The man who sent you here obviously forgot to mention that he ceased being a father to me long ago. And I am sorry to say that you have come a very long way for nothing, Captain. Now get out!"

Draper stood staring down at Quintana Wade. He wasn't sure just what he'd expected to find upon his arrival in London, but it hadn't been the headstrong young woman with eyes like quicksilver and hair like pale winter sunlight, glaring up at him now as if she'd like to cut his heart out.

Her anger, strangely, did not repel him.

Indeed, it seemed to breathe life and energy into her face . . . a face that before had seem almost too delicate, too cold, remote, and aloof . . . a face that had seemed carved from lifeless alabaster.

She was lovely, the colonel's daughter.

Her fine arched brows were drawn into a furious line above her slim straight nose, and a blush of cold rage bloomed upon her gently curving cheeks, turning her lush lips a deep becoming shade of dusty rose.

Hers were soft-looking lips, Draper thought, the sort to part reluctantly beneath a man's insistent kisses, then blossom with sweet unexpected response . . . and he found himself wondering how long she would resist him if he took her in his arms and sampled their honeyed sweetness . . .

"Well," she demanded, effectively shattering the spell Draper had been under, "do you intend to heed my demands, or must I have you thrown bodily into the street?"

Draper's hard mouth curled in a lazy, seductive smile. "You may try it, if you like. But I'll tell you now, it won't be easy. I gave my pledge to bring you back, and I don't make commitments lightly."

"Very well then." Quintana rose stiffly from her chair and stalked to the walnut kneehole desk that was positioned against the wall.

In the topmost drawer of the desk was Winston's dueling pistol, looking strangely out of place amid the foolscap, sealing wax, and quill pens.

Quintana's fingers curled around the weapon's worn mahogany grip. She'd never had the occasion to use it until now, and she was amazed upon lifting it from its bed just how heavy it felt in her hand. She concealed it in the folds of her jade velvet skirts.

Captain Draper Boone was proving as persistent as he was well-favored, and if he spoke the truth, his allegiance lay with her father. He was an American rebel, her enemy sworn, and unless she wished to find herself aboard a ship bound for America, she would have to deal with him accordingly.

Arms crossed before his chest, he stood contentedly toasting his backside before the fire and watching her with a look of mild amusement. He displayed no signs whatsoever of leaving.

"You are making a terrible mistake, Captain," Quintana said. "Are you quite sure you will not reconsider?"

Draper was still thinking of her lips when she spoke. Her voice amazed him. Her tone was clear and crisp, every syllable enunciated with the utmost precision, and he thought with an inward smile that she would doubtless rather die than drop a *g*.

"Quite sure, m'lady," Draper replied. She moved, almost imperceptibly, and her hand emerged from the deep folds of her plush velvet skirts . . . a hand far too small, too finely boned, to be holding so large and lethal a weapon.

The gaping black bore of the pistol made a

slow circuit of his breastbone, then wavered and dipped to his abdomen and the general vicinity of his masculine pride. He mouthed a curse and his eyes widened as he slowly raised his hands before his chest. "Damn it all, woman, can't we talk about this?"

"The matter is not open to further discussion," she replied. "I believe I asked you to leave here. Now I am telling you."

The barrel of the flintlock dipped, made a small circle in the air, and unerringly came back to point at his vitals.

"*Jesus H. Christ.*" Draper swallowed hard. She was damnably unsteady, and his mouth was suddenly dry. "Do me a courtesy and point that thing a few yards to the left. You're likely to do someone irreparable harm, and I've this sick feeling it's going to be me."

Her father's hard silver eyes glared down the barrel at him. "You won't come to harm if you set aside this foolish notion you have and go," she said.

Draper moistened his lips with a flick of his tongue. He was feeling rather ill. A fine sheen of sweat had broken out on his brow, and his stomach was busily trying to tie itself in a knot. "I gave my word."

"Your word means nothing to me," Quintana said.

The pistol dipped again, then righted itself. "You can threaten me all you like, but if you squeeze the trigger, it will be cold-blooded murder."

"A trespasser," she said with unnecessary

relish. "An American rebel who forcefully entered my home and is armed to the teeth—"

"There was no force involved," Draper argued. "I knocked at the damnable door, and your spindle-shanked maid let me in."

"Perhaps. But who do you think the authorities will believe? A wounded intruder, who also happens to be an American rebel? Or a poor, defenseless young woman defending her hearth and home?"

Draper gave an inward wince. She had him dead to rights, and she knew it. "Are you always this cold and calculating?" he questioned.

"I prefer to think of it as a means of protecting myself," Quintana said. "From you, and from the machinations of a father I happen to despise. Now keep your hands in plain sight, and back slowly away from there."

Quintana saw him hesitate. She'd hoped the sight of the pistol would be enough to frighten him off, but it was becoming obvious that Draper Boone was more thickheaded than most.

He stood his ground by the hearthside, watching her warily, seemingly in need of some gentle persuasion.

Quintana raised her thumb to cock the piece, but the lock was stiff from disuse, difficult to maneuver.

"Easy with that," he said. " 'Tis liable to go—"

Quintana threw him an irritated glance, and

as she did her thumb slipped off the lock. There was an ominous click as the goose-shaped hammer fell and flint struck steel with a host of sparks.

The piece bucked and roared, spewing fire and acrid smoke from the muzzle . . . rocking Quintana back on her heels with a startled cry.

She'd been stunned by the explosion, but not half as stunned as Draper Catworth Boone. She could see him through the grayish-white haze of sulphurous smoke that hung suspended in the air, and he was curiously ashen beneath his healthy tan.

He turned, staring at the impressive hole she'd blown in the handsome oak paneling, just three inches to the left of his head, and his color came back in a furious rush.

"You foolish little wretch," he said with a terrible softness. "You nearly blew my goddamned head off."

He started forward, stalking her, a demonic light in his eyes.

Quintana backed away. She thought she heard footsteps at the rear of the house . . . or was it merely the thunderous pounding of her heart? She had meant only to frighten him, and it seemed that she had succeeded. "I gave you fair warning!" she insisted. "You brought the entire episode upon yourself!"

"Fair warning!" he snarled. "If you ever try something like that again, I'll personally see to it that you don't sit down for a month of bloody Sundays!"

Quintana shrank back against the wall, and still he stalked her, pure menace in deerskin. There was nowhere to go, and no escape.

The lumbering footfalls were coming closer; Tilly's voice, alarmed and imploring, sounded just outside the double doors. "Have a care with your safety, Nigel! The villain is heavily armed!"

Draper shot an irritated glance at the doors, and in that instant when he looked away from her, Quintana bolted. She threw the empty pistol at Draper's head, and when he ducked the missile, she darted around him and made straightaway for the doors.

He grabbed for her and she felt his fingers brush her shoulder. His touch was incredibly warm on her bare skin. Quintana gasped, shocked by the brief contact. She was almost there. Another few inches!

Breath sobbing in her throat, she grappled for the door handles and felt the cold brass at her fingertips . . . At the same instant the hard hands of the frontier captain seized her trim waist, lifting her off her feet, dragging her back . . .

Chapter 2

Quintana was picked up and pulled against a long lean body that was as warm and hard as living stone. She was acutely aware of the sinewy arms that encircled her, precariously close to her breasts, and the hard-muscled chest at her back. She found his nearness strangely stirring.

Her reaction to him was instinctive, and totally unacceptable. It caused her to struggle all the harder to break his steely hold. *"Colonial devil! Let go of me!"*

"All in good time, m'lady," he said, grunting in pain as she kicked his shins. "I'll release you, and gladly, just as soon as I've secured my position and whittled down the odds a bit. For now you'll be much safer if I can keep an eye on you."

Quintana cursed beneath her breath and jammed an elbow into his midsection, but his stomach was as hard as iron, and her blow had little effect on him. "Keep still!" he growled, tightening his hold on her and snatching a pistol from his belt just as Nigel Bird burst through the drawing room doors.

Nigel, five feet nine inches and seventeen stone, glared at Draper. " 'Oo the bloody 'ell are you, and 'ow did you get in 'ere?"

From the corner of her eye, Quintana saw the frontiersman incline his dark head. The gesture was cocksure, the light in his clear golden eyes frosty. "Draper Boone of the Seventh Virginia," he said. "And I came through the friggin' front entrance. Now be so kind as to back off."

"Cheeky bastard," Nigel muttered. He flexed his hands open and squeezed them again into fists, and looked longingly at the frontiersman's corded throat.

The feeling of hostility, verging on open warfare, was thick in the room. For the first time since the captain's coming, Quintana felt a thrill of genuine fear. Nigel had been with the family for years. He was a good loyal servant, a family man. She didn't wish to see him hurt . . . and the captain looked capable of anything.

"Nigel, please," Quintana said. "Do as the captain asks."

"Don't let 'im frighten you, miss. I'll snap his bleedin' spine for 'im, *then* I'll call the watch!"

"You will do no such thing," Quintana replied. "Have you given a thought to what Sarah will do if you are hurt?"

At the mention of his young wife, Nigel hung his head. Quintana felt a fraction of the tension drain from the man at her back, though he still held her tightly against him.

He fixed her with his inscrutable gaze. "You like him that much, do you?"

"Nigel is Tilly's nephew," Quintana replied, "and has been in my service for years. He's very much like family."

"Then the good Nigel here is a fortunate man." Draper smiled, looking slightly demonic. "It wouldn't be advisable, however, to push your luck too far. It's been a difficult day, and my patience is worn precariously thin."

"You needn't worry," Quintana assured him. "Now please put your weapon away, Captain."

"Not quite yet."

"Precisely what are your intentions?"

The frontiersman shrugged; Quintana felt the sinuous ripple of muscle against her back and shivered. "There must be some place where Nigel can while away the next week in relative comfort—some place that will keep him out of trouble, away from my sometimes uncertain temper . . ."

"A week?" Quintana was appalled.

"Aye," he said. "Unless you're impatient to begin your new life and wish to depart immediately for the coast."

She closed her eyes and sought for some way around his demands. With Nigel under lock and key, there would be no way to thwart the brash young captain, and despite his having gained the upper hand so quickly, Quintana had no intention of accompanying him from the house, let alone from England.

A glance at the capable hand that held the huge black pistol, however, reminded her that this was not the most opportune time to resist. It was imperative first to gain his trust, lull him into complacency so that she would be able to set her scheme into motion—whatever scheme that happened to be. It would require some thought . . . planning . . .

"M'lady," her adversary prompted.

"There is only the storage room in the cellar, but I suppose it will suit your present needs."

He grinned wolfishly down at her and said softly, "Let's go then, shall we?"

"We?" Quintana was shocked. "You surely aren't suggesting that I accompany you to the cellar alone?"

"There's no cause to fret, m'lady," he informed her. "I'm not about to carry you off to some darkened corner and ravish you." His wicked grin deepened, revealing groovelike dimples in his unshaven cheeks. "Hell, if I wanted to ravish you, I'd do it right here."

Quintana's cheeks burned scarlet. "Are all your countrymen as arrogant and insolent as you, Captain?"

"Not all," he said with a laugh. "I like to think I'm—"

"Conceited?" she supplied.

"Unique, m'lady," he said. He stepped back, taking hold of her arm.

Quintana was free of his unwelcome embrace, but far from relieved. She could still feel the ripple and play of the supple male body

beneath the shirt and leggings he wore ...
still smell the faint scent of leather, the cool
smoky damp of London fog, the sweet pungent scent of tobacco, pleasant and masculine
all, strangely alluring.

The thought of being alone with him in the
damp dusty cellar, away from the prying eyes
and constant supervision of the household
staff, unnerved her. Yet the strong hand grip-
ping her upper arm, urging her from the room,
gave her no choice but to accompany him.

They passed Tilly Bascombe in the foyer.
Wide-eyed, she stood watching, a thin blue-
veined hand at her mouth. "You won't make
the mistress go down to the cellars," she said,
plucking at the fringe on the frontiersman's
sleeve. "There's spiders down there, and Miss
Quintana doesn't like spiders."

Draper glanced at the older woman. "I'll
look after your mistress's welfare," he said.
"What is your job here?"

"Sir?" Tilly said.

"What is it you do?"

"I'm Tilly Bascombe, maid to the mistress,"
Tilly said, coming back to herself with a sniff.

"Do you know your way around a kitchen,
Tilly Bascombe?"

"Enough to get by, an' that's for certain!"

"Good. Find me something to eat," Draper said, "and bring it back here. I'm hungry
as hell."

Tilly gaped at him, then, catching sight of
her mistress's nod, she ambled off to the kitch-
en, grumbling to herself, "Men! It makes no

matter if they're good or if they're evil, they all expect to be waited upon!"

Tilly's muttering died away. Quintana took a lamp from the table in the foyer, and she and Draper fell into step behind the sulking Nigel.

They made their way in tense silence down the long dim hallway, passing through a door on the left and into the kitchen pantry.

Draper studied his surroundings. It was not so far removed from any kitchen pantry in America, except that for the most part, m'lady's shelves were bare.

It was obvious that the colonel's daughter was having money troubles, and he couldn't help but wonder how she'd come to this pass.

Perhaps as he himself, she'd simply experienced a run of bad luck that had yet to right itself . . . It was something he could understand.

A year ago he'd have never believed that today he'd be in bloody England, or that his own life would have grown so completely out of hand . . .

His difficulties had started early in 1777 with the opening of the spring campaign by British forces, and the breaking of the blockade on the St. Lawrence River—a turning point on the western front, and in Draper's life.

During the first twenty months of the conflict between Britain and her colonies, the blockade and a shortage of ammunition had kept the British allied Indians in check.

Then in 1777 the blockade was breached, and an unlimited supply of powder and lead was funneled into the British outpost of Detroit, and in turn to the Wyandot, Mingo, Chippewa, and Ottawa tribes, who for years had gradually been pushed from their homes and hunting grounds by the land-hungry Americans.

The sudden influx of ammunition, combined with the encouragement of the British government, had resulted in a frontier aflame from the Hudson Valley to Can-tuck-ee . . .

"This way, Captain," Quintana said, rousing Draper from his musings. The shelves he had previously noted lined three walls from floor to ceiling; in the middle of the fourth wall was a door, which Nigel held open.

A cool draft wafted up the dark stairway, like smoke rising up a chimney. The candle flame flickered and danced.

Quintana Wade looked at Draper. Her small face was a pale golden cameo in the lamplight; her eyes seemed large and luminous, startlingly silver. "He'll catch the ague if left down here for long," she said anxiously.

"Your maid can bring him down a blanket or two, to feather his nest and to fend off the chill."

"A blanket or two will hardly prove sufficient against the draft, Captain," she said, a look of irritation playing over her delicate features. "But since there has been no reasoning with you thus far, I suppose I am wasting my breath by arguing."

"Better the draft than a hot dose of lead," Draper said softly. At his prompting, Nigel plunged through the black rectangle of the open doorway; Draper followed, warily keeping Quintana close by his side.

The burly-bear Englishman was not to be trusted, and if the worst happened and it came down to a fight, he wanted the girl out of harm's way.

"The steps are steep, and crumbling in places," Quintana said. "You'll need to watch your step."

"My thanks for the warning," Draper replied.

"It's not for your benefit that I mentioned it, Captain, but for Nigel's. I wouldn't want you to stumble and discharge your weapon accidentally."

Draper laughed low. The sound, echoing down the steep passageway, was hollow and distant.

The light from the lantern stretched along the hand-laid stone walls of the corridor, driving the obsidian shadows before its cheery yellow flood.

At the foot of the stairs was a long, narrow room and a heavy oaken door, black with age and slightly ajar, set into one wall. Quintana shrugged off Draper's hand and went to Nigel. "It's only for a little while," she said. "I'll find some way out of this, I promise you."

"The key, m'lady?"

Reluctantly, she placed the large iron key into Draper's outstretched hand, then watched her last and best hope of having her unwelcome guest ousted locked safely away.

"I hope that you are satisfied," Quintana said, once they'd returned to the comfort of the drawing room.

"I won't be satisfied until I quit these crowded shores," Draper Boone replied. He glanced around, chafing his bearded cheek with his knuckles. "Where is that maid of yours? I'm starving."

"Oh?" Quintana said with feigned sweetness. "Is there any chance you will expire soon?"

To her disgust, he chucked her beneath the chin. "I'm glad to see you have a sense of humor."

Tilly's soft steps announced her return. "I've brought the tray you wanted, Cap'n. I'll just leave it on the desk."

"That won't do," Draper said.

Tilly stopped in her tracks and slowly turned, biting her lip. "But, sir, 'tis good, solid English fare. An' I even brought a pint of ale to wash it all down with."

Draper didn't reply. He simply took the tray from the maid's hands and placed it on the small piecrust table beside Quintana's wing-back chair, then positioned another chair companionably near. "I mean that I never eat alone when I can sup with a beautiful lady," he said. "Bring your mistress a plate."

"Yes sir." Tilly returned to the kitchen to do his bidding.

"That's quite unnecessary, Captain," Quintana said. "I have already eaten."

"I insist." When Tilly returned, he cut up some of his dinner, putting it on the extra plate for Quintana.

She watched as he sank into the chair with an audible sigh, stretching his long legs out before him. "Stir the fire, will you, Tilly Bascombe?" he asked. "I'd like to see what it is that I'm eating." As he turned his attention to the plate, Tilly caught Quintana's eye with a vigorous shake of her head. Tilly's gaze slid pointedly back to the plate of boiled beef, cheese, and bread positioned between them.

Quintana's eyes widened. *Dear God, Tilly had put something in the food.* She watched as he speared a small piece of beef with the tip of his knife and brought it to his mouth . . .

"Is something amiss, m'lady?"

Quintana started. "What? No, of course not. Why do you ask?"

"You haven't touched the food or drink."

She forced a shaky smile and hoped he could not see her upset. "You'll understand if I have no appetite, and no urge to join you, sir. It isn't every day that a stranger calls and lays siege to my household."

He smiled a reply, taking up the tankard of ale. He'd consumed the last morsel of food, and seemed none the worse for wear for having eaten it. Quintana breathed somewhat more easily.

She wanted him gone, but she didn't want him dead.

The captain brought the tankard to his lips, but he didn't drink, and after a moment's hesitation, he lowered it again. "I've never had the stomach for ale," he said, turning to look at Tilly, who craned her neck anxiously. "Why don't you drink it, Tilly Bascombe?" The maid hesitated, looking alarmed. "Come now," he drawled softly. "You've earned it. Besides, a moment ago you seemed intent on looking it down my throat."

He held out the pewter tankard, but Tilly shrank back. "*Take it!*" he thundered.

"Really, Captain! I suppose that for the time being I must tolerate your presence in this household, but I won't have you intimidating the servants for the sake of your own amusement! You have wreaked quite enough havoc here already!"

He turned on Quintana, a black scowl on his face as he thrust the tankard into her hands. The ale washed over the rim, wetting her plush velvet lap. "Then you drink it, m'lady. And we'll bloody well see who's amused."

Quintana's heart fluttered madly in her breast. She slowly raised the tankard, defiantly meeting his gaze over the rim. The cool bitter ale wet her lips . . . but before she could drink, Tilly sprang forward, knocking the vessel from her hands.

"Perhaps you'd enjoy spending the next few days locked in the cellar with your cow of a nephew," Draper said with a terrible softness.

"It wasn't nothin', really," the maid said, wringing her hands as she spoke. "Just a powder to help you to sleep . . ."

Draper stared hard at Tilly; the older woman seemed to shrink. "You wouldn't lock me old bones away in the damp, now would you, Cap'n? The mistress has need of me services."

Quintana's heart went out to the older woman. She rose to put an arm around her thin, shaking shoulders. "That's quite enough."

The intended victim of Tilly's scheme pushed angrily out of his chair. "Enough, you say? She tried to poison me." He paused and calmed himself by dint of will. "Listen well, the both of you. You have five days in which to ready your things for the journey to America. On the morning of the sixth day we depart for the coast. The time between can be as pleasant, or as miserable, as you wish to make it." He paused, and his gaze slid from Tilly's frightened face to the cool placid face of her mistress. "Have I made myself clear to you?"

Lifting her chin, Quintana met his gaze without flinching. "Abundantly so, Captain," she said.

Indeed, her present predicament was all too clear. Captain Boone had been sent with her father's blessings to kidnap her, and she had just five days to thwart their plans.

Chapter 3

Quintana was not a habitual early riser, yet the next morning she was awake and dressed by six o'clock.

The presence of a stranger in the house was vastly unsettling; the knowledge that he'd spent the night standing guard outside her chamber door, infuriating. Because of that knowledge she'd slept but fitfully, and awakened in an impatient frame of mind.

She rifled through the wardrobe, looking for a gown to set him back upon his heels, but nothing seemed to suit.

She settled for her much-worn favorite, a morning gown of rose silk with a full skirt tucked up over wide panniers and adorned with tiny rosettes of pale pink ribbon. A petticoat of pale pink silk overlaid with Venetian lace showed beneath the divided skirt.

The gown had belonged to Rowena. Quintana, with the help of her deft-fingered maid, had altered it to fit, adding the lace and tiny ribbon rosettes.

Tilly helped her to dress and to don the elaborate white cadogan style wig that had also belonged to Rowena. The sausage curls at the side, the tucked tail in back, and the ribbon and jaunty plume made Quintana feel fashionably elegant. The wig was certain to shame the wretched colonial for his total lack of refinement.

With one final glance at her reflection, Quintana opened the door and stepped into the hallway, coming face to face with the bane of her existence.

He was lounging against the wall, a study in indolence, yet when she emerged from her chamber, he came instantly erect and stood waiting, his hands at his hips and a slight smile playing around the corners of his hard mouth.

Quintana gazed at him with narrowed eyes. His rough good looks, his thoroughly American lack of refinement, should have repelled her . . . yet strangely it didn't.

Draper Catworth Boone was unlike any man she had ever met, striking, flamboyant, half-wild . . . possessed of a raw, innate sensuality that she found every bit as maddening as it was hard to resist.

The longer Quintana's gaze lingered, the broader his smile became. "Mornin', m'lady."

"Captain," Quintana stiffly replied. He was looking exceedingly well this morning—too well, Quintana thought.

In the course of a single afternoon, he had managed to complicate her well-ordered life, and it was small compensation that he stifled a yawn as he pushed away from the wall against which he'd been leaning and fell into step behind her.

Head high, she made her way to the dining hall, the slightly rumpled captain dogging her every step.

The long board was spread with a fine linen cloth, the table set for two.

She turned and shot him an irritated glance. "I suppose this is your doing."

He regarded her with an upraised brow and said nothing.

"I am accustomed to dining alone."

He stared pointedly at her elegant silver head and curled his lip. "I shouldn't wonder. That thing on your head is enough to frighten anyone off."

Quintana looked down her nose at him. "It is not a *thing*, Captain. It is a wig. Wigs are an essential part of an English gentlewoman's wardrobe, but I wouldn't expect a provincial like you to know such things."

He rudely continued to stare, his dark brows drawn down in speculation. "Are you sure it's a wig?" he asked at last. "It looks to me as if a family of possums have perched on your head."

Quintana stiffened and her face grew hot beneath its thin film of ceruse. She sought for something to say, something to set him back upon his arrogant heels, but she couldn't think of anything cutting or sarcastic enough.

"Will you linger all day in the doorway?" he asked, a bit too casually. "I'm hungry, and you could do with a bit of fattening up."

"I beg your pardon?"

"You're far too thin, m'lady."

"My figure, sir, is hardly your affair!"

"Your health became my affair the moment your father appointed me to the post of nurse-maid. You may take me at my word when I say 'tis a task I do not relish."

Quintana stalked into the room, Draper close behind her. She seated herself at her usual place at table; he stood at a little distance, staring imperiously down at her.

Martha, the cook, had gone to market early that morning for fresh hens' eggs, tripe, and clotted cream. Quintana, distracted by the presence of the tall frontiersman, had little appetite. She chose a kippered herring and a hot buttered scone, but could eat no more than a few mouthfuls with the captain observing her so closely.

She tried to ignore him, but he would have none of it. "You pick at your food like a bird," he said. "And that ceruse you have smeared on your face—"

She gasped. "If you cannot control your insolent tongue, sir, then kindly take your meals in the kitchen with the servants."

Draper smiled grimly. "Your pardon if my bluntness has offended m'lady's sensibilities, but bluntness is my way."

"It is nothing to take pride in, Captain."

"A silken word is far too often ignored, Quintana. I succeeded in gaining your attention, and it's come to me recently that's no mean feat."

"I cannot imagine that anything *you* would have to say would interest me." She put her elegant nose in the air.

"It would interest you greatly if you cared at all for your health. The cosmetics you are wearing will ruin your complexion and ravage your health. They have already diminished your appetite, and it's a wonder you've a tooth left in your lovely head; you cannot afford to be frail where we're going. The journey from Williamsburg to Fort Pitt is an arduous one. The country doesn't coddle those who are weak, and neither do I. Think of that, Miss Wade, if not how it makes you appear."

"And how does it make me appear, Captain Boone?" Quintana wasn't sure why she was asking. She shouldn't care a fig for his thoughts or opinions.

"Ghastly," he said. "You're white as a sheet."

Her chin came up defensively, and he softened his tone. "The lass I saw last night had no need of artifice. Indeed," he said, "I found her quite fetching."

The sudden warmth in his voice, the unexpected compliment, disarmed Quintana. "You confound me, Captain. You say you find me attractive, yet at the same time you profess an intense distaste for all things English. Are you certain you know what you say?"

Without warning, he reached out, covering her hand with his. Quintana was shocked anew by the incredible warmth of his touch, the way his skin, so strong, so brown and weathered, contrasted vividly against her own. His hands, despite their roughness, were elegantly formed, his palms broad and callused, his fingers long and tapering. Capable hands, Quintana thought, but not the hands of a gentleman.

He was overstepping the bounds, and she knew that she should reprimand him, send him off with a scathing reproof. Yet she sat transfixed as he brought her fingertips to his lips. "English?" he said, so softly that she unconsciously strained forward in her chair. "Where were you born, Quintana?"

She saw the trap too late. He'd caught her handily. "In Philadelphia, Captain. It hardly matters, I am English to the core."

"It matters a great deal," he said. "You're an American born and bred, Quintana. Just like me." He squeezed her hand; she pulled it from his grasp, then wondered at her fleeting sense of disappointment that he let her go so easily.

He moved to his chair, all male arrogance and catlike grace. "We're kith and kin, you and I," he said. "And more alike than you care to admit at present."

"You are a rebel, sir," Quintana said emphatically. "A traitor to the Crown. Gallows bait! No better, surely, than the man who sent you here."

Her statement brought the smile back to his mouth, causing the outer corners of his eyes to crinkle pleasantly. "You, of all people, should understand the rebel mind, m'lady . . . currently being involved in a small rebellion of your own."

Quintana threw down her napkin. "There are no similarities in the two situations. Fifteen years have passed since I last set eyes upon my father, yet quite suddenly he decides to reenter my life! My mother died last year, Captain, a broken woman, torn by the shame of the choices he'd made. And every single day that she grew weaker I reminded myself that it was Winston Wade's abandonment that crushed her spirit . . ."

Quintana's hands were shaking. She hadn't intended to discuss Winston with Draper Boone, or with anyone, for that matter. Thinking of the father she had never known only served to bring back the memories, the childhood hurt, things that were better left in the past . . .

Quintana thought back on Rowena's stories, of how Winston, as the younger son of an old and revered family, had stood no chance of inheriting, and so could ill-afford his taste for high living.

Within six months of Winston's and Rowena's marriage, Winston's father presented him with an ultimatum: a cell in Newgate Prison for his mounting debts from the gaming tables, or a career in the military. Winston chose the latter, and was promptly packed off to the colonies with his newly purchased commission in hand and Rowena by his side.

The journey to America was to be a turning point for both of them.

The regimented life of a military man suited Winston perfectly. When removed from the excess and debauchery of life in London, he proved hardworking and ambitious; his rise in the ranks of His Majesty's Colonial Forces was swift and startling.

By the time Quintana was born, Winston had been promoted to major, and just three years later, he was granted a colonelcy and his first command at a tiny isolated outpost in the vast Allegheny wilderness called Fort Ligonier.

Rowena remained in Philadelphia until such time as Winston could safely send for her and their young daughter. Yet oddly enough, that long anticipated day never arrived.

The months and years that followed were lonely ones for Rowena. Winston's frequent letters told of hardship and the rigors of daily life beyond the boundaries of the civilized world. But tales of another sort arrived with alarming regularity from the West as well, related by the harried survivors of Indian raids upon unprotected settlements, of scalpings and torture and wanton cruelty . . . tales that haunted the anxious days and lonely nights of the fragile Rowena.

Weekly, she wrote her husband feverish missives begging him to resign his post, to return with her to England.

But Winston refused. There was nothing left for him in England. In the new land lay opportunity, and he vowed to send for her soon.

Rowena, impatient with waiting, began to see the underlying truth in his replies, and recognized in the vast unsettled land her rival.

The trackless forests teeming with adventure, the fertile river valleys, the rugged mountains had woven their primeval spell around Winston; the England he remembered was far too tame.

At last Rowena recognized defeat. Her rival for her husband's heart was too alluring, too powerful, for her to fight. And so in June of 1764, just three days before Quintana's fifth birthday, Rowena Wade and her young daughter went home to England.

Neither of them saw Winston Halcourt Wade again.

Oh, there had been letters, of course, increasingly infrequent missives that, as Quintana recalled, made her mother weep.

Rowena soon faded, withdrawing completely from family and friends. And Quintana, closely observing her mother's decline, nurtured the hatred she felt for the man who had sired her. But the crowning blow had come on the winds of rebellion.

After fifteen years of distinguished service in His Majesty's Colonial Forces, Colonel Winston Halcourt Wade had been offered a position of equal rank with the rebel army, a command at the wilderness outpost of Fort Pitt, west of the Allegheny Mountains. He had accepted—and was publicly denounced as a traitor to the Crown.

The news had come as a shock to Rowena, one that brought shame and eventually death.

Quintana alone was unsurprised that her sire could shed old loyalties as easily as he had shed commitment and responsibility.

On New Year's Day of the previous year Rowena Wade had taken to her bed with a fever, and precisely one year ago yesterday she found a permanent release from her earthly shame.

At the age of eighteen, Quintana had few prospects for marriage, for whenever a potential suitor discovered that she was in fact "Quintana Wade, traitor's spawn," he tucked tail and ran.

Not that it mattered to Quintana. Marriage had ruined her mother, and Quintana felt that it was useful only as a means of survival.

Yet agreeable to the idea or not, she would soon be forced into some sort of action. Her mother's family consisted of two aging, impoverished aunts who had already suffered greatly because of Rowena's scandalous match and who could not afford to grant her the smallest stipend on which to live.

Winston's family had seemed embarrassed by Rowena's return to London. Her presence and that of her child was a constant reminder of Winston's traitorous bent, something the Wades had preferred to forget. Samuel Wade, Winston's father, had gone so far as to deed the house on the Strand to Rowena, but this was as far as the bounds of his generosity had stretched. He had refused to contribute so much as a farthing to their meager income, and Quintana refused to beg.

Thus far they had survived on Rowena's sparse savings, but the money was almost gone, and Quintana had been left to manage on her own.

Quintana paused to get hold of her raging emotions. When she continued her voice had softened, but the hatred she felt for Wolverine Wade was still underlying . . . indeed, it never seemed far away. "Have you any idea how much I loathe Winston Halcourt Wade?"

"Perhaps as much as I loathe England," Draper replied. "I'm willing to concede that your feelings toward your father are warranted. God knows, he's not an easy man to like. Still, it doesn't change the facts. He's given me the task of delivering you safely into his hands, and that's precisely what I intend to do."

"Why must you be so obstinate?" Quintana cried in exasperation. "It is not as if you have a personal stake in this! What can you possibly hope to gain by dragging me half the world away?"

She'd spoken rhetorically, out of frustration, not really expecting an answer. But there was something in the way he looked at her that turned her cold, raised new suspicions.

Quite suddenly it all began to make sense. "There is something, isn't there, Captain? What has my father offered you? At what price can I buy your compliance?"

The warmth left Draper's expression. Suddenly he was cold and aloof. "Redemption," he said flatly. "Tell me, my dear Mistress Wade.

Can you give me back what I have lost? Can you give me back my life?"

Quintana tried to ignore the knot in the pit of her stomach. "Give you back your life?"

"Restore my rank, dispel the doubt and suspicion with which I've dwelt this past year? Can you aid me in proving wrong the charges pending against me?"

Quintana wet her lips, prepared to bargain with the devil's envoy who sat down the board. "You know I can't, but perhaps there is another way for you to mend your difficulties. You could stay here, in England. Start anew—"

He looked at her, amazement on his dark, handsome visage. "Have you not been listening to a word I've said, woman? I'd rather slave in hell than live a life of luxury in bloody England!"

"You speak from prejudice—"

He laid a fist upon the table, the knuckles showing white, and his eyes flashed golden in his tawny face. "Aye," he said. "A prejudice well-founded. My father's family came from the Highlands, near Loch Maree, in Wester Ross. To a man, they supported Charles Edward Stuart's bid for the bloody throne, and near to a man, they perished.

"Those who had the temerity to survive fled the field, but were soon run to ground by the British cavalry. They rounded them up like cattle, my grandfather and his three surviving sons, and brought them to England to trial. The old man turned seventy-three the day he mounted the scaffold and watched as two of his sons were hanged, their bowels torn from their bodies while they still lived and roasted before their very eyes . . ."

Quintana sat perfectly silent. There was nothing she could say that would lessen the venom in his voice, cool the fire of hatred a generation old that flashed in his golden-brown eyes.

"The only one to survive that day was Dewar Boone, my father. The noose was about his neck when the news came that his death sentence had been commuted to transportation and seven years of enforced slavery in Virginia."

Draper paused, shuddering from the effort to control the emotion roiling inside him, while Quintana looked on, as cool and emotionless as a pale marble statue.

He'd been terribly wrong in his assumption that because they were American by birth, they were therefore alike. The woman seated down the board was every inch the English beauty in her sumptuous gown of rose-colored silk awash with ecru lace and dainty pink ribbons. And he could no more understand the fascination she held for him than he could control it.

He heaved a sigh and ran a hand across his face. He was weary and desperately needed to sleep. Perhaps sleep would help to dispel the images that haunted his thoughts . . . images of a spirited young woman whose glorious flaxen hair swirled to her hips . . . of quicksilver eyes narrowed in warning . . . of an overly large pistol clutched in a too small fist.

Overlapping that thought was another one, infinitely more disturbing to Draper. It was the face of a youth, gaunt and careworn despite his tender years, his features marked by pain . . .

Draper ran a hand over his face, trying to force the image away. Hamlin had trusted him, believed in him, and Draper had failed him. He would not fail again. This was his only chance to restore in part that which he'd lost—his confidence . . . his honor . . . his name.

Bridgett Tanderlay entered the room, the pert little wench he'd met late last night on the servants' stair. She poured Quintana's tea and moved to Draper's chair, holding the teapot poised above his cup. He covered it with his hand and shook his head. "Be a good lass, and ask Cook if she's got a bottle hidden somewhere in the kitchen. I don't give a damn if it's Irish or Scotch, so long as it's whiskey."

Bridgett looked to Quintana, who gave a brief nod of permission. The servant left, and Quintana turned once again to Draper. "There is something else, isn't there, Captain? Something you aren't telling me?"

Bridgett came with the bottle he'd asked for. Draper pulled the cork with his teeth and spat it on the floor. "You might want to fortify yourself first," he said.

He held out the bottle, but she declined with a wave of her hand. So he tipped it and drank, tasting the smoky flavor of Cook's good Scotch whiskey. After a long and satisfying draft he lowered the bottle and again looked at Quintana.

She gave the appearance of waiting patiently, but he could almost feel the tension that coiled tightly in her lithe form. "Your father has decided you should marry. The man he's chosen is Lieutenant Uriah Bell, a prosperous farmer with family and land in the Wyoming Valley. I am escorting you to the fort, where you will be reunited with your father, and then given into your betrothed's keeping."

Quintana said nothing.

Draper sat watching in grim silence as the blood slowly drained from her face. It was odd, he thought. He'd anticipated flinging this piece of news in her teeth since the previous evening when she'd attempted to have him thrown into the street. Yet now that the long-awaited moment had arrived he felt only disgust, with Uriah Bell for agreeing to take an unwilling woman to wife, with Winston Wade for arranging both of their lives with such cool detachment, and with himself for being the instrument of her discomfiture.

Throughout the morning Quintana labored over the household accounts, irritatingly aware that the colonial captain lounged just outside the counting room door, so that he might at his convenience observe her movements and those of the household staff as they went about their duties.

For the third time in ten minutes she tallied up the column representing the previous month's expenditures, and for the third time her thoughts veered stubbornly away from the sum total of mutton, flour, sugar and salt to the specter of Lieutenant Uriah Bell, the man to whom she'd been betrothed without her knowledge or consent.

Betrothed.

The word provoked a veritable tide of anguish within her breast.

While other young maidens sighed and dreamed girlish dreams of husbands, home, and children, she'd looked upon marriage with an intense aversion.

Marriage, as she well knew, did not bring happiness, but loneliness and pain. And while her pragmatic mind told her there must be some whose lot in matrimony had improved, her heart insisted otherwise.

Uriah Bell.

She closed her eyes and shuddered, and when she opened them again a large dark blot had appeared to mar the ledger where her quill had come to rest.

Uttering a soft oath, she laid the quill aside and closed the ledger.

Things couldn't be worse, she thought, rising from her chair.

The sound of feminine laughter and the impudent voice of Draper Boone drifted in from the hallway. Curious, Quintana made her way to the door.

Bridgett Tanderlay stood in the hall with an armful of much-mended linens, her path blocked by Captain Boone. As Quintana watched, the Virginian touched the girl's throat and said something low and unintelligible.

Bridgett's eyes widened and her mouth formed an *O*. And then his dark head was descending, and he covered the girl's willing lips with his own . . .

"A word with you, Captain," Quintana said sharply.

Bridgett jumped at the sound of Quintana's voice, flushing guiltily. Averting her eyes, she dropped a curtsy and turned, fleeing down the hall and out of sight.

"It's about Bridgett."

Draper watched her go before returning his attention to Quintana. "She's a cant lass, that Bridgett. I wonder if she's ever thought of going to America."

His words turned Quintana cold. She amended her earlier thoughts that nothing could be worse than an unwanted marriage to Uriah Bell. She could think of one thing that was infinitely worse: marriage to this insolent man.

"Though 'cant' she may be, she is also a member of this household, and as such she deserves my protection and vigilance."

"Protection from what?" he coolly inquired.

"Protection from you. I won't have you mauling the serving maid at every turn. It is unseemly and unacceptable."

He braced a brown hand on his hip and grinned down at her from his great height. His dark face was devilish, his golden eyes glinting with a humor Quintana did not understand. "I didn't maul the girl, Quintana. I kissed her."

"I fail to see the difference, Captain—" Quintana began, but Draper cut her off.

"Oh, but there is . . . a very great difference indeed." He came slowly forward, closing the little distance between them, moving with a predatory grace, maneuvering her up against the wall. "Perhaps," he said in a voice that was silken and low, "you'd like me to demonstrate?"

"Demonstrate, Captain?" Quintana asked, striving to keep her tone cool and light. "What is it you are suggesting?"

"I am suggesting that you might be curious . . . and that your blood doesn't run as cold as you'd like me to think . . ." His voice was soft, his manner beguiling, so different from the stranger who had refused to leave her house last evening, from the dictatorial man who had been so brusque, so insulting at breakfast . . .

Quintana was wary and at the same time intrigued by him. She could not turn away.

"I've been kissed before, Captain," she said with feigned bravado. "I'm not as inexperienced as you seem to think."

"Indeed?" he said, reaching out to tease the curling tendrils that had escaped her chignon and fell forward to frame her face. "And how have you been kissed, m'lady?"

She looked at him uncomprehendingly.

"How, m'lady? Have you been kissed by a fine upstanding English gentleman . . . or by an unprincipled rogue . . . hmmm?" The hand that had toyed with her hair a second ago caught at her own hand, bringing it to his mouth. "A gentleman might brush his lips ever so lightly against your knuckles..." He demonstrated. "Or perhaps he'd buss your cheek..." His dark head dipped and he lightly saluted her upon her cheek. "But he wouldn't seduce you with slow heated kisses... the kind of kisses that leave you weak and trembling, crying out for something more..."

Bracing both hands against the wall on either side of her shoulders, Draper touched his mouth to Quintana's... gently, so tenderly that Quintana found herself straining upward on her toes to fit her mouth to his.

The instant Draper felt the change in her, he broke the kiss. He had been deliberately taunting her, knowing the icy demeanor she affected was but a protective shell designed to shield the vulnerable woman inside, to hold him at bay, and, perversely, he'd been wanting her to respond.

Yet somehow in the midst of his sensual teasing everything had changed... and during the brief instant when his lips had melded with hers, when she strained upward to intensify the contact, he'd become lost in the innocent charms of Quintana Wade.

And she was innocent... a spoiled womanchild. She needed a man to show her what she'd been missing... She needed kissing... someone patient, tolerant, kind... not a callous frontier rogue with too much time on his hands and a deep-seated hunger he couldn't quite seem to control.

No, she didn't need him . . . and he couldn't afford to lose sight of his goals. He was here in Winston's stead to find and escort her to the fort. And given his uncertain future, he could not afford to become romantically involved with the daughter of Wolverine Wade.

Reluctantly, he pushed away from the wall and stared down at her, a look of mild amusement on his dark, handsome face. "You could use a sound kissing, my dear Mistress Wade. And I've little doubt that one of these days you'll find a man who'll kiss you so thoroughly that he'll take some of the starch from your stiff petticoats." He reached out and ran the pad of his thumb across one velvety cheek. "My only regret, m'lady," and here his smile turned slightly, inexplicably sad, "is that I won't be around to see it. I'd be most interested to know just how it all turns out."

With that, Draper Boone, brash young frontiersman and irrepressible rogue, turned and slowly walked away.

Quintana, still feeling shaken and strangely vulnerable, was shocked to find that she shared in Draper Boone's regret.

Chapter 4

Quintana's steps dragged as she made her way from the kitchen. Her lack of sleep, the strain of the American's presence in her household, the constant battle of wills being waged between them, all combined to fray her nerves and shorten her temper, until she wondered just how much more she could stand.

The sound of the captain's booted steps on the inlaid floor was a constant reminder that she was nothing more than a pawn in her father's chosen game.

As she progressed along the hallway, she tried hard to ignore the irritating sound, but when she reached the stairs, her frazzled nerves snapped. With her hand resting on the newel post, she turned to him. "Must you dog my every step? I am only going up to sleep!" Her strident tone magnified her headache. To ease it, she pressed her fingertips to her temples. "With any luck," she continued more softly, "when I awake I will discover that you are nothing more than a terrible nightmare."

"I know a trick or two to rid you of that headache," Draper said with an impudent grin. But before he could elaborate, an impatient pounding sounded at the door. "Will you answer it? Or shall I?"

Exasperated, Quintana made her way to the door. Cook was busy in the kitchen, and Nigel was locked away downstairs. To ensure Bridgett's safety, the girl had been assigned to help Tilly upstairs, which left only Quintana, mistress of the manor, to put an end to the nerve-jarring noise.

She opened the door a crack to peer at the rangy character slouched on the stoop. He was dressed in tattered garments of dubious origins: dark breeches that were torn at the knee, through which a hairy leg protruded; gaiters; and a shirt the shade of butternut, topped by a faded blue doublet, a woolen coat, and a dusty black hat.

He was one of the most disreputable beggars Quintana had ever seen, but looks aside, she could not turn him off without the promise of a meal. "Go by the back door if you want to eat," she said a bit too sharply. "Cook will give you bread and mutton before she sends you on your way."

The beggar's black eyes flashed under bushy brows, and his fierce red beard parted to reveal a toothy snarl. "I dinna cum for no handoots, woman. Noo, step aside and let me pass. I'm expected within the hoose!"

By now she'd lost all patience. "If you're expected, then I'm the ruddy queen!"

She tried to shut the door in his face, but he was quick, and caught the panel's edge with a knotted brown hand, levering it open. Quintana fell back in alarm. She gaped at Draper, who stood off to one side, a look of mild amusement on his handsome face. "Will you do something?"

He moved to the door, but instead of ejecting the beggar, he helped him with his gear.

"Dear God," she said as realization dawned. "You know this man, don't you?"

"This is Corporal Absolute Farquar," Draper replied easily. "Acting as my reinforcements. Absolute: Quintana Wade, Wolverine's cub."

"Can't say as I'm pleased, yer ruddy highness," Absolute grumbled.

Reinforcements. Quintana regarded the Scot with ill-concealed contempt.

She was no longer dealing with a single trespasser. Dear God in heaven . . . she'd been invaded.

"Some distant Highland cousin who escaped a Tyburn noose by the skin of his teeth, I suppose?" she said.

The hoary Scot replied with a grunt. "I'm here to watch oot for the laddie's back. In case ye haven't noticed, there's Sassenach aboot."

"Sassenach indeed!" She was acutely aware of the Scot's penetrating gaze resting upon her. "I've had all of this that I can stand. I'm going to my chamber now, Captain, and trust you have no objections."

Draper gave a curt nod, then watched as she gathered her skirts and stiffly climbed the stairs. "How is your sister Fiona?"

The Scot grunted softly. "As cantankerous as ever, but nonetheless, glad to see me. She sends her best." He inclined his shaggy head toward the stair Quintana had so recently mounted. "Full o' sass, ain't she?"

A moment passed and a door closed in the distance. "She's headstrong, and impeccably cool, with a spine as unbending as iron . . . just like her old man."

"Ye daen't get on verra well wi' the lass. Per'aps ye ought to make the effort. She is the colonel's bairn. A word frum her could ease yer plight, daen't ye think?"

Draper snorted. "I will not kiss her highbred ass just to save my neck!"

"Then ye won't be envyin' the lieutenant his good fortune?"

Draper pushed a weary hand through his unruly black locks. "Uriah Bell is welcome to her, and be damned to both of them. I like my women warm."

"What aboot the hoose? Is it secured?"

"For the present," Draper replied. "They gave me the very devil of a time when I came yesterday. I had to lock the footman in the cellar storage room."

Absolute digested the information, surveying his surroundings with a keen black eye. "What odds?"

"The cook and the chambermaid are biddable enough, an Irisher and a Highland lass. And then there's Tilly Bascombe, the girl's maid. She may look harmless, but don't be fooled. She has a mean left hook and is intensely loyal to her English mistress. She isn't to be trusted."

The older man clapped Draper's shoulder. "Gae on, lad. Find yersel' a hole to burrow down, and dinna worry. I'll stand the first watch."

Draper turned and mounted the stairs.

He hadn't closed his eyes in two days, but the previous night hadn't been a total loss. While keeping watch he'd scouted the second floor, familiarizing himself with his surroundings.

What he'd found in his search was room upon sumptuous room, the likes of which he'd never before encountered, not even in Williamsburg. Silks and brocades abounded, aging but still rich. There were fading velvet hangings and feather mattresses soft enough to swallow a man, paintings with vast ornate gilt frames.

The house had once been a veritable palace, and he was a backwoodsman, a man more accustomed to a bed of leaves and clothes of rough-cut leather, to jerked venison and good Monongahela whiskey, than to satins, silks, and laces.

The fine dainty furniture, the gleaming floors of inlaid mahogany and teak, made him feel sadly out of place. Everywhere he turned he was painfully reminded that he did not belong here . . . and that Quintana did.

He went quietly up the stairs and traversed the hall to the master bedchamber, passing a small wooden table with spindle legs. On the gleaming top sat a delicate porcelain vase. It jarred slightly as he sauntered past; frowning, he softened his steps.

Quintana had come to womanhood in these very surroundings, Draper thought, glancing around.

He tried to imagine the haughty young woman he knew as a child with soft golden curls, running like a hoyden down this very hallway, bouncing on the big feather beds . . .

It was difficult.

He entered the master bedchamber, closed the door behind him, and leaned against it, thinking of his own youth.

As a lad, he'd never been content with the endless chores that were so much a part of a struggling farm, and so he'd spent his days roaming the wooded valley and surrounding mountainsides, as wild as any Indian.

On his eighth birthday—and despite his mother's objections—he'd been presented with his first rifle, a gift from his Uncle James, and though he'd been tall for his age, he'd still had to stand on a stump to push the ramrod home . . .

The cost of the great feather bed on which he lay, with its ornately carved headboard and tall spiral posts supporting the plush red velvet canopy, would have paid for his father's farm. And Draper mused as he slowly drifted off to sleep that there was little wonder he and the colonel's daughter couldn't seem to agree on anything.

He'd come from poverty, she from wealth, and the disparities between their worlds were simply too great to find a common ground.

For the remainder of that day and early into the next, Quintana stayed in her chamber and seethed.

It was difficult to believe that just two days ago life had been comfortably dull, her most pressing worry having been how to get on once her mother's savings ran out. With the captain's arrival, however, all of that had changed.

The problem of her dwindling funds seemed suddenly inconsequential, paltry indeed when compared to the difficulties she must now face.

It was eight o'clock on the morning of the third day, and Quintana sat by the bed-chamber window, staring out at the bustling city that had been home to her for the past thirteen years. It would be difficult to leave it, but leave it she would if she didn't do something to stop Draper Boone, and soon.

A light tapping sounded at the door. "Come in," Quintana said, not turning from the window as the door softly opened and closed. "You may take the tray. I'm finished with it."

"The cook will be worried. You've barely touched your food, and she works hard to please you."

At the sound of Draper's resonant voice, Quintana turned to face him. He stood just inside the door of her bedchamber, his tall, proud form bathed in the diffused morning light. There were subtle differences in his appearance this morning: the freshly brushed buckskin clothing, the plain black hair ribbon that secured his neatly combed locks at his nape. He was looking fit and well-rested, she noticed; indeed, he was looking quite handsome.

"I'm heartened, m'lady. Being welcomed into your bedchamber is more than I'd hoped for." He left the door ajar and sauntered into the room.

Quintana was almost grateful for his comment. For an instant she had been so taken by his appearance that she'd forgotten his unmitigated arrogance. Deliberately, she looked away. "Had I known it was you, Captain, I'd have bolted the door. I thought you were Tilly."

"And I thought that perhaps you'd finally come to grips with your situation."

Quintana lifted her chin. "It seems we were both mistaken. What is it you want?"

"Are you always so brusque? It's a most unseemly trait in a woman."

Quintana raised one fine arched brow and smiled at him. "Was I being brusque, Captain? I hadn't realized. Your pardon. Now please get out."

Draper ignored her request, moving instead to the large cherry wardrobe that occupied the westernmost wall. Quintana watched him warily.

His stride was lazy and catlike, so supreme-
ly confident, so graceful.

"There's no need to apologize, Quintana. I'm
beginning to see that your rapier-like tongue is
part of your charm." He smiled at her over his
shoulder, his amber eyes dancing in his tawny
face. "Besides, it helps to cover your fears."

"Fears indeed," Quintana said with an irate
sniff. "What would you know of them?"

"I'm a damned good judge of character,"
Draper replied with a wink. "And an even
better judge of women."

Quintana had to suppress a smile. He was
cocksure, she'd give him that . . . and charming, after a dark, somewhat devilish fashion.
But she was determined not to succumb to his
teasing advances again.

Of necessity she must keep her distance,
must keep her vulnerability hidden. And so
she dragged out her oft-used prickliness, the
stiff outer shell she'd worn like armor for so
many years.

"I don't care a fig for your approval, sir,
or lack thereof. I've never been afforded the
luxury of weakness that most women enjoy,
since there has been no man in my life to lean
on. I suppose that if my solitary life has made
me strong and invulnerable, then that is one
thing for which I can thank Winston Wade."

"Rigidity is often mistaken for strength,"
Draper told her. "Take the oak, for instance.
It's one of the giants of the forest. And once
seasoned, there is not a sturdier wood to be
found . . . yet the limbs of the living trees are

brittle. In a storm wind they snap like the most fragile twig."

"What is your point, Captain?"

He shot her a level look over one broad shoulder. "I would have thought that obvious. You have to learn to bend m'lady, or you're liable to break."

After opening the doors of the wardrobe, Draper thumbed through her gowns. Satin, silk, brocade, and velvet . . . and not a single garment that would hold up to the rigors of travel through the wilderness. "These will have to suffice until we reach Williamsburg," he said, choosing a few of the heavier garments and tossing them onto the bed. "Once we're there, I'll purchase something more suitable."

The sight of his strong brown hands crushing her gowns roused Quintana's anger. She rose from her chair and stalked to the wardrobe. "What on earth do you think you are doing?"

"I'm helping you pack."

She grabbed up the gowns Draper had flung on the bed and tried to push past him. Without the white ceruse, her skin had lost its deathly pallor, and the delightful rose of a burgeoning anger glowed high upon her cheeks.

She was even lovelier in this natural state than Draper recalled. He felt a familiar catch in his loins, the answering stir of blood in his veins . . .

The bed was close. And for a fleeting instant he thought of urging her down and kissing her into compliance. A kiss or two and she would thaw, another and she'd melt. With a little effort he could have her writhing beneath him in no time, moaning his name . . .

The concept was tempting, and he'd even started to reach for her when Absolute entered, carrying a medium-sized trunk on one shoulder.

Tilly followed close behind him, carping all the while. "That won't be sufficient to hold Miss Quintana's things," the maid was saying. "Now be so good as to fetch up the other one. It's in the corner of the storage room— and bring up the rest of the hatboxes too!"

Absolute glared fiercely at Tilly, then turned around and stomped to the door, grumbling about the "pushy ways of city-bred Sassenach women."

"Leave them," Draper said. "We travel light." He turned back to the wardrobe, intending to sort through her underthings, but Quintana blocked the way.

"Out! Both of you! Get out this instant! If there is any packing to do, then Tilly and I will do it!"

"Left to your own devices, I can well imagine what you would pack," Draper said.

She looked silver daggers at him. "Left to my own devices, sir, I would not pack at all!"

Draper frowned down at her. She was the most obstinate young woman he'd ever had the misfortune to meet, and without a doubt the most dangerous. And he wondered, not for the first time since his arrival two nights ago, what had possessed him to take this particular assignment.

Desperation. He'd been just desperate enough to agree to anything . . . and more than a little surprised that Winston Wade would entrust his daughter to him.

And then there was the guardhouse, a subterranean hell that made a midwinter voyage on the stormy Atlantic a journey through paradise by comparison—incentive enough to keep his lust for Quintana Wade under control.

She was, after all, the colonel's chit, he reminded himself. And he would languish the rest of his days in a lightless, airless hole if he as much as showed an interest in her that might later be misconstrued.

Yet even more than that, she was Uriah Bell's woman, and Bell alone would have the honor of relieving her of her precious virginity.

But when he thought of the trouble and strife that he must go through just to deliver her into another man's hands, the outcome seemed grossly unjust.

With an oath he stalked away from the wardrobe, away from the golden temptress, to the window, where he leaned against the sash.

"I think this saffron silk will suit very well," said Quintana to Tilly, holding a gown before her. "If I must be forced into meeting my father, then I will do so on my own terms. Oh, and Tilly, be sure to put Mother's wig in one of the boxes. I will have need of it as well."

"The wig stays behind," Draper said emphatically.

"Don't be ridiculous, Captain. It won't take up a great deal of space. I see no reason why—"

"These are turbulent times in America. Longtime residents suspected of having British sympathies are being drummed from the settlements, hassled, and sometimes hanged. And while it may be a common occurrence to flaunt such ridiculous folderol in your fashionable circles, in the backwoods settlements it will only draw unwanted attention, ridicule, and perhaps even trouble. And I've trouble enough, to be sure."

She faced him squarely, the light of rebellion burning bright in her pale silver eyes. "I don't care a fig for your trouble, Captain. That wig belonged to my mother, and whether you like it or not, I'm taking it with me."

Quintana moved to the dressing table that held her powders and perfumes, brushes and wig, intending to take up the disputed headdress, but Draper was swifter. He snatched it from its stand and opening the window, quickly hurled it out.

She gasped and flew to his side, leaning through the open window.

Far below, an ancient crone scooped up the treasure that had fallen at her feet. Clapping it on her head, she cackled with glee. "Thankee much, gov'nor. Goes well with my duds, don't ye think?" She spread her rags luxuriously, dipped a curtsy, and danced a little jig.

"Wear it in good health, madam," Draper called down to the retreating hag, then slammed shut the window. "The matter is settled," he said to Quintana.

"You unfeeling, despicable bastard!" Quintana brought her hand back to slap his handsome face, but he deftly caught her wrist.

His black brows lowered ominously. "You'll find I'm more than willing to negotiate terms, to compromise. But know this: you cannot possibly hope to win against me." He let go of her and walked to the door. "I suggest you keep that in mind."

Quintana stomped her slippered foot in rage. But Draper Boone had gone.

Chapter 5

When she entered the dining hall, he was standing by the great bank of windows, gazing out upon the smoky London night . . . the man Quintana intended to betray.

Her decision to go to the authorities had not been made lightly. The consequences of her plan were far too serious for that.

Draper Boone was a rebel, a traitor to king and to country, a threat to all Quintana held dear. She realized now how wrong she had been to allow him to continue to dwell in this house, undetected and unchallenged, while he plotted and planned to abduct her and carry her off to a foreign land.

That the authorities must be alerted now seemed quite clear.

There was no other alternative, yet Quintana found herself strangely reluctant to think about what would happen to him once he was apprehended.

Pausing in the doorway of the dining hall, she studied his straight back and knew in her heart that they would try their level best to break him.

At the very least, he would be clapped in

irons and carted off to rot in prison. Or, if anti-rebel sentiment was running high, there was a chance he'd earn a goodly length of Tyburn hemp.

In her mind's eye she saw him mount the cart outside Newgate for the long ride to Tyburn Hill . . . a shadow of the man who stood before her now . . .

"Is it always like this?" he said, breaking into her musings.

The sound of his voice was oddly welcome and helped somewhat to dispel the ghostly image of the gallows cart and Tyburn Tree, but as Quintana entered the room she couldn't quite shrug off the cloak of melancholy her imaginings had evoked. She tried to harden her heart against him, to push his future— or the lack of it—from her thoughts, to say it didn't matter, but it was one of the most difficult things she'd ever had to do.

She finally gave up the fight and moved to her place at table. "Like what, Captain?" she asked.

"London—such hazy sunsets," he said. "A faint touch of color taints the mist, but all too soon it fades to black, and there's nothing. There aren't any stars in the night sky, nothing to see beyond the roofs of a million houses and a veritable sea of chimney pots."

"London is a great sprawling city, Captain. It has endured a thousand years, and will likely endure a thousand more. Surely you have cities in America?"

"Aye, we have cities. But nothing to compare to the squalor, to the abject misery I've seen here. I confess that I find your homeland oppressive, Quintana. I can't tell you how glad I'll be to see the last of it."

She gave a soft laugh. "No gladder than I shall be to see you go."

At that moment he turned to face her, and Quintana caught her breath. His leather garb was the same in which he had arrived two nights ago, but he'd obviously taken considerable pains with every other aspect of his appearance.

The unruly raven locks that always seemed to be falling forward onto his brow had been brushed neatly back, caught at his nape with a leather thong. It accentuated the lean planes of his face, the stubborn jaw and clefted chin, scraped meticulously clean of the short dark beard.

The change wrought in his appearance was startling, and Quintana acknowledged uneasily that if before she had thought him handsome, he was now arrestingly so.

"Your eagerness surprises me," he said. "Especially since when I depart London, it will be in m'lady's company."

He helped her into her chair before taking the seat beside her. The simple act of courtesy surprised her, and she wondered for the first time where the rogue with whom she'd been at odds had gone. Draper then bent, lifted the linen tablecloth, and peered suspiciously beneath.

"Why, Draper Boone, whatever are you doing?" Quintana demanded.

"Just trying to determine if you've got a howitzer hidden away beneath your skirts. I find this lull in the hostilities damnably unnerving."

"I could insult you if you'd like, but I find the idea of setting aside our differences for the duration of the evening an intriguing prospect." The last evening they would be spending together, she thought.

Draper looked wary. "You're proposing a truce?"

"Call it what you like, Captain. I think we both can use the rest."

"My Christian name is Draper. Since we're about to enjoy a temporary lull in the fighting, I see no reason why you shouldn't use it."

"Very well, then, Draper," she said, shocked at how easily it slipped off her tongue. "You said your father's family was from the Highlands. Is it a Scottish name?"

He shook his head. "Irish. My mother's name was Catworth before she met Dewar Boone. I'm named for her eldest brother. The family hailed from Killaloe, near Loch Derg." He paused and, golden eyes glinting, sipped his amber brew. "What of you? Have you family hereabouts?"

Quintana shrugged. "Two aging aunts on Mother's side, and their scattered offspring. We were never very close. My father's family resides just outside of Tonbridge at The Willows, the family seat. Grandfather died years ago, after willing us this house. Uncle William, the eldest son and heir, refuses to recognize me as kin. My father has seen to that."

"It must have been hard for you growing up without him." It was an observation, not an inquiry.

Quintana merely sipped her wine, unaware how tightly she gripped the glass. "My life has not been easy, Cap—" She stopped herself, amending, "Draper. My mother's health was failing upon our return to England. I was only five years old, but I remember creeping from room to room, speaking to Tilly in whispers, afraid I would disturb her. Those were not happy times."

"Surely you can't blame your father for your mother's frailty?"

Quintana's laugh was scornful. "I do indeed blame him. If not for him, she would still be here."

"You cannot know that, lass."

"I do know it! Here!" Eyes flashing silver fire, she placed a hand upon her breast, so white and lush above her gown of dull golden Chinese silk. Draper watched her intently, thinking how he envied that small hand the uncontested right to rest upon her pearly bosom, envied the gown that lay intimately against her sweet young form.

"Winston Wade robbed her of her life, the same way he now seeks to rob me of mine!" Her breathing had quickened apace with her temper. With each breath she drew her breasts swelled alarmingly above the daring decolletage of her gown, threatening to burst free.

Draper gave an inward groan and forced

his gaze up to her face. "The betrothal rankles deep?"

She nodded, and he thought he saw her small rounded chin quiver. "Do you know this Lieutenant Bell?" she asked.

"Aye, you might say that."

"Will you tell me what you know?"

Draper grew uncomfortable. "Perhaps I'm not the one to ask."

"You are the only one available to me," she said. "It is my right to know about the man I am to wed."

Draper conceded silently that he owed her that much. It was indeed her right. "What do you wish to know?"

"Is he young or old? Tall or short? Fat or thin? Is his disposition kindly, or is he mean-spirited? Why did my father choose him over you, or anyone else, for that matter?"

Draper shifted in his chair and wondered how much he dared to tell her about Uriah Bell. He thought of lying out of spite for Bell, but she continued to stare at him with those great luminous eyes, a look of expectancy on her face. She appeared so young, so completely and unexpectedly girlish in that moment, that he couldn't deny her anything.

"He is twenty-six, younger than me by three years, short and fairly thin, with dark hair and eyes. He's passable to look at, I suppose, if you don't mind the hint of the weasel about his eyes and mouth."

"Weasel?" she asked, her eyes sparkling with amusement and interest. "Fie, Captain! From the way you said that, it's easy to see you do not like Lieutenant Uriah Bell. Now why is that, I wonder?"

Draper's mouth hardened to a thin line. "No, I do not like the lieutenant, any more than he likes me. As for why your father chose him over me . . . it just so happened *he* was willing."

She tilted her head and smiled sweetly. The wig was gone, but she'd still managed to dress her blond curls with a silver-gray powder that perfectly matched the color of her eyes. "And you were not?"

"I'm not looking for a wife, Quintana," he answered tightly. "Not that it would have made a difference. Your father would never agree to such a mismatch. The prospect of owning a man like me as a son-in-law is doubtless the colonel's worst nightmare."

"You are not overly ambitious," she mused aloud. "It seems to me the man I wed stands to gain a great deal more than just a wife. Power, influence, and connections will come his way through so strong a link with the notorious Winston Wade."

"I only want what's due me, " Draper said.

"And what is that?" she questioned bluntly. "I asked you once before what you stood to gain by coming here to England to do my father's bidding. You answered cryptically; perhaps now you will explain. What did you mean when you said you wanted redemption? When you said you wanted back your life?"

"What difference does it make? My life, my trials, mean less than nothing to you."

"I think you will agree that I have a vested interest."

He snorted derisively. "A vested interest! What hardships do you face, truly?"

"Marriage to a man not of my choosing! Unwanted interference by a man I hate!"

"Marriage is a woman's lot," Draper said harshly. "If anything, your father's interference will make your life simpler . . . while it's made mine a living hell."

"A telling choice of words," she said. "What does he hold above your head, Draper? And pray, do not try to beg off with an evasion. I know there's something. I want to know what it is."

He sank back in his chair with an exasperated sigh. "Have you any idea what it is to lose face, Quintana? To lose one's credibility? To see the doubt in the eyes of your fellow men when they look at you?"

"I know scorn firsthand," Quintana replied. "I know what it is to be shunned by your peers and considered unacceptable because of circumstances beyond your control."

"Then perhaps you can understand my determination to make good now . . . to prove wrong my accuser."

Quintana went still. "Your accuser?" she said.

He tossed back the last of his whiskey, then stared broodingly into the empty glass. "There are charges pending against me."

Quintana frowned. "Charges? What exactly have you been accused of, Captain?"

He glanced up at her, and there was not a single ounce of contrition in him as he answered, "Disobeying a direct order, desertion, insubordination, attempted murder. Take your bloody pick."

Quintana was taken aback. "And I am to assume you are guiltless of these supposed crimes?"

"Think what you wish," he said flatly. "I didn't desert my command."

"You didn't desert," Quintana said warily. "What about the other accusations you mentioned? Did you really try to kill someone?"

"I had my hands wrapped 'round his scrawny neck when they pulled me off him, if that's what you want to hear. To say I made an attempt upon the man's life is insulting. I promise you, my dear Miss Wade, I'm more adept than that. Had I truly wanted the pompous incompetent ass dead, he would be."

"My father?" Quintana asked, shocked by his bluntness.

He grinned at her then, wolfishly. She felt a chill chase up her spine.

"Your intended," he replied. "The honorable Lieutenant Uriah Hampstead Bell."

Draper's revelations at dinner had been shocking indeed, and gave Quintana a great deal to think about. Her opinion of her father had always been unfavorable, yet until this evening she'd never had cause to question his sanity.

Discovering, however, that he'd placed her

life in the hands of a man who freely admitted having made an attempt on the life of another, his slated victim her betrothed, prompted her to wonder if Winston's judgment was faulty, or if perhaps he, suspected there was more to this situation than met the eye, as she did.

Whatever Draper's faults, he did not seem capable of cold-blooded killing. He had a vile temper, it was true, but even when enraged he was not without restraint.

She thought back to the night of his arrival, how he'd entered bone-weary and miserable. She thought of the reception he'd received, and his reaction to it.

He'd bested her. He'd let her know she couldn't win against him. But she couldn't say with honesty that he had caused her any harm . . . despite the fact she'd nearly shot him, and tried to have him beaten and thrown into the street.

His actions hardly seemed those of a would-be assassin, Quintana thought, and as the evening wore on, she found herself speculating more and more as to what Uriah Bell could have done to provoke him to such violence.

They had repaired to the drawing room soon after dinner, and now Quintana sat in the large wing chair drawn up close beside the cheery fire that blazed upon the hearth, her sewing spread across her lap.

Draper sat on the floor at the opposite end of the hearth, patiently etching a design onto what appeared to be a powder horn with the tip of his hunting knife.

For a long while Quintana watched him, wondering at the silence that stretched between them. It was strangely pleasant, being in his company, and as she turned her attention to her stitchery, thoughts of his arrest were far away.

She stitched awhile, her needle flashing intermittently before it poised above the cloth, and her gaze again wandered unerringly up to the frontiersman's dark enigmatic face . . .

"What is it that troubles you?"

His voice made Quintana start. She flushed a guilty pink, knowing she'd been caught staring. "I didn't mean to be rude," she said. "It's just that your talk at dinner intrigued me."

"Oh?" he said. "How so?"

"Though it pains me to admit it, I find I'm curious."

Until now he'd been totally absorbed in his task, but at her admission he raised his whiskey-colored gaze to hers. "What is it you wish to know?"

"What is he really like? My father?"

There was a catch in her voice as she posed the question. Quintana clearly heard it, and from the soft patience in his voice as he replied, she knew that Draper had heard it too. "Your resemblance to him is uncanny. I knew the moment I laid eyes upon you that you were the one I'd come seeking."

"He must be nearing his fiftieth year."

He ran a thumb across the place where he'd been carving. "Fifty-five, I think. But the years, for the most part, have been kind to him. He's a tall man, and well-favored, with a soldierly bearing, and a bit of gray at the temples. Not elderly by any means."

He deepened one particular cut, then held it to the firelight for a close examination, while Quintana battled with her emotions.

Tears pricked behind her eyes. Irrational tears, a purely feminine response. She fought down the urge to give in to them and pushed doggedly on, certain that it was only knowledge she wanted, that Winston Wade didn't matter to her in the least. "You seem to know him very well. Have you been with his command for long?"

"My," he said, "you're brimming with questions this evening . . . a fine indication that you are either growing quite at ease with my company, or suddenly developing an interest in something other than England."

He sent a smiling glance her way that caused Quintana's heart to turn over in her breast. "You'll forgive me if I flatter myself and claim the former," he said.

More from habit than hauteur, Quintana elevated her slim nose. "I haven't the least bit of interest in you," she lied adroitly. "But since it seems to please you so, think what you will."

"I've been with the Seventh Virginia since '75," he said, going back to his work on the horn. "The war had just begun. Some of the lads from the settlements thought that picking off a few Englishmen might be fun, and they decided to join the militia. I went on up the valley with them, but I quickly found that life within the fort just didn't suit. So I signed on as a scout instead. It gave me a measure more freedom than the regular military."

"And did you? Pick off a few Englishmen?" Quintana asked.

He sighed, laid the knife and horn aside, and rubbed the knuckles of his right hand along his cheek and jaw. "It wasn't any fun, if that's what you're asking. Warfare rarely is. What's happening along the frontier is particularly brutal. Unfortunately, it has also become an inescapable facet of life on the bounds of civilization.

"It started during the time of King William's War, and the French were the first to employ this kind of skirmish warfare. The Comte de Frontenac called it *la petite guerre*, the little war. The concept is simple, really. A combined force of Indian warriors, led by an officer, rains terror down upon the settlements, and destroy most everything in their path. The old and infirm, the babes too tender for travel . . . the women. Precious few of those targeted are spared.

"It's a war of annihilation and retaliation, of strike and revenge. And only one thing's changed in almost ninety years. The French have left the continent. And the officers now leading the tribes against us are wearing British red."

"How do you fit into all of this?" Quintana found herself asking. He'd told her of her father; she now wanted to know of him. Perhaps it would help to erase him from her thoughts if some of her questions were answered. Perhaps her curiosity concerning him would dim.

His gaze turned brittle. "As captain of the scouts, it was my job to carry 'the little war' to the villages of the Six Nations, the allied tribes of the northern lakes region, to bring back the captives whenever possible . . . to avenge the dead. It wasn't a pleasant task, or one I took pride in, but one in which I happened to be skilled."

"You spoke in the past tense, sir. Am I to assume you no longer serve as captain of scouts?"

She thought she saw his face flush dark, though with the shifting shadows cast by the firelight it was difficult to tell. "Astute of you to notice. I've been demoted until such time as I can prove myself, assigned to a prolonged stint as guardian to a headstrong young Englishwoman."

Quintana gave a soft laugh. "The way you say it, one might think you far prefer facing down a Mingo warrior than a simple English miss."

"At least when I run afoul of a Mingo warrior, I know what to expect while you, Quintana Wade, remain a mystery."

"Surely you aren't serious, Captain! How could I possibly intimidate you?"

His cool gaze swept over her, lingering on the soft white expanse of her breasts swelling above the square neckline of her golden silk gown. "An icy beauty with a penchant for pistols, fetchingly gotten up in a gown that would easily cost me a full year's wages . . . a woman I ache to touch, but one I'm sworn to protect, my superior's only daughter . . . and I a self-professed womanizer and all-around rakehell." He paused for a moment while she caught her breath. "My dearest Quintana," he admitted softly, his eyes glinting in his shadowed countenance, "you scare the living hell out of me."

Quintana searched without success for some appropriate reply. When Absolute came to the door to summon Draper and he rose to quit the room, she was oddly grateful.

There was something occurring between them this evening she didn't understand, something unexpected but not at all unpleasant . . . something that made her ill-at-ease, stretching her nerves taut.

Setting aside her sewing, she rose from her chair and made her way to the hearth. The shining dark horn lay upon the bricks. Even from a distance, Quintana could see the intricate patterns Draper had so painstakingly carved into its highly polished surface.

She'd watched him as he'd worked, watched his hands.

He had such wondrous hands . . . hands that were brown and hard and callused, yet capable of guiding the tip of the blade across the horn with uncommon skill and delicacy.

She bent to retrieve it. A pattern of vines had been etched in an oval shape, conforming to the curve of the horn, and forming a cameo slightly smaller than her palm. Here and there among the intertwining vines, a rose had been lightly outlined . . . and in the very center of the cameo she saw herself with tresses tumbling, a wistful smile upon her face.

" 'Tis but a humble rendering," he said softly, close by her ear.

"It's lovely," Quintana replied. "The workmanship, I mean."

"You sound surprised, m'lady," he said. He was gazing steadily down at her, a slight smile curving his firm sensuous lips.

Quintana was suddenly, acutely aware of hisnearness.Sheshouldturnawaynowandleave him to his own devices, beat a timely retreat to the safety and solitude of her chamber. And yet she lingered, feeling exhilarated by his presence. "I suppose that I hadn't expected—"

"You hadn't expected a man like me to appreciate the finer things life has to offer," he softly supplied. "A sumptuous dinner, soft candlelight, the company of a beautiful woman." He took the hand that held the horn and, as he spoke, drew her in so that they stood very close to each other.

Quintana gazed down at the strong hands that held hers. "You mistake my meaning, Captain. I was about to say that I hadn't expected, when I picked up your handiwork, to see my likeness gazing back at me."

She raised her gaze to his, and suddenly felt shy in his presence. "Why? Why would you do this? We are adversaries, you and I . . . and under the circumstances, I cannot foresee us ever being anything else . . ."

Draper's left hand still cradled Quintana's right, but his free hand slid along her wrist and the upper curve of her arm. His voice when he spoke was low and seductive. " 'Tis you who's mistaken this time, m'lady. For you and I are so much more than simple adversaries."

"What else could we possibly be?" Quintana said with a laugh; inwardly she shivered.

Draper's fingers curled around the curve of her elbow, moving continually upward, drawing her closer, into his embrace. "The possibilities," he said, "are endless."

"Endless?" She moistened her lips with the tip of her small pink tongue, and felt a strange thrill unfurl in the pit of her belly. She really should go . . . She'd stayed much too long as it was . . . far longer than was proper for a young woman of quality . . . but the light in Draper's clear amber eyes intrigued her . . . he intrigued her. She wanted to understand what it was he was saying . . . She wanted . . .

At the moment, she was not at all sure what she wanted.

"Endless . . . m'lady," Draper avowed.

"How very intriguing," she murmured. "Can you name them for me? Not all, if indeed, as you say, they are endless. Just a few, Captain, off the top of your head."

"Our time, I think, would be far better spent in *exploring* the possibilities." What Draper had in mind was dangerous. Yet at the moment, he didn't seem to care.

Quintana was the very embodiment of temptation, soft and desirable, teasing and sweet. He'd kissed her once, but the contact had been so brief, so damnably unsatisfying. He wanted to savor her honeyed lips, to test her pliancy.

Then perhaps, just perhaps, he'd at last be able to put her from his thoughts.

It seemed the perfect plan, but just as Draper's dark head descended, Quintana turned her head.

Draper was not deterred. Bringing one hand up to cradle the back of her head, he kissed the petal-soft cheek she offered, and then in a slow and leisurely fashion, worked his way to the corner of her mouth.

Quintana closed her eyes. His kiss was slow but searing, a passionate assault upon her senses she had no will to resist.

He kissed her until all conscious thought deserted her, until she moaned and wrapped her arms about his neck . . . then kissed her again and again, urging her lips to part, exploring the silken recesses of her mouth.

The moment Draper's mouth met hers, the world outside the drawing room doors ceased to exist, and for Quintana there was only the strength of her buckskin-clad lover's embrace.

She swayed in his arms and melted against him, giving herself up totally to her impetuous desires . . .

Draper felt her will dissolve and knew that he had won. With a sense of triumph he listened to her soft moan as he blazed a heated trail of kisses down her throat and beyond.

Her breasts were soft and white and fragrant.

She smelled of sunlight on roses . . . pink velvet petals damp with morning dew . . .

He caught a ragged breath and worshipped the pearly flesh that showed above the gown, gilded by the firelight, so warm and enticing.

The ache in his loins was becoming unbearable, and he was certain that she felt it too. Until tonight he'd thought her stiff and prudish, but he'd been wrong. For beneath that prickly English hide of hers beat the heart of a wanton woman.

What a pleasant discovery that had been, he thought, wondering what other secrets she was keeping.

Another moment, and everything between them would be laid wonderfully bare. He'd take her here, before the fire, and not a man with a bloody pulse would blame him . . . save one.

As swiftly as it had mounted, Draper's desire dwindled away. Winston Wade would not thank him for deflowering his precious chit. Indeed, he would be furious, and rightly so.

Sighing his deep and abiding regret, he kissed her fragrant flesh a final time, lifted his head, and released her.

Wavering slightly on her feet, she touched wondering fingertips to lips that were rosy and swollen from his kisses. The gesture was so innocent, so childlike, that Draper felt his stomach clench and he had to look away.

"For Christ's sake," he said, raking a hand through his hair. "Go to bed. And lock your door, before I change my mind."

Quintana couldn't look at him. Her face crimson with embarrassment, she turned and fled.

It was all Draper could do to keep from calling her back. His self-control was slipping. He crossed his arms before his chest and stared into the fire, willing her from his thoughts.

But to forget the feel of her body pressed tightly to his, her lightning-swift response, the wondrous smell of roses that clung to her soft white skin, was a virtual impossibility. And in that moment, as he listened to the sounds of her tearful retreat, he was horribly aware of just how precariously close he had come to disaster.

Chapter 6

The cadence of the drums was slow and steady, a relentless pulsing beat that filled the darkness behind Draper's closed lids, bringing with it a certain sense of trepidation, anger, an inescapable mounting dread.

The court-martial proceedings.

He'd forgotten them somehow—he must get up and face them squarely—no time to lie here feeling ill.

Lying prone and stiff from sleep, he turned to rise, and fell off the divan onto the cold, hard drawing room floor.

He'd been mistaken. There were no drums, except inside his head. And he was still in England.

For a long moment Draper lay on the carpeted floor with his eyes shut, clutching his skull and wondering what had possessed him to try and drown himself in Martha's good Scotch whiskey.

When he opened his eyes, he found the answer to his question lying inches from his nose. The likeness of Quintana Wade smiled at him from the gleaming surface of the powder horn, her lips curving impishly.

She'd been so very warm last night, so accessible, so willing. So unlike the thorny young Englishwoman with whom he was accustomed to matching wits.

The change had been so abrupt . . . and he'd been captivated.

With a groan, Draper came to his knees and sat patiently waiting for the furor inside his skull to die down.

He walked to the window and stared glumly out at the teeming street. Then he paced to the divan and back again. He was filled with a sudden restlessness. Boredom and inactivity were taking their toll upon him. He had to move, and soon. He had to get away from this house, away from the strangling confines of London.

Once they reached the coast it would be easier to avoid Quintana and her charms, and thus avoid temptation, he half-convinced himself.

The long days with nothing to do, the longer nights in her company, would not press so unbearably down upon him as they seemed to do now . . . and she would be easier to control, out of her natural element.

It counted as nothing that two days remained until their scheduled departure. He'd find Absolute and have him hire a carriage immediately. He was taking her out of here, out of this house and away from London, within the hour. They could wait out the two days until the ship sailed in a nearby inn.

With purposeful strides Draper walked to

the drawing room doors and flung them open, stepping into the hall.

Bridgett was there, dressed in a dark woolen cloak with a deep cowled hood. "A word with you, Cap'n, sir," she said, an anxious expression on her pert face.

Intent upon finding Absolute, Draper walked past her, but she tugged at his sleeve to bring him up short. "What is it?" he asked impatiently.

She caught her bottom lip between her teeth, looking somewhat nervous. "It's me mum. A lad came by with a message this mornin'. She's taken to childbed, and I was wonderin' if you'd mind if I just went on home? There's little ones to look out for, so I'm needed."

Draper saw her wring her hands and sighed. "I won't detain you if you're needed. Have you informed your mistress yet?"

She shook her head, then reached up to adjust the cloak's hood when it fell forward. "I thought it best to ask you first if it was all right."

"Go on then," he said, and chucked her chin. She smiled at him timidly, then headed for the stairs. "Bridgett?"

"Aye, Cap'n?"

"Have you seen Corporal Farquar?"

She bobbed her head and the cowl fell forward over her face. "Aye, sir. He's in the kitchen havin' a cup of tea with Cook."

When Quintana heard the light, quick step of the chambermaid on the stair, she opened the door, took her hand, and pulled her into the bedchamber. "Did he see you?" she asked.

The girl shrugged off the woolen cloak and handed it to Quintana. "I sought him out, just like you said. He was on his way to the kitchen to speak with Mr. Farquar."

"Pray God it's a lengthy discourse! If he stays in the kitchen, I can slip out unnoticed." She draped the cloak about her shoulders, tying the strings in front.

Clucking anxiously while she worked, Tilly tucked Quintana's golden curls beneath the cowl. "Now, remember, miss! Go direct to Seamus Gotfried. He's a God-fearing man who'll give you shelter while you await the authorities."

Looking on, a worried Bridgett wrung her hands in earnest. "Oh," she moaned, "I wisht I hadn't done this! It isn't right to betray him when he's been naught but kind!"

Tilly rounded on the girl, who cowered back. "Hist, girl! Where does your loyalty lie? With Miss Quintana, who's buttered your bread all these years, or with a handsome rogue, who for a ruddy farthing would steal your heart and leave you cryin' on your pillow?"

Tilly's sharp reprimand silenced Bridgett and made Quintana wince. She and the girl might be separated by a wide chasm of class distinction, education, and refinement, but they shared a common bond in their weakness for the rakish frontiersman.

Last night Draper Boone had uncovered a side of her she hadn't been aware existed, a woman who failed to think beyond the moment, beyond the next sultry kiss. A woman who had reveled in the embrace of a man whom by rights she should scorn.

To remain cool and aloof in his presence was impossible. She could no more resist the attraction she felt for him than she could fathom its origins.

She only knew that slowly, inexorably, she was being drawn into his world, a world that both terrified and repelled her . . . and because of it, she was being drawn to her own destruction.

What was occurring between her and the frontier captain was all too familiar to Quintana. For it had happened once before a long time ago, when the luckless Rowena had fallen in love with the handsome young rakehell Winston Halcourt Wade.

Once drawn, the parallels between her infatuation with Draper and Rowena's with Winston seemed too blatant to be ignored. She had indeed cried into her pillow late last night, just as Tilly had said. But when she awakened this morning it was with a new resolve, for she possessed something her mother had never had in abundance: the strength to carry on with life and do what must be done, no matter how objectionable the task might be, no matter how frightening . . . no matter how the image of Draper on his way to Tyburn Hill haunted her thoughts . . .

The choice was hard. It was his survival or hers, for if she remained in his company she feared she would be lost.

"Take care to keep the hood down," Tilly said. "If he gets the smallest glimpse of your face—"

The maid broke off, but there was no need for her to finish. Quintana, more than anyone, knew how much she stood to lose. With a whispered word of thanks she hugged Tilly and Bridgett in turn, then, holding her breath, opened the door.

From deep within the manse came the murmur of voices. As quickly as she dared, Quintana descended the stairs, pausing for the barest instant to glance down the long dim hallway. The drawing room doors were slightly ajar, but there was no one in sight.

She took a deep steadying breath, hoping to slow the racing of her heart, then spun and dashed to the door.

"Bridgett! I'm glad I caught you!"

At the sound of his voice, Quintana froze, and her racing heart plummeted to the tops of her soft kid slippers peeping from beneath her voluminous skirts. She shot a desperate glance at the door and bit her lip.

Confound him anyway!

The door was close, but Quintana knew there was precious little hope of reaching it before he caught her. His legs were long, his indolence a sham. He doubtless spent his days dashing through the wilderness forests, running from dusky-skinned savages seeking his scalp.

What chance did she stand of eluding him, burdened as she was by her cumbersome layers of petticoats, skirts, and woolen cloak?

Listening to the ring of his boot heels on the shining floor come closer, Quintana gritted her teeth and did silent battle with her frustration. There was no help for it. She would simply have to try and brazen it out, hoping the hood shielded her face.

Draper came to a halt beside her. "I was hoping you hadn't gone home yet. I have something for you before you go."

Pray God it was not a kiss in parting!

He was infuriatingly free with his kisses, she thought, watching warily as Draper reached into his shirt and produced a coin that he pressed into her palm.

His touch was her undoing. The heat of his skin as it pressed against hers, well-remembered yet unexpected, sent a strong tremor through Quintana. Instinctively she pulled away, and the coin fell from fingers suddenly nerveless, landing very near her slippered feet.

Draper bent to retrieve it. "Good luck to you, lass," he said, returning the coin to her. "And to your ma as well. I hope the babe's a strapping big lad."

Not daring to risk a reply, Quintana gave a quick bob of her cowled head and turned away.

He followed her to the door and stood leaning against the jamb as she hurried down the steps and up the walk to the wrought-iron gate. Each step was a step closer to the success of her plan, yet freedom seemed very far away. With each shallow breath she took, each swift jerking beat of her heart, she anticipated hearing the sound of his running footfalls behind her, his angry shout that would signal she'd been caught.

Curiously, it did not come. She reached the gate, and after a second's nervous fumbling with the latch, pushed her way through into the street and to safety.

When at last Quintana risked a hasty glance backward at the house along the Strand, she saw the front door was closed . . . and Draper Boone had gone.

A quarter of an hour later, Quintana hurried up the walkway of Seamus Gotfried's half-timbered house and noisily plied the brass wolf's head knocker that graced the front entrance.

No answer.

She rapped again, feverishly.

A second floor casement window slid open at the north corner of the structure and Seamus Gotfried thrust out his graying head. "For God's sake, will you cease that infernal racket! The servants have the day off, and there is no one downstairs to hear you!"

"Mr. Gotfried," Quintana called up to him, "it is I, Quintana Wade. Rowena Chamberlain Wade's daughter. Please, sir, will you come down and let me in? I must speak with you immediately about a matter of dire importance!"

Gotfried frowned fuzzily down at her. "Rowena's gal? Haven't seen you since you was this big." He made a motion with his hands, and then the window slid down, bumping his head and wringing a curse of annoyance from him.

"Yes, sir. Please, will you speak with me now? I'm in terrible trouble, and I desperately need your help and advice."

"What manner of trouble?" Gotfried asked vaguely. "Oh, never mind. Wait there. I'll come in a moment." He disappeared inside, and the window slid closed.

A few moments later, Quintana was seated on the edge of a garish red and gold brocade divan in the front salon of the half-timbered Tudor house.

Gotfried, seated comfortably near the blazing hearth, cleared his throat. "Now then. What sort of trouble brings you out on such a day as this?"

Quintana related the recent events that had caused so much upheaval in her household, beginning with Draper's unexpected arrival, and ending with her recent escape. She touched upon the important fact only—her desire to rid the premises of his unwelcome presence—and left out the intimate details of their brief time together.

When she'd finished, Gotfried sat back with a low whistle. "A colonial, you say? Your father's man? Shocking! Though knowing your father as I do, I can't say I'm surprised that he might try something like this. He always was a hand at getting what he wanted."

Quintana took a deep breath and fought to maintain her dwindling patience.

She was so close to victory. If only she could convince Seamus Gotfried, Draper would soon be out of her house, out of her life . . . and her days would once again take on some semblance of normal life.

"Can I prevail upon your friendship with my mother, sir?" she asked at last. "Will you help me get rid of this wretched colonial?"

Seamus ran a stubby forefinger across his receding chin. "Well, I've kept in close contact with my old regiment, and as a retired major I can doubtless pull a few strings." He shook his head and uttered a low humorless laugh. "Can't say I envy the poor bugger, though. I was in Falmouth a few years back when the *Adamant* docked and that fellow Allen was brought ashore. Not a pretty picture, I can tell you."

Quintana frowned. She had nearly forgotten about Ethan Allen's arrival in England several years before. Allen, rebel leader and frontiersman, had been captured in Canada and brought in irons to England, then paraded through the streets like an animal before being imprisoned.

At the time, the faceless Allen's misfortune had meant little to Quintana, yet confronted now with the thought of Draper sharing a similar fate, she quelled inwardly, and for the first time since leaving the mansion, she wondered if perhaps she had acted too hastily.

"No need to fret, m'dear," Gotfried was saying. "We'll apprehend the rascal and have him safely tucked away in Newgate in time for tea." Chuckling, he got to his feet. "I'll just pen a note to Sergeant Trevelyn of His Majesty's Twenty-first Regiment of Foot, and then we'll be on our way. Trev can meet us at your residence. He owes me a favor."

Gotfried went out, all pomp and assurance, leaving Quintana alone with her rising confusion and her doubts.

She had managed to convince Seamus Gotfried to help her, to use his friends and influence to rid her home of the frontier usurper. She'd matched wits with the wily Draper Boone, and she'd won.

She waited for the sense of wild elation that should have come with the knowledge of certain victory over a worthy opponent, waited for the joy, the satisfaction she knew were rightly hers to claim, yet all Quintana felt was a deepening sense of dissatisfaction, of unease, and, oddly, of remorse.

She rose slowly from her seat on the divan and made her way to the window. Outside, a fine snow was falling, dusting the grounds with powdery white, swirling around the horse's hooves and the wheels of a passing carriage.

Quintana closed her eyes and, sighing, leaned her brow against the cool glass of the windowpane.

In the house on the Strand, her father's emissary was biding his time in relative comfort, secure in the knowledge that there were only two days remaining until their scheduled departure and completely unaware that he'd just been betrayed by the very woman he'd sworn to protect.

Seamus Gotfried was true to his word, for when his black lacquered coach rattled to a stop before the Wade manse, the scarlet-coated soldiers of the Twenty-first were already there and milling over the grounds.

A dozen sleek horses stood at the gate, cared for by a fresh-faced private of Quintana's years. The young man smiled a greeting to Gotfried and Quintana and rushed forward to open the door of the coach.

"Private Pitts," Gotfried said in an amused voice. "Good afternoon, sir! How goes the hunt?"

"Well enough, I think," Pitts replied. "They haven't found the foxy fellow yet, but Sergeant Trevelyn has every confidence that we'll run our quarry to ground very soon."

Gotfried chortled as he stepped from the coach to the street. "Indeed, indeed!" he said. "I'll wager you haven't had such good sport in years."

Quintana's quicksilver glance slid from one man to the other. She had paused in the open door of the conveyance, but as her escort and his young companion came forward together to help her down, she shrugged them off and stepped to the street unaided. "There is something you gentlemen seemed to have forgotten."

Both men stared at her quizzically. Gotfried spoke. "Indeed? And what might that be, m'dear?"

"The 'quarry' you seek to run to ground," Quintana said stiffly, "is a man, not an animal, and as long as you are on my property, you will treat him as such. I want him removed from the premises; I do not want him broken or beaten or harmed unnecessarily. Is that quite understood?"

Her query was met with disbelieving silence. Private Pitts stared at her as if she'd taken leave of her senses.

Gotfried's reaction was no less irritating. Clucking his tongue, he took her elbow in a firm but gentle grasp and guided her up the walkway to the door. "I'll see you settled comfortably, m'dear, and have Miss Bascombe bring you a nice soothing cup of tea. Too much excitement is no good for a woman, and I fear you're overwrought. Then once you're settled, you may instruct the servants to pack your clothes and necessities in a trunk, and you and Miss Bascombe shall stay the night in the guest house at Gotfried Manor. Not that I don't have faith in Trev and his men, but there's no sense in taking chances."

Quintana started to retort, then thought better of it. Perhaps after all Gotfried was right, and the events of the past few days had simply taken their toll on her. What other explanation could there possibly be for this sudden wellspring of concern for a man whom she detested?

There seemed no ready answer, and no time to ponder the true cause of her conflicting feelings toward the Virginian, for when Quintana and Gotfried stepped over the threshold, they entered into a scene of utter chaos.

The house was swarming with soldiers, upstairs and down. Several scarlet-coated figures could be glimpsed from the open drawing room doors. Two were going up the steps as one was coming down. A private stood sentinel just inside the door, another down the hall.

"Ah, Gotfried, there you are!" The officer who spoke appeared to be in his early to middle thirties and was ruggedly attractive, with sandy hair and blue eyes. He came forward quickly.

"This is Sergeant Arthur Trevelyn," Gotfried said to Quintana. "Trev, Miss Quintana Wade, the daughter of an old and dear friend."

"Ah yes, the *demoiselle* in distress," Trevelyn murmured over Quintana's hand. There was something in Trevelyn's smile that she didn't like. The unnatural thinness of his lips seemed to suggest a cruel bent, a lack of all but the most superficial warmth.

Quintana ignored his remark, wanting this unpleasant business concluded as swiftly as possible. "Have you found him, Sergeant?"

Trevelyn's blue eyes turned chill. "Not yet, but we will. My men will ferret him out, rest assured, dear lady."

One of the infantrymen brushed past with a respectful nod and mounted the stair. The bright steel of the bayonet affixed to his Brown Bess musket gleamed lethally in the half-light.

A cold dread closed slowly around Quintana. She couldn't seem to tear her gaze away from the deadly length of steel. "Is that truly necessary?" she asked, inclining her head in the direction of the weapon.

"The man we're hunting is a traitor, and he shall be treated as one."

"But surely there is no need for such drastic measures!" Quintana said.

"My men and I are due to ship out a week from today," Trevelyn said crisply. "We're headed to Philadelphia, and from there, God alone knows where. Should the worst happen and this interloper of yours bring about his own untimely demise, then I for one shall not be sorry. He'll simply be one less rebel we shall have to face once we reach America."

"Sergeant, sir," a soldier called from the drawing room doorway. "A word with you at your convenience."

"Your servant, Mistress Wade," Trevelyn said. He bowed to Quintana, turned smartly on his heel, and crossed to the drawing room, where he stood conferring with his man.

Quintana watched him go. His hardness had shocked her. Draper Boone was indeed a colonial rebel, and she wanted him out of her home, out of her life.

But she did not want his death.

She was still standing in the hallway, staring after Trevelyn, when Tilly came down the stairs, followed closely by Bridgett. Tilly looked concerned, Bridgett fearful.

"Are you all right, miss?" Tilly asked.

"Yes, Tilly. I'm fine," Quintana said. But it was far from true. She was worried. How would she live with herself if she brought about Draper's demise, however inadvertently? She shot a wary look at Trevelyn, who was still deep in conversation, then, confident that she would not be overheard, she turned to Tilly. "Where is he?"

"Upon me sainted mum's grave," Tilly whispered. "I haven't seen hide nor hair of either of them since the soldiers first pulled up outside. It's like they up and vanished."

Quintana turned her silver glance on Bridgett, who shook her head. "I don't know where the cap'n's gone to, miss! I swear I don't."

"If he has any sense of self-preservation he'll have abandoned his plans and fled London." Quintana sighed, and, taking Tilly's hand and Bridgett's in her own, she gave them a reassuring squeeze. "At least we can hope that he is. No matter how I detest him, and everything he represents, I would not want his death upon my conscience."

The men who had gone upstairs a few moments ago now returned. "All clear upstairs, Sergeant!"

"What about the cellars?" Trevelyn demanded. "Has anyone searched the cellars?"

Those loitering about exchanged blank looks. Trevelyn lost his temper. "What in Hades are you waiting for? The bloody beggar has to be here somewhere, and by God, we aren't leaving until we find him!"

Quintana drew a deep steadying breath and released it by degrees. She could feel her own anger and frustration building, though she wasn't at all sure with whom she was more put out, Draper Boone for disappearing so precipitously, Sergeant Trevelyn for his wicked disposition and unmitigated arrogance, or herself for thinking that she could contain so volatile a situation.

Laughter drifted from the drawing room, punctuated by a small crash as one of Trevelyn's men backed into the low table in the hallway, knocking over a pale green porcelain vase.

Quintana gritted her teeth. "This is no longer my home," she muttered to no one in particular, "it's Bedlam." Turning abruptly, she stalked along the hallway toward the back of the house.

"Miss?" Tilly called after her. "Where are you going?"

"To the garden," Quintana replied. "I need quiet. I need to think, and I cannot manage it amid all this blasted confusion!"

The angry glitter in her pale gray eyes allowed Quintana to pass through the hall unmolested. She entered the kitchen and saw Martha, the cook, peeling potatoes for dinner. "Martha," Quintana said. "Have you seen anyone pass this way?"

Martha replied without looking up from her task. "One or two of them redcoats, but they left almost as quick as they came. I s'pose it's this here toad sticker." She brandished her knife. "D'ya want me to throw a few more spuds in the kettle fer the sergeant and his men?"

"That won't be necessary, Martha," Quintana said. "As soon as the house is secured, they'll be on their way once again."

Seeming satisfied, Martha returned to her work. She paid little heed to her mistress, who pushed through the back door into the cold.

For a moment, just a moment, Quintana leaned back against the door and closed her eyes, savoring the cold caress of the softly falling snow upon her heated face.

The crisp winter air felt refreshing in comparison to the stifling atmosphere of the house. Quintana breathed deeply, filling her lungs, allowing the relative quiet of the garden, the unearthly stillness of the early winter eve to seep into her careworn soul.

The past days had been one long ordeal, but it was over now. The frontiersman had fled, and the moment he'd taken to his heels her private travail had ended.

Relief would come in a moment . . . contentment . . . and while she was awaiting the gladness of her triumph, there was the beauty of the winter garden to enjoy.

Stepping from the shelter of the house, Quintana moved along the garden path. In summer the garden was lush and green, heady with the sweet mingled fragrance of Rowena's pale pink roses, lavender, and mint . . .

But the verdant green of summer seemed a lifetime away. The garden today was still and lifeless, sleeping, secure and lovely beneath a thickening blanket of pristine white. Across that new-fallen snow, the indigo shadows slowly crept, silent precursors of the coming evening.

Soon it would be dark. She really should be getting back.

Turning to the house, Quintana saw a soldier standing on the path, facing half away, a tall, well-built man in scarlet coat and snowy breeches, powdered peruke, and tricorn hat set rakishly upon his head. The shoulders of the scarlet coat were liberally dusted with snow; it was obvious that he'd conducted a thorough search of the garden, Quintana thought, and the poor man must be chilled to the bone.

As if to confirm her suspicions, a shudder passed through his long-boned frame. Quintana quickened her steps. "You, there! Private! There really is no need for you to remain out in the weather. Go inside and warm yourself. The man you've been searching for so valiantly is gone."

He stiffened slightly at her words, but he didn't reply, didn't turn. Quintana frowned, and as she came abreast of the man, stole a glance at that shadowed familiar face. Draper . . .

Realization dawned upon Quintana, a blazing sun of recognition that crushed her hopes, revived her fears. "Dear God," she groaned aloud, "it's you."

Quintana tried to back away, but the fugitive was faster. His arm snaked out, and steely fingers closed around her wrist. "Not so bloody fast, m'lady. You've set your British hounds on me, and you're going to help me elude them, whether you like it or not. I didn't travel all this way for a length of friggin' hemp."

His iron grasp cut into Quintana's tender flesh. She winced and tried to pull away. "Why didn't you flee while you had the chance?"

"My orders, m'lady. They won't have been carried out until I deliver you to Fort Pitt."

"But Sergeant Trevelyn and his men are in the house and on the grounds—"

"Aye," he growled, "and seething for my head. I was standing on the topmost cellar stair, and I heard his ruddy tirade. I also heard him order his men to search the cellar. That's how I came by the uniform." He grimaced at the scarlet coat and white breeches, a shudder of revulsion running through his lean hard frame. "Who'd have ever imagined that *I'd* be wearin' British red?"

"You didn't kill those men?" Quintana asked.

"There was no need," Draper replied. "The first one took his lumps and is probably still napping. His companion was most eager to cooperate after that. He's keeping Nigel company."

Some of the tension drained out of Quintana. She was disappointed at falling back into his hands, yet a small secret part of her was also glad . . . glad that he was alive and unhurt,

glad to see the strong clean lines of his face
in profile, the dark amber gleam of his eyes.

"Come, m'lady," Draper said, urging her
along the path. "Absolute is waiting, and
we've no time to lose."

"Why don't you just go?" Quintana asked
quickly. "You can slip away unnoticed if you
leave immediately, before the men you tricked
are discovered. I'll help you. I can distract the
sergeant, keep him here a bit longer so that
you can have a good head start—"

Draper's gaze slid to hers. His whiskey-
colored eyes were cold and fathomless. "I listened to your siren's song last night, and look
where it's got me." He seated the pistols he
wore more securely into his belt, and pulled the
tricorn low to shade his face. "You've betrayed
me once, and I like my neck too well to give
you another chance."

When they reached the front lawn, Draper slowed his pace. Twenty feet lay between
them and Gotfried's coach . . . fifteen . . . ten.

From the tail of her eye, Quintana saw the
front door open and Trevelyn emerge. Draper must have seen him too, for she felt him
tense, felt his grasp tighten so that his fingers
bit into her wrist. Quintana cast an anxious
glance back over her shoulder.

Trevelyn came down the steps at a bound
and started after them, his long strides carrying him quickly across the snowy lawn. "Hold
up there, Private!" he called to Draper.

"Captain, please!" Quintana hissed. "You
cannot hope to get away with this!"

They reached Seamus Gotfried's black lacquered conveyance just as Sergeant Trevelyn came through the gate. Draper jerked open the coach door, seized Quintana by her trim waist, and thrust her inside.

Trevelyn strode boldly up to Draper. "Damnit, Private, I ordered you to halt!"

Draper said nothing by way of reply, which seemed to enrage the sergeant. Trevelyn grabbed the frontiersman's right arm, bringing him around to face him.

"Pitts, what the hell is wrong with y—" Trevelyn's mouth dropped open as he gazed up into that taut shadowed visage, those smoldering topaz eyes. "You aren't Pitts!" he said.

"No," Draper drawled, "I'm not." Before the sergeant could react, Draper's left fist arced up with lightning speed and smashed into his chin. The vicious blow sent Trevelyn sprawling unconscious in the snow.

A shout went up from the dooryard of the manse. At the same instant, the coachman hurled a broad Scots oath at the soldiery and cracked his whip above the horses' heads.

Draper leaped into the conveyance as the coach lurched forward, settling himself onto the seat opposite Quintana. "You might untie her now," he suggested, inclining his head to indicate the figure bundled into the corner of the forward seat.

With a closer look, Quintana saw that it was Tilly, bound at the wrists with a strip of cloth, a rag passing between her jaws and tied behind her head to still her tongue.

"What manner of animal are you?" Quintana demanded hotly. She hurried to remove the linen gag from Tilly's mouth.

Draper's gaze was cool. "A cornered one, m'lady."

"There was no need to bind her!" Quintana freed the knot and drew the rag away from Tilly's mouth.

"I saw the need," Draper snapped. "I couldn't take the chance that she might alert your friend back there, and though I wished simply to leave her, Absolute had some fool notion that you might value her presence during the coming months."

"He is not my friend," Quintana said softly. "And you might have left us both."

A muscle worked violently in Draper's tawny cheek. "It's over now," he said harshly. "The struggle is ended, Quintana, and you have lost. Get used to it."

"I cannot," Quintana whispered into the gathering purple dusk, but even as she spoke the words, her shoulders sagged, and she sank back against the padded velvet seat.

Her sense of defeat was almost overwhelming, and she had the sickening feeling that London and all things familiar were already a part of her past, and that Draper Catworth Boone, who lounged on the seat opposite her and Tilly, his black hair framing a face that was brooding and tense, was very much the harbinger of things to come . . .

Chapter 7

Williamsburg, Virginia
May 5, 1778

Quintana stood before the cheval glass at the dressmaker's shop, garbed in a drab gray linsey-woolsey gown, a look of horror stamped upon her features. "You can't mean to make me wear this hideous rag! It gaps at my bosom and gaps at the waist, and it scratches! Why, I'll be chafed raw before we reach the outskirts of town!"

Draper looked her up and down, a slight smile on his sensuous mouth. "Your bosom looks fine to me," he said.

Quintana felt her cheeks grow hot. During the ten weeks at sea they had seen very little of each other. Draper had kept to his cabin during the day and had spent his evenings in the company of the ship's officers, gaming and drinking, while Quintana strolled on deck when weather permitted or sat with Tilly in their cubicle of a cabin when it did not.

There had been nights aboard ship when she'd lain on her bunk, thinking of Draper, wishing for his company.

Two days before, they had docked at Yorktown, and with each moment she had spent in the frontiersman's company, it had become increasingly clear that nothing had changed between them. He was still just as obstinate and opinionated as ever, callous, arrogant, fractious and rude . . . and she was still attracted to him.

It was a knowledge that grated relentlessly on Quintana's pride, since he seemed able to dismiss her from his thoughts so handily. The entire situation was intolerable, and Quintana did not have a clue as to how she might resolve it.

"Do you care nothing at all for my comfort?" she demanded.

"It's your comfort I'm thinking of."

"Liar. Had you the least consideration for my feelings, you would not have kidnapped me. And I would still be in England."

Draper paid the seamstress, who looked on with bright-eyed interest. "I'll send someone by later for it," he said. Taking up his rifle, he went to stand before Quintana. "You can nurse that grudge you've been carrying all the way to the three rivers, or you can ease your plight by taking my advice. I'm only trying to help you through a difficult time—"

"You're trying to humiliate me by forcing me to wear this . . . this . . . peasant's garb!" she said. "And I will not stand for it!"

He turned and sauntered out to the street, as if he hadn't heard a single word she'd said, while Quintana seethed.

"Swaggering, pompous beast of a man." She huffed and stomped her foot, then underscored her contempt for him by putting out her tongue. It was a childish gesture, but it gave her a tiny bit of satisfaction all the same.

The seamstress sent her a disapproving look, but Quintana deftly ignored her. After all, the woman was only a seamstress, and Quintana didn't care a fig for what she thought.

A few moments later Quintana emerged from the shop. Draper pushed away from the building where he'd been leaning and came to stand beside her. "Don't think you have won, Captain. I do not surrender so easily."

"Suit yourself, m'lady. But don't bitch to me when your stubbornness comes back to haunt you. Consider yourself forewarned." Without another word he settled the rifle in the crook of his arm and started across the street.

Quintana watched him with narrowed eyes as she followed along behind. He'd undergone a subtle change since taking ship from England. The wariness was gone now, and there was an ease about his movement, his speech, even the way he looked at her, that had been missing before. Until this moment she'd wondered at the change in him, but now she felt she understood.

He was in his element . . . and she was sadly out of hers.

She picked her way precariously across the muddy street, around the steaming clods of horse dung. Williamsburg was a world away from London.

It was much smaller than she had imagined, and hardly appeared at first glance the hotbed of sedition she'd always heard it to be.

Shading her eyes against the bright glare of spring sunlight, she gazed at her surroundings.

The quaint houses with their steeply gabled roofs and neat kitchen gardens, the shops and ordinaries that vied for space along the wide tree-lined Duke of Gloucester Street, the steady pulse of daily life that was everywhere, lent it an atmosphere that hardly differed from that of any market town in England.

Quintana found it surprisingly pleasant, and difficult indeed to believe that such notorious revolutionaries as General Washington and Patrick Henry had sown the seeds of rebellion in the grand brick capitol down the way.

What was it about this land that nourished the radical spirit? she wondered. But even as she posed the question, she knew she could no more hope to understand this strange land than she could hope to comprehend the enigmatic frontiersman who had brought her here against her will.

Fate had firmly pitted them against each other, a rebel and a loyal subject to His Majesty, King George. And Quintana truly doubted *that* much was destined to change.

When they entered the Raleigh Tavern, Tilly was waiting. She nodded and smiled at Draper before turning her attention to Quintana. "A word with you, miss, if you don't mind."

"I'll find a table," Draper said. "You may join me when you're through."

It was an order, not a request. Quintana felt herself bristle. "I do believe he lies awake at night trying to think up ways to infuriate me."

"I don't believe that's true at all, miss. The captain has personal difficulties awaiting him when we arrive at the fort. I think he's worried about the future, and so does Mr. Farquar."

Pursing her lips, Quintana said nothing. She wasn't ready to sympathize with his "difficulties," and perhaps she never would be. "What did you want to speak to me about, Tilly?"

"Oh, well. I was wonderin' if you'd be needin' me this evening? Mr. Farquar offered to show me the town, and I thought it might be nice to look around."

Quintana frowned. She was not overly fond of Corporal Absolute Farquar. In fact, she thought him a Scottish rogue. But Tilly seemed set upon going, and since the voyage had been particularly taxing for her, Quintana thought that her loyal maid deserved a reward for her unflinching selflessness. "I can't imagine there is anything I will be needing," said Quintana, somewhat grudgingly. "Go on and enjoy yourself. But tell Corporal Farquar to be on his best behavior, or he'll answer to me."

"Bless you, miss!" Tilly said, hurrying off to join Absolute, who loitered by the door.

Quintana reluctantly joined Draper at the table by the window. "I'm not sure I like the idea of them spending time together," she mused aloud.

Draper had been contemplating the dregs of his whiskey, but now he looked sharply up. "And why is that, m'lady?"

She sent him a cool silvery glance. "Tilly may not be of gentle birth, Captain, but she should set her sights higher than Corporal Farquar."

"Absolute's a good man," Draper replied. "Tilly seems to recognize it, and I admire her ability to look beyond a man's outward appearance to the heart that lies within. You would do well to try to emulate her."

Upon hearing the word *heart*, Quintana narrowed her eyes. "Precisely what are you implying, Captain? Has Corporal Farquar behaved inappropriately toward Tilly? For if he has—"

Draper sighed and tossed back his whiskey. "I'm not 'implying' anything. I'm merely saying that while you were sulking in your cabin aboard ship, they were keeping company. They seem to enjoy each other, and I'm telling you to leave them be."

"Well, I never!"

"She's been there all your life to look after you. Don't you think she deserves some happiness?"

"With him?" The very words were distasteful.

"Aye. And why the devil not, if that's what she wants?"

Quintana glared. "I shouldn't wonder that you would encourage your partner in crime to despoil my maid."

"Despoil? Tilly Bascombe?" He lowered his glass and laughed outright. "Somehow I doubt that at her age she's innocent!"

"You are base and vile, sir," Quintana said stiffly. "And if I am to sit here and sup with you, then kindly abandon this topic for something more suitable."

"You didn't think me base and vile when you all but gave yourself to me that last night in London," Draper said.

Quintana blushed to the roots of her powdered hair. "A temporary lapse," she insisted. "And characteristically rude of you to remind me of it."

The grinning devil leaned back in his chair and regarded her with lazy interest. "What say we put it to the test, Quintana? Another kiss, and we'll see if you're all bluff and bluster. Hell, I'd even be willing to make it more interesting by wagering a month's pay against your chemise that you can't remain unaffected."

Quintana was trembling as she answered him, but whether from simple outrage or the thought of his kisses, she could not tell. "I was raised according to a strict moral standard, Captain. And for you to even suggest that I could—that I would—with any man other than my husband is a mean attempt to bring me down to your own level!"

Draper raised his glass in mock salute, and his golden eyes glinted above the rim. "To m'lady, and her priggish young lieutenant! May you live long, live well, and bear him many priggish sons!"

Quintana sat with her spine ramrod straight, glaring at him. "You are drunk," she said flatly.

The serving wench came to the table, carrying a steaming plate of stew in each hand, which she set before them. Draper caught her eye, and with a broad flirtatious wink, asked her to bring more whiskey. She dimpled at him prettily and flounced away. "A likely lass," he murmured. From the corner of his wandering eye he saw Quintana bristle, and smiled to himself.

She could pretend all she liked that she was invulnerable to the desires of the flesh, he thought. That she was not possessed of a sexual self, that she was above it all . . . unreachable, cold, aloof. But she was deceiving herself, for he knew that beneath her cool facade she burned every bit as brightly as he.

He'd felt the fires banked deep within her secret self that night in London when he'd held her tightly against him and kissed away the last remaining shred of her resistance . . . and the notion continued to lurk in the back of his mind that, brought together, they would kindle a white-hot blaze of seething, writhing passion . . .

The impulse to seduce her into willingness was strong—difficult for Draper to ignore. It had kept him from enjoying her company on the long ocean voyage, for only by avoiding the object of his ungovernable desire could he avoid temptation.

The serving wench returned with Draper's whiskey and plunked it down before him. "If there's anythin' else you're wantin' sir, just let me know," she said coyly. "I'm Betsy."

Draper dropped a coin in the girl's low-cut bodice, chucked her chin, and sent her on her smiling way.

Quintana, meanwhile, turned her attention to her food. Gingerly she took a bite. Then another. "This is passing good," she said after a time. "What is it?"

"Brunswick stew," Draper replied. "It's made with squirrel, and a favorite around here."

Her spoon was poised in midair. She stared at him, aghast. "Squirrel?"

Draper gave a nod. "Aye. Furry little bastards with big bushy tails. They dwell in the treetops and generally make nuisances of themselves, except when they're placed in the stew pot."

Quintana carefully lowered the spoon to her plate and looked a little green beneath her powder and paint. She closed her great gray eyes and sipped her golden wine, the same tawny shade as her curling tresses, gleaming from underneath the dusting of powder.

Draper continued to watch her. "Was it something I said?"

"You might have told me there was squirrel in the stew," she said in a small strangled voice.

"I saw no need to mention it, since it's of no consequence."

Quintana gritted her teeth. Although she had no proof, she was certain he had done this on purpose, knowing how she would react. The past two days, no! the past two and a half months, had been one long struggle for supremacy . . . and she had the disconcerting notion that the brash frontiersman was winning their ongoing battle of wills.

When at last she replied, it was apparent in her voice that she had reached the end of her patience. "We too have squirrels in England, Captain," she said tightly. "In the parks and in the country. I've seen them many times, but never once in all my life did I consider eating one!"

"You can't afford to be so choosy," Draper said. "And there will be a hellish lot of things you'll do in the coming weeks you never considered doing in bloody England. Scarfing down a squirrel or two will likely be among the least objectionable."

Her hiss of disgust didn't faze him. "You've been spoiled," he went on doggedly. "By your mother, and by Tilly. Rowena Wade did you a very great injustice by dragging you back to England at such a tender age. And I've come to believe that you would have been better off to have remained in your father's care. At least you would have lived your life, instead of being cloistered away in an environment that proved every bit as sterile as a nunnery."

Quintana shot from her chair and would have fled the table but for the steely fingers that closed around her wrist and brought her forcefully back. "Let go of me this instant!"

Draper's dark face was hard, impassive. "Sit down and finish your dinner, Quintana."

"If you think for one instant that I will sit docilely supping on stewed rodent while you insult my mother's memory—"

"I'm not insulting anyone," he insisted. "I'm merely stating some very hard truths."

"You may keep your damnable truths, sir!"

"This is our final night in civilization, and I won't have you going off to bed with nothing but anger in your belly!"

"What do you care?" Quintana demanded. "You only want to see me made miserable!" She sank her nails into the hand that held her and heard him curse. With one fluid motion he was out of his seat and towering over her, a menacing, hard-bitten backwoodsman with little love for all things English, and less sympathy for her plight.

With incredible ease, he caught her other wrist and held her still, pinned against his chest. "I do care, goddamn it. But I can't help you if you refuse to let me."

He was asking her to let go of her anger . . . the very thing that had sustained her all the many difficult miles from London.

He was asking too much; Quintana was consumed by anger. Indeed, it had begun the moment he had walked in the door at her London residence, and had been steadily mounting ever since. Through the two and a half long months at sea when his neglect had cut so deeply, through the ordeal of the past two days, the fittings for that wretched gown, the squirrel stew, through all of his many attempts to humble her, to drag her off her pedestal—her fury had been constant. She would not be bullied or coerced into letting go of her anger, and she kept her head high even when he pushed her down into her chair.

"It is not cooperation that you want from me, but complete capitulation! And I will tell you now, Captain Boone, that it is the one thing you shall never have from me!"

Draper snorted, splashing a generous amount of whiskey into his glass. "If you don't learn to bend, the land will break you." He jerked his raven head toward the door and his whiskey-colored eyes took on a harsh glitter. "Out there your pride will only bring you trouble, your stubbornness will bring contempt. Being a woman won't entitle you to any favors, Quintana, and one miscalculation will earn you the same grave whether you're English born and bred . . . or something less refined."

"My father appointed you to get me safely through the wilderness. Are you telling me you intend to shirk you duty?" she replied flippantly.

His grim smile didn't reach the chill depths of his eyes. "I'm telling you that things can go awry unexpectedly, and I may not always be there to save your precious English ass. Consider yourself forewarned . . . *m'lady*."

Chapter 8

Draper squinted at the sun showing just above the eastern horizon, then threw an impatient glance at the second floor bedchamber window. They'd been waiting half an hour and there was still no sign of Quintana.

"Looks like ye got yer work cut oot for ye," Absolute said, stating the obvious. "Unless I miss my guess, she's set to stall every step o' the way."

"Aye," Draper growled, his scowl growing blacker by the moment. "So it would seem."

"D'ye want me to go an' fetch her doon for ye?" the older man asked.

"She's my responsibility," Draper said. "And I'm the one who'll have the pleasure of bringing her to heel." He started toward the Raleigh, but was stopped in mid-stride when his recalcitrant charge at last appeared in the doorway of the Raleigh Tavern.

Draper looked her up and down, his mouth thinning to a grim line in his hard face.

She was painted and powdered and impeccably coiffed, done up in a riding habit of salmon-colored velvet with contrasting collar and cuffs—every inch the spoiled English beauty, from the rakish black tricorn and its jaunty salmon plume perched high upon her silvery curls to the self-satisfied smile that curved her rouged lips when she saw his reaction to her outfit.

"You're late, Quintana," Draper said. "Your blasted primping has held us up for half an hour."

"I am here, Captain," Quintana countered. "And it seems to me that your churlish mood is now responsible for our delay."

"That's not the gown I purchased for you."

"Indeed, it is not," Quintana said, spreading her full skirts with dainty black gloved hands. She was still piqued with him for his contemptibility at dinner the previous evening and bent upon having her revenge, no matter how paltry it happened to be. At the moment, this one small act of defiance was all she could afford. "This belonged to my mother, and it's one of my most prized possessions."

"Is there a reason you're wearin' this getup?" he asked. "Or are you defying me for the sheer thrill of it?"

With her slim nose up, Quintana gave him a look of defiance that had been rehearsed to perfection. "Neither," she answered imperiously. "I merely decided that if I'm to be forced into meeting my father, I shall do so on my terms. Get used to it, Captain. You cannot change me, no matter how hard you try. I want no part of your country or your quaint provincial ways. I'm English to my very bones, and I fully intend that I shall remain exactly that."

"A pretty speech, m'lady," Draper said. "But are you certain that's what you want?"

"I have never been more certain of anything in my life," Quintana replied stiffly.

She saw him set his jaw and he bowed mockingly. "As you will, m'lady."

"Come again?" Quintana said, instantly suspicious. "No insults? No arguments? No reprimands, threats, or warnings? Not the slightest attempt to bully me into wearing your peasant's gown and clumsy leather shoes?" She peered at him with narrowed gaze. "You worry me, Captain. Are you certain you're feeling quite well?"

Draper's answering smile held no humor. Despite the weight of the velvet gown, despite the warm promise of the rising sun, Quintana felt a chill creep up her spine.

"You've obviously gone to great pains to prepare for the trek north," he said. "And if this is truly what you want, I wouldn't dream of interfering." He turned his back on her, swinging into the saddle with ease. "Well, don't just stand there gaping, woman! We've wasted a good portion of the morning as it is. The gray's yours. She's a sweet-natured little thing, so be easy on her."

Something was not right, Quintana thought. He had acquiesced too easily. "Aren't you going to help me find my seat?" she called after him.

He gave her a dark meaningful look, turning the roan into the street. "At the moment it might be safer for you if your 'seat' is well beyond my reach. If you find you cannot mount of your own accord, Absolute will help you."

Quintana glanced around. "What about my trunks? How shall we transport them when we have but three horses?"

"We take only what we can carry on our backs," Draper said, "and not a damned thing more."

"But what about my gowns, my necessities!" Quintana cried.

His expression was as hard and unyielding as stone. "Tilly Bascombe packed all that you'll require under my direction. The rest will come up over the mountains by pack train in a week or two."

"A week or two! Are you mad? You can't expect me to wear the same gown for a week! It's barbaric, it's ... preposterous, it's mean and cruel and—"

"It's necessary," Draper put in flatly. "We're traveling as fast and light as possible, Quintana. The horses will have enough difficulty just carrying us into the mountains, and I'll be damned if I'll burden them with all of the folderol and foolishness you would drag along if I let you have your head! As for wearing the same gown for an entire week, that won't be necessary. I instructed Tilly to pack the linsey-woolsey. If you've any sense, you'll save that rag you're wearing for your arrival at the fort, and wear something more durable for travel."

She was set to argue, but Draper, impatient to be gone, was in no mood to lend a willing ear. He booted up the roan, cantered down Duke of Gloucester Street, and left Quintana in his dusty wake.

"Well, yer ruddy highness," Absolute said, presenting her with a feral grin. "What'll it be? D'ye need a leg up, or no?"

"I shall manage, thank you," Quintana said stiltedly. Unable to shed the feeling that the two men shared some secret jest at her expense, she led the gray mare to the mounting block and, minus a proper sidesaddle, settled herself as best she could astride the animal.

Draper set a relentless pace, and when Quintana questioned him he would only say that he intended to push the horses hardest where the country was flat.

They traveled thirty miles that first day, past sprawling manor houses flanked by tobacco fields where Negro servants labored, past swampland and long stretches of dense forest, and when at last they drew rein in the dooryard of a wayside inn late that afternoon, Quintana and Tilly were precariously close to exhaustion.

The ordinary itself was small and shabby, with sagging shutters and greased paper instead of glass windowpanes, but Quintana was too weary to care or complain.

She ate her dinner in silence, still feeling the jogging motion of the mare beneath her long after she tumbled into the big bed she shared with Tilly.

Quintana fell asleep almost instantly, but was awakened sometime later by the sound of voices nearby. *Someone had entered their room.* "Who's there?" she demanded, sitting bolt upright in bed.

"The innkeeper's wife, mistress." The woman raised the lantern she carried; light streamed across the bed.

Shielding her eyes with her hand, Quintana groaned aloud.

The day had been a particularly grueling one for both her and Tilly, and when Draper had told her to be ready before daybreak she knew that tomorrow would be no different.

She needed desperately to sleep, and her resentment of this woman's intrusion was clearly evident in her voice. "What on earth are you doing here?"

"Why, I'm showing this good woman up to bed, that's what! Scoot over deary, an' make room."

The innkeeper's wife turned the lantern slightly so that the light fell on a thin, rabbity woman with large lashless eyes and protruding front teeth. "This here's Mistress Hettie Muldoon, sister to the Reverend Ellis Muldoon, from Fairfax. Perhaps you've heard of 'im?"

Quintana was fast losing what little patience she possessed. "Surely you must have someplace else you can put her up."

The woman waggled her mobcapped head. "We only got four beds to let, besides the mister's an' mine. The other three's full up with gents."

"My good woman," Quintana said, "we can't possibly sleep three to a bed."

"Three to a bed's our policy, miss," the woman said. "Now move your arse over or hie yourself out to the barn and sleep with your mister!"

Quintana frowned at the blowsy woman, who stood with a fist propped on her ample hip. The timid Mistress Hettie Muldoon stood beside her. "I'll just sit on one of the benches downstairs," Miss Hettie offered.

"Nay! I'll not have that!" the innkeeper's wife protested. She looked to Quintana, her dark eyes beady in the lantern light. "Well, miss, what'll it be? A cozy bed or the hayloft?"

Sighing in defeat, Quintana moved to the middle of the bed, muttering to herself, "Pray God she does not snore."

She turned her back to Miss Hettie and the innkeeper's wife and, after punching her fist into her pillow several times, settled down once again to seek her rest.

Draper was eating his breakfast when Quintana came down the next morning. He looked particularly well-rested, she noted with irritation, and greeted her with unaccustomed good cheer.

"Good morning, m'lady," he said, looking up from the copy of the *Virginia Gazette* he'd been reading. "How did you pass the night?"

"Horribly," Quintana replied, seating herself opposite him. She inclined her head to indicate Miss Hettie Muldoon, who sat yawning by the hearthside. "That wretched woman has elbows like pikestaffs," she whispered. "And I swear, she kicks like a bloody mule! Between her incessant pokes and jabs and Tilly's snoring, I barely got a moment's sleep the entire night."

"Indeed?" Draper folded away his paper. "I'm sorry to hear it. I slept like the dead myself. The hay in the stable loft was soft and sweet." The gaze he raised to hers, the devilish smile that played about the corners of his hard mouth, made Quintana shiver. "You should have sought me out, Quintana. You could have shared the loft with me. I don't kick, and I don't snore, and I'd have done my level best to make you welcome."

"I must confess the thought occurred to me more than once," Quintana said, blushing furiously at her own admission.

Draper's smile grew broader. He leaned across the table and touched her cheek with gentle fingers. "My invitation stands," he said in a soft voice. "I can think of far worse ways to spend the night than in your sweet arms."

Quintana's cheeks burned in earnest. She covered them with her hands in a vain attempt to cool them, even as she chided him for his boldness. "You're wicked to tease me when I've already endured so much torment!"

"There are certain instances when wickedness is an attribute rather than a flaw." He raised a mocking brow. "Since I cannot seem to pique your curiosity, you might as well have some breakfast. Perhaps a full stomach will help you put things in perspective."

Quintana did eat—despite the dangerous white lead she stubbornly insisted upon wearing, which often destroyed one's appetite—with far more enthusiasm than she had displayed thus far in their brief acquaintance. Fried speckled trout and hominy, boiled ham and beaten biscuits, all found their way onto her plate, and were dispatched beneath Draper's watchful and approving eye.

When the innkeeper's wife came to offer warm ginger cake, Quintana sat back in her chair. "It smells heavenly, but I couldn't possibly eat another mouthful."

Draper smiled to himself. They'd made landfall just four days ago, and already he could see subtle changes in Quintana. Oh, she was still determined to have things her way, and she clung to her "Englishness" as if her very life depended upon it, but she displayed a resiliency he grudgingly admired.

It would be interesting indeed to see how she reacted to the challenges they would face in the days and weeks ahead. And as he watched her sip her peppermint tea, Draper found himself speculating if, given a little time, the forces of nature and the unforgiving character of the land might not accomplish with comparative ease what he'd been unable to do in weeks of heated conflict.

On the third day out of Williamsburg, Quintana first glimpsed the land that for so much of her adult life she had detested.

The hazy blue line drawn at the horizon at

first resembled thunderheads, yet as the day wore on, she realized her mistake, and despite the cloying warmth of the sultry afternoon, her flesh grew chill.

Shadowed and mysterious, more threatening than any looming storm could be, it was the western mountain barrier, the Great Blue Wall that Winston had mentioned in his numerous impassioned narratives so many years ago.

Shuddering, Quintana forced her gaze away, but she could not seem to rid herself of the feeling of trepidation that had infected her at the first sight of Rowena's rival.

It quickly became obvious that Draper did not share her lack of enthusiasm.

He pushed them on relentlessly through the early afternoon, and only halted briefly in a wooded copse to dine on jerked venison and the ginger cake he'd purchased from the inn-keeper's wife the previous morning. The fare was far from adequate, but Quintana was grateful for the respite.

Three long days of being bounced about on the back on the mare had taken a heavy toll on her. She was battered and bruised and sore in every muscle and joint, and convinced that her posterior would never be the same.

Draper seemed impervious to her sufferings. Indeed, he seemed impervious to everything save his unwavering quest to reach Fort Pitt and clear his name of the charges brought to bear upon him by Lieutenant Bell.

As soon as the last crumb of ginger cake was

eaten, he rose and made his way to the shade of a huge chestnut tree, where the horses stood lazily swishing flies.

Watching, Quintana gritted her teeth. The last thing she wanted was to get back on that horse. "Must we leave so soon, Captain? We've been riding for hours, and we all need to rest."

He stroked the bay's flank and gave the animal an affectionate pat. Quintana thought darkly that this was more attention than he had ever given her. "I want to push on. If we travel hard, we can reach Chitakawa Creek before nightfall, and make camp there," he answered.

"But we are tired now, and need to stop and rest," Quintana persisted. A large brown fly buzzed annoyingly close to her cerused cheek; she slapped it away before giving him her full attention. "Captain, please. If you care nothing at all for my sufferings, then at least think of Tilly. She hasn't the stamina of youth to sustain her that you and I have. Would you have her fall ill because of your impatience?"

Draper studied the older woman, who sat at a little distance, chatting contentedly with Absolute. "She's a long way from a state of collapse, and so are you. Now come. On your feet."

He grasped her hands and pulled Quintana upright while she huffed beneath her breath. "You're being hardheaded and stubborn, sir. It's only a small delay."

Draper replied with forced and unaccustomed patience, for all the world as if he were addressing a willful child. "The sooner we bridge the mountains, the sooner we'll reach Fort Pitt. I'm anxious to arrive, m'lady, anxious to clear my name. And while I don't expect you to understand or to sympathize with my predicament, I fully expect you to get back on that horse when I tell you to."

"Upon my life," Quintana said aside, moving slowly toward the mare. "I cannot comprehend how a man who loves his freedom so intensely that he would rebel against the dictates of his king, could turn into such a bloody tyrant."

She placed her foot into the stirrup, then gasped aloud when Draper's hard hand settled on her derriere. "How dare you take such liberties!"

Ignoring her protest, he lifted her into the saddle and grinned up at her. "If you're going to name me a tyrant, then I might as well reap some of the rewards." He returned to the roan.

"Of all the unmitigated arrogance!" she said, unwilling to admit, even to herself, how deeply his words, his bold touch, had affected her.

In the hours that followed, they headed into the foothills of the Blue Ridge Mountains, laboriously picking their way along paths too narrow and treacherous for two to ride abreast, through thick tangles of thorny bramble bushes and clinging vines that snatched at Quintana's plush velvet skirts.

After what seemed an eternity of battling the nearly impenetrable underbrush, they finally emerged into a wide valley, the floor of which was level and carpeted with a sea of tall waving grasses.

In places here, the ground was wet, and the horses's hooves sank deep. Draper dismounted and, dropping his reins, allowed his horse to graze, making his way back to the others.

"What is it, Captain?" Quintana asked. "Are we stopping here for the night?"

He shook his head. "The ground's too soft to ride, the footing precarious in places. We'll have to walk a ways."

Quintana frowned down at him. "I don't understand why we can't ride—"

"It's too chancy to ride through this kind of terrain," Draper explained. "There's no telling what's under the marsh grass, so we'll have to go slowly and feel our way along. Could be there's uneven ground."

"Can't you find some way around it?" Quintana asked. The idea of wading through the damp morass was repugnant to her.

"This is the most direct route—and the driest," Draper replied, tilting back his head to meet her gaze. "We've only half a mile to go, m'lady," Draper said.

"But if it's too difficult a terrain for the horses, then surely it's too difficult for us as well," Quintana countered.

"Just hold tight to the halter, walk her slowly through it, and you'll both be fine." After helping her down, he turned back to the roan.

Grasping the horse's reins, he started off.

Quintana took a tentative step and sank into the cold ooze up to her ankles. She gasped and scrambled back, coming away without her ankle boot. " 'It's just a little water,' " she said in scathing tones as she bent to search the spongy soil for her boot. "A little water indeed!"

Gathering up her trailing skirts, she started off again, gritting her teeth and seething as she followed in Draper's footsteps.

The ground grew softer, the going far more difficult. Sweat trickled slowly down Quintana's temples. She blotted the moisture with the tail of her skirt and allowed her mind to wander.

How she longed for a bath!

Not the damp rag and pitcher full of tepid water provided to her thus far, but a full hip bath of steaming water and scented soap. Roses . . . soap that smelled like great bouquets—no—gardens filled with English roses!

For a long moment she drifted, caught up in her daydreams, numb to the real discomfort, to the degradation she must suffer at the hands of Draper Boone, to the horrible sensation of mud squishing up between her bare toes . . .

A sharp pain in her cheek jolted Quintana from her musings.

Bringing up her hand, she brushed away a large brown deerfly. It buzzed annoyingly close to her ear; cursing, she swatted at it again.

Another stab, this time on her neck, like that of darning needle piercing her flesh.

Quintana cried out, dropping her skirts, slapping madly at her throat.

Tilly saw what was happening and rushed forward to help her, but for every insect they managed to kill, two more seemed to materialize.

Finally, in desperation, the older woman turned to Absolute. "Oh, Mr. Farquar! Do something! She'll be eaten alive!"

"There's naught to be done *here*," Absolute said sternly. "That stuff ye wear on yer face and in yer bonny hair's what draws 'em. Ye'll have to wait till we get to yonder stream an' warsh it awa'."

He pointed toward the distant tree line, and in that instant Quintana saw it . . . a faint glimmer of silver visible through the trees near the western edge of the valley, five hundred yards away . . . salvation.

Slogging through the mire at a snail's pace, she thought it might as well have been five hundred miles.

The insects buzzed persistently around her, biting her cruelly until Quintana felt that she would lose her mind if she could not escape.

Letting go a low and desperate sob, she grabbed the mare's reins and dragged herself up and into the saddle, oblivious to Absolute's strangled curse as he rushed forward to stop her. With a kick and a wild cry, she pushed the mare into a startled lunge across the uncertain terrain.

At the same instant, Draper turned and dropped the roan's lead, moving to block her path. "Quintana, no! Wait!"

Insensible to all save her own desperate need, Quintana dug her heels into the mare's sides and drove her forward, pushing her into a deadly gallop across the marshy ground.

Draper lunged for the bridle as she raced past, but Quintana hauled the reins to the right and veered the horse away. He sprawled on his face in the murky water and came up cursing. "Goddamn it, woman! Rein her in before you break your goddamned neck!"

Quintana heard, but did not heed him. If she halted she'd be eaten alive! She had to reach the creek!

The silver glimmer of the creek beckoned in the near distance. She could almost feel the cool refreshing water on her hot, stung face. A hundred yards, no more. Then a shrill-sounding scream issued from the valiant little mare, and Quintana went tumbling through the air.

She hit the ground hard, and for a few seconds lay stunned. The strange suck and plop of Draper's footsteps, the labored breathing of an animal in distress, and Tilly's anxious voice—she heard all these sounds. Gathering her strength she struggled to rise, but the sight that greeted her made tears well up inside her.

Not far away, Draper knelt beside the gray's sleek head. With his left hand he held the horse's bridle, in his right his scalping knife.

"Draper, please, no," Quintana said in a small voice. Her tears were flowing freely now, racing down her pale cheeks. "She'll be all right. I'll help you. We'll get her on her feet."

Draper only shook his head. "Her forelegs are broken, and I don't have a choice."

Quintana swallowed hard. "If you must put her down, then surely there's another way. Can you not at least use your rifle? It would be more humane—"

She heard him grind his teeth, and a muscle leaped convulsively in his tawny cheek. "More humane perhaps, but a waste of precious powder and lead I cannot in good conscience make. Besides," he said, glancing pointedly around at the wide valley, "the sound of the shot would carry for miles, and there's no telling who might hear it. It's safer this way."

His blade bit deep, ending the dispute and the mare's life while Quintana stood openly weeping, the pinkish water staining her skirts.

She felt terrible remorse at the senseless loss of the mare, and she badly needed comforting. No gesture of forgiveness, of conciliation, however, was forthcoming from the hard frontiersman, who without a word turned his back on the scene, on Quintana, and walked quickly away.

Quintana watched him go, wishing that he would rail at her, curse, or tell her what a fool she had been, *anything* to break the terrible silence that now lay heavily between them.

Chapter 9

"Won't you come and have a bit of dinner, miss? It's getting late, and Mr. Farquar says it's not fitting for you to be out here all alone."

Quintana pretended interest in the glorious sunset, struggling to keep her voice level. "I'm not hungry, Tilly. But please thank the corporal for thinking of me," she said. "And assure him that I'll be along in a little while."

In truth, she could not bear the thought of facing the others, of sitting near the fire where all could plainly see that she'd been crying.

Once her pride had served her well, helping to conceal the wounds inflicted by a father's abandonment, giving her the strength to hold her head high and carry on with her day-to-day existence when Rowena had taken to her bed.

Yet quite suddenly, when she most needed its cold familiar comfort, that same staunch pride that had been her mainstay and her strength all her life deserted her, stripping away her cool and aloof facade, laying bare her vulnerability for all the world to look upon, making her feel painfully exposed.

Another tear trickled down Quintana's cheek

132

as she listened to Tilly's sigh of resignation. The older woman did not argue, just turned and slowly made her way back to the campfire that glimmered at a distance of fifty feet through the trees.

The glory of the evening sky above the western mountains was fading. The pale saffron hue tinged with rose, the yellow-white, the soft gray-blue gave way by gradual degrees to a violet dusk . . . and with it came the creeping chill of evening, accentuated by the waters of the nearby creek.

Still Quintana stood, searching for the remnants of her tattered pride to draw around her, protection against the censure she was sure she'd face from Absolute and Draper upon her return.

Draper's was a cold and silent fury, the lash of which stung more acutely than any heated accusations, threats, or insults could, and all the more difficult to bear because Quintana knew in her heart that he was justified.

She had acted impetuously, without any thought beyond her own comfort, and the outcome had been disastrous.

Not so long ago in Williamsburg he'd named her a spoiled child; she now saw with shameful clarity that he was right.

The hot flow of her tears increased as she thought of the valiant little mare who had given its life so selflessly, and though Quintana covered her mouth and tried to contain it, the miserable sound of her remorse escaped in the form of a heartfelt sob.

"It's a lovely evening, m'lady," Draper said, "but growing chill. You shouldn't be out without a wrap." He was leaning on his rifle a few yards away, not far from the great spotted bole of a sycamore tree. A brace of hare and a single woodcock lay at his feet, the fruit of his evening's labors.

When she made no reply, he propped his rifle against the sycamore and came to stand beside her. "Come, I'll see you back to camp."

"I thank you, sir, for your kind concern. But I assure you I am fine."

Her voice broke on the last word; Draper took her by the arms and turned her to face him. "What is it, Quintana? What's wrong?"

She should have held fast to what little strength she had left, should have declared that all was fine, but the strength in Draper's hands was one Quintana couldn't hope to equal. "Everything," she blurted out. "This land, this awful place, you . . . and me. I am unsuited to life in your wilderness. It is too strange, too foreign, too deadly."

"Ah," Draper said. "It's because of the gray that you're out here alone in the dark courting the wolves and pneumonia."

"I'm s-sorry," Quintana cried brokenly. "I should have listened. I sh-should have—"

Draper gathered her against him, kissing the soft strands of hair that curled at her temple. She'd washed away the powder that turned the sunlit gold to silver, scrubbed her alabaster skin free of the deadly ceruse. "You're frightened," he said, tipping up her chin and smoothing away her tears with his fingertips. "But you're far stronger than you know."

"Why are you being kind to me?" Quintana asked.

"You've been punished enough," came his soft reply. "And because I hate to see you cry. No more tears—promise me—and I'll get you something to ease the sting of those welts."

Quintana sniffed back her tears, searching his face for signs of anger, but saw instead quiet concern. As she watched he reached down to gather a fistful of small oval-shaped leaves, then crushed them in his hand to extract the juice, which he applied to the welts that marred her tender skin.

"What is that?" Quintana asked. It felt cool and soothing to her skin.

"Plantain. The Indians call it white man's foot because of its tendency to crop up near the settlements." The task was completed; Draper dropped the crushed leaves, but he didn't lower his hand, didn't move away. Her eyes were a soft melting silver, and though he wondered if it was merely an illusion of the dim purple twilight, they seemed to beckon to him.

Draper could not resist her for long. He bent his head slightly, the better to savor her fragrance. Gone were the harmful cosmetics, the powder and paint. She smelled of wood fern and mellow spring sunlight, fresh and sweet, intoxicating. Draper filled his lungs with her essence. He knew in his heart he should escort her back . . . back to the campsite, to safety.

Whether or not she was aware of it, she was not safe here with him. The thoughts he had for Quintana were not the wholesome thoughts a guardian had for his ward.

"We'd best be getting back," he said half-heartedly.

"So soon?"

"There's danger in the night, Quintana. You shouldn't linger long so far from the fire—"

"But I'm not alone," Quintana said quickly. "You're here with me."

Draper smiled down at her, a trifle wryly, and took her by the shoulders. "I can protect you from what's out there . . . but who will protect you from me?"

"At the moment, I fear you much less than what I must face when I return to camp." She caught her bottom lip between her teeth. "Humor me, Draper, please. Stay here with me a little while."

It was what he wanted most, exactly what he'd been hoping for. He led Quintana to a log and sat, drawing her down onto his lap, kissing her damp cheek with unaccustomed tenderness. "Quintana," he murmured. "My sweet English rose. What am I to do with you?"

"Talk to me," Quintana said with a sniff. "Tell me again that it will be all right."

Draper chuckled darkly. "Are you certain that's what you want? The reassurance of your father's lackey?"

Quintana sighed and pressed closer to his chest. Tonight she needed to be close to someone, desperately craved a human touch. Draper was warm and he was hard, oh so pleasant to hold and to be held by in return.

"Tell me of this place," she asked him. "You are familiar with it, aren't you? Tell me of your home, your family. Tell me anything. Your voice rumbles so pleasantly in your chest when you speak, and my mind craves a diversion this evening."

He chuckled softly and hugged her closer. "It rumbles, does it?"

Quintana frowned up at him.

"Your pardon, m'lady. But a compliment of any kind coming from your luscious lips is bound to be met with some astonishment."

Refusing to be baited, Quintana continued to press him. They'd been together for almost three months, and she still knew very little about him. "Is your home very near here?"

"My home is in the Valley of Virginia," Draper replied. "Or was."

"Did your family move on?"

He shook his head. "I'm all that's left. The last of my line. My father died of typhus when I was fifteen. Garrick was the oldest son, five years my senior. He was quiet and reserved, a good and honest man, with a greater fondness for the Bible than for the pleasures of the flesh. When I went off to fight in '75, Garrick stayed behind to provide for Mother and my other brother Hamlin and to tend the fields."

"What happened to Garrick?" Quintana asked. "Did he change his mind and join you?" She tried to imagine what he might have looked like . . . if he was as handsome as Draper, with hair as dark and glossy as a raven's wing, and eyes like amber fire . . .

Unaware of the direction of her thoughts, Draper smoothed the hair back from her face and smiled sadly. "No, Garrick never went to war. He didn't have my restlessness, and never ventured farther than Williamsburg. He drowned in the Rappahannock River in '76. He'd been to the Tidewater on business, and was on his way back home. They said he tried to ford the river after dark, and lost his footing. Garrick never was much of a swimmer—"

"It must have been very difficult for your mother," Quintana said, watching him closely. The last of the light had faded, and darkness held sway over the land. His features, so strong and arrogant in the bold light of day, seemed almost sinister, but she was not afraid.

"Aye, it was difficult. She couldn't work the land alone. My younger brother, Hamlin, helped her some, but he wasn't content to stay there on the farm. Damned young hotspur he turned out to be . . . had some fool notion about goin' up the valley to pick off a few bloody Englishmen . . ."

There was a note of melancholy in his voice. He sighed and stroked the hair that tumbled freely down her back, pausing to nuzzle the sensitive hollow beneath her ear, to bury his face in the curve of her throat.

Quintana arched her neck, turning slightly away, but he was not discouraged, and gently nibbled the tendon that joined her neck to her shoulder.

A pleasurable jolt coursed through her, and it took every ounce of strength she possessed to pull away, to hold him at arm's length. With hooded eyes he watched her, a strange half-smile upon his face. "You would avoid the issue, sir," she said. "We have not finished our discourse, nor is my curiosity concerning you in the least abated."

"Tell me, lass," he said, his smile turning wicked, his gaze intense. "Would your curiosity about me extend to *other* things?"

Quintana frowned at him. "Perhaps it would be best if we held strictly to safer subjects."

"Faith, woman," Draper said with a dark laugh. "Where's your spirit of adventure?"

"Draper Catworth Boone! You are incorrigible!"

"I'm also highly entertaining when I've a mind to be."

He made to pull her close again, but Quintana braced her palms against the solid muscular wall of his chest, gazing up into his face. "You were telling me of your home, I believe," she said with determination.

With a noise of disgust, he passed a hand over his features. "If not for the fact that you are such a delectable little piece, I'd leave you for the wolves."

"What became of your mother? And Hamlin? You said you were the last son surviving. How did his life end?"

Draper didn't answer. Instead, he pulled her to him, kissing her lips with a hunger he could no longer repress, and bore her slowly to the ground . . .

In that instant, with the cool grass for her bed and Draper's warmth to shield her from the crisp night air, all the questions, all her curiosity concerning Draper's background fled Quintana's thoughts.

Draper's mouth, so hot and demanding, the hands that slid slowly down her spine to cup her derriere and bring her closer to his swollen loins, the breathless way he made her feel, were all that mattered now.

With wild abandon, she kissed him back, giving freely of herself as she had never thought to do before this rapturous moment.

A silvery excitement threaded through her veins, racing to her vitals, making warm molten pools in her lower belly. She wanted to be closer, to feel his vital warmth. She wanted to . . .

"Miss?"

Draper went rigid. He leaned his cheek against her throat, and Quintana felt his muscles tense, heard him curse low through his teeth.

"Quintana? Are you there?" Tilly paused at the edge of the clearing. "Mr. Farquar, she must have wandered off. Perhaps you'd best go look—"

Draper raised his head and shot a glance in the direction of the camp. "Go on back. Before they come and find you here with me."

He kissed her once more, then quickly stood up.

"Aren't you coming?" she asked.

He snorted in reply and swept a hand downward to indicate his breechclout. "If I saunter into camp in my current state of frustration there'll be no doubt in anyone's mind as to what's kept you."

Quintana's gaze wandered downward. His manhood strained against the soft cloth covering, and she saw that he was very well-endowed. "Oh," she said, averting her gaze while her cheeks suffused with the hot blood of embarrassment. She would have spun on her heel, but Draper caught her arm and brought her back around to face him.

"Quintana," he said urgently. "Let's finish what we started here. Walk out with me tonight beneath the stars."

Quintana hesitated. With her lips still tender from his passionate kisses and her blood running high, she felt reckless, unafraid.

But what about tomorrow?

What would the wilderness dawn bring to her if she gave herself to Draper, as he urged her to do?

To openly declare themselves lovers could prove disastrous. She was pledged to another; he was dependent on her father's continued good faith to free him of the charges.

Quintana's head waged a fierce battle with her heart. He wanted her for his paramour, yet there had been no talk of marriage, not a single word to indicate that she was more to him than just a passing fancy.

Quintana shook her head to clear it. Passion

had him in its grip; he was not thinking clearly. "I don't know," she said.

"When the moon is high," Draper said. "I'll
wait for you at the edge of the clearing."

Quintana broke away then, hurrying to
camp. When she reached the clearing she
glanced back. Draper was standing where
she'd left him, a shadowy figure silhouetted
by the silvery light of the rising moon, as mysterious and savage, as suddenly frightening, as
the black bulk of the mountains looming in the
distance.

"My, this does bring back memories! Why,
I remember when I was just a girl, long before
Mother passed away and I had to seek work in
the city, I used to pluck chickens of a Saturday
evening for the next day's dinner. How me
brothers used to taunt me!"

Tilly raised a damp hand slick with fine
gray pinfeathers, and dabbed at her eyes with
the back of her wrist. The woodcock lay before
her on a flat rock, looking very little and pitiful
without its plumage.

Seated cross-legged on the ground on the
opposite side of the small blaze Absolute had
kindled, Draper skinned the final hare and cut
it into quarters, snapping the tiny spine easily
in two. "Had I known you'd wax nostalgic
over plucking a few feathers, Tilly Bascombe,"
said Draper, "I'd have bought you a damnable
chicken in Williamsburg."

Tilly pulled a face at the frontiersman. "I
never said I enjoyed the task! Only that it

brought back memories of me youth. Truth to tell, I hated havin' to pluck those stinking birds. Always made me angry enough I'd start to cry. 'Twas why me brothers poked such fun."

Draper laughed at that. "You should have said something. I could have made short work of it for you."

Tilly tossed the feathers into the fire and placed the bird before him. "From time to time, we all must do things we don't especially like, sir. And I'm glad to help out when I can. Why, we Englishwomen are a hearty breed, for the most part, able to withstand whatever comes our way. Isn't that so, miss?"

Quintana smiled and said nothing. At that moment, she was feeling terribly unsure of herself. She had displayed this day an unsettling facet of her nature she hadn't known existed, a reckless impetuosity that could lead her into trouble if she allowed it to take control.

Basking in the warmth of the fire and observing Draper at his work, Quintana was aware of how perilously close she had come to forfeiting her virtue to the handsome rogue across the way.

He seemed to have some hold on her, some dark seductive power she couldn't understand or resist. In the past she had depended on her fortitude and indomitable will to help her through difficult times, yet one touch of Draper's callused hand, and that same once indomitable will was no longer her own. Truth to tell, Quintana Wade was terrified.

Absolute put the finishing touches on the half-faced camp he'd been constructing for Tilly and Quintana, a hastily built structure with a great fallen log as its back. Poles had been driven upright into the ground ten feet in front to support the roof poles, and the top and sides were covered with blankets. "It ain't nothin' fancy, but it'll help to keep ye warm an' dry and fend away wolves an' sich, if they should wander into camp."

Absolute dusted off his breeks and sat down next to Tilly, who promptly cuffed his shoulder. "That's wasn't funny, Mr. Farquar!"

"I wasna tryin' ta jest wi' ye," he said with a smirk. "There's wolves an' bears aboot always. An' other creatures just as deadly, more so mayhap! Just ask the lad if ye daen't believe me. Why, they've got so bad up near the fort that a man mus' watch his back when in the woods. The carrion from Braddock's defeat made 'em fat an' lazy, an' give 'em a taste for human bein's."

"Oh, that's a terrible tale!" Tilly said. "One you must recant!" She looked immediately to Draper, who stared into the fire. "It's not true, now is it, Cap'n?"

"Predators have always been a problem," Draper said.

Indeed, Quintana thought. But at this moment wolves and bears did not concern her. The predator that filled her heart with trepidation walked tall and straight and dressed in supple deerskin.

"Don't let it frighten you, Tilly," Draper

went on. "Just use the common sense God gave you, and you'll reach the safety of the fort unscathed. Don't venture off alone, and never leave camp after dark unescorted. Aside from that, just cry out if you spy a carnivore. We'll feed 'im Absolute."

There was general laughter and the conversation turned to other things. Draper pierced the plump sections of the hare and the breast of the small woods fowl with a skewer he'd fashioned from a birch rod and placed the spit in the fork of two sharpened sticks thrust into the ground.

Draper's kill roasted slowly over the fire. Quintana grew drowsy as she watched the dancing flames. The smells of wood smoke and roasting meat wafting on the chill night air were exotic and new after the noisome odors of London. Her stomach rumbled loudly; she caught Draper's gaze, so pagan gold, so unreadable, across the fire.

"Hungry, m'lady?"

"More so than I realized," she replied drowsily.

"A hard day's ride and the cold night air promote a healthy appetite," he said, glancing at the angle of the newly risen moon. "I find that I myself am not immune."

Quintana ate her portion of the hare, then, saying good night, walked slowly to the three-sided shelter.

"Rest well, m'lady," Draper called softly after her.

Quintana did not rest at all. For hours she

lay upon her bed of leaves, watching the pale light of the moon as it seeped through the cracks in the roof of the half-faced camp, shifting, changing, growing brighter as it moved higher overhead.

Somewhere in the shadows, beyond the perimeter of the clearing, Draper awaited her coming . . . waited in vain . . .

Quintana's decision had not come without difficulty. Tonight her fear had won out, but as she closed her eyes and turned her face into the curve of her upraised arm where the silver beams could not reach, she knew that it might not always be so.

Chapter 10

Quintana awoke next morning to Tilly's soft humming. Seated near the fire, the older woman smiled at Quintana when she appeared and called a cheery morning greeting.

Quintana glanced around. There was no sign of Draper; even Absolute was conspicuously absent. "Where is everyone?" she asked with as much nonchalance as she could muster.

"Why, the cap'n's gone off hunting," Tilly replied. "And Mr. Farquar saw some nice black birch he says makes a delicious tea."

"I'm surprised," Quintana said. "I thought he would be eager to be on his way this morning."

"Aye, and so I thought too. But Cap'n Boone says it's bound to rain near noon today. The goin' will be slow in any case, and he wanted to scare up some game before it sought shelter from the storm."

Quintana frowned, glancing at the sky. "It doesn't look like rain to me. But I shan't complain about this small reprieve." She rubbed her hip. "My derriere can use the rest."

"Your derriere looks fine to me."

147

Quintana's heart leaped into her throat. She slowly turned.

He was standing at the clearing's edge, a yearling buck draped across his shoulders. For a long moment, he stood motionless, his warming gaze traveling over her, while Quintana's cheeks grew slowly pink beneath his leisurely perusal.

Feeling suddenly and inexplicably self-conscious, Quintana lifted a hand to smooth the tousled locks that lay across one shoulder and saw his lazy smile.

Tilly broke the tense silence that stretched between them. "My," she said, "what a nice little deer! He does look tender, doesn't he, Cap'n?"

Coming forward, Draper laid the deer at Quintana's feet and sketched a courtly bow. "M'lady's dinner," he said with mock humility. "I hope that you approve."

Quintana gave an answering smile and watched his whiskey-colored eyes crinkle pleasantly at the outer corners. He was a rough-hewn rogue, a bit ribald at times, savagely handsome . . . and altogether irresistible.

Draper dressed the deer while Tilly prepared breakfast. There was little for Quintana to do, and so she sat observing Draper at his work.

Moving surely and swiftly, he slipped the scalping knife through the skin and split the hide from hoof to hoof inside the hind legs, then working with a skill she found surprising, he stripped the hide away from the carcass.

"Come lend me a hand here, would you, lass?"

Quintana had been so absorbed in the motion of his hands, the fascinating ripple and play of his muscles beneath the brown skin of his forearm, that she was stunned. "Come again, Captain?"

"Would you lend me a hand, m'lady? It isn't difficult. Just grasp the hind legs there, above the hoof, and hold tight while I make short work of this."

Quintana stared at him, aghast. "You can't mean that you want me to—to touch that dead thing?"

Draper looked at her, the corners of his hard mouth lifting slightly. "That 'dead thing' is dinner. You want to eat, now don't you?"

"But I couldn't—I've never—" Quintana broke off and looked hopefully around. "I'm certain Absolute will help you."

"Absolute has gone downstream a ways to scout around. He won't be back for an hour or two. This can't wait that long. Now come."

Quintana looked from the small white-tailed deer to Draper, who patiently waited, and back again. She could simply refuse, turn around, and walk away. Yet Draper hadn't refused her last night when she'd asked him to stay. He'd been strangely compassionate at a time when she most needed sympathy and understanding, not offering a word of reproach, despite the role she'd played in the loss of the gray.

With a curl of her dainty lip, she approached him, and at his direction took hold of the fragile-boned legs with her fingertips. She closed her eyes and waited, but nothing happened.

A moment passed. Quintana opened her eyes the smallest crack, peering at him through her tawny lashes.

The look on his dark handsome face was one of incredulity. "M'lady," he said, "if you truly mean to assist me, you'll have to do better than that."

Quintana frowned, closing her hands around the deer's hind legs just above its small black hooves, and shut her eyes tight once again.

"Brace yourself, and don't let go," Draper said, then began to pull the deerskin.

Quintana dug in her heels in an effort to gain some leverage. The hide let go all at once, and with the sudden slack between them and a squeal of surprise, Quintana sat down hard.

Draper laughed as she rubbed her derriere. "You might have warned me," she said.

"How was I to know you'd close your eyes?" He extended his hand with an impudent grin. "Here, let me help you."

For an instant, just an instant, Quintana stared at the appendage held out to her, hesitating. It was not the pale, beringed hand of a gentleman, swimming in a sea of pristine laces . . . it was possessed of a raw and potent power, a savage elegance Quintana found irresistible.

Something shattered inside her in that moment while she sat there staring, and a large part of the cool and brittle shield she'd employed all her adult life to protect her from the world crumbled to pieces and fell away.

She reached out and, with a tremulous smile, placed her small hand into his keeping, watching, fascinated, as his fingers closed around it.

Draper pulled her to her feet. "A job well done, m'lady. Thank you for lending your assistance."

He dropped a kiss on her cheek and turned back to his task, leaving Quintana to marvel at the gentle glowing warmth that filled her at his simple praise.

Draper packed the venison in the salted hide and lashed it to the saddle for the long trek up the mountainside. The trail was narrow and treacherous, winding steadily upward, snaking back upon itself at times to avoid deadfalls or boulders so huge that they proved insurmountable.

Before noon it began to drizzle. By early afternoon the mist turned into a deluge from which there was no escaping.

Draper led the way, for once without his long rifle. The weapon was thrust into the leather scabbard attached to his saddle and covered with an oilcloth to keep the powder dry.

Quintana, slogging along behind him as they inched their way upward, doubted its effectiveness.

Everything was wet.

Water dripped from the boughs overhead and sluiced down the brooding gray stone face of the mountain. It soaked Quintana's velvet gown, weighing down her skirts, making every step she took a chilly damp misery.

The lowering skies quickened the coming of evening. By the time they reached the summit it was gathering dusk.

Absolute set about constructing the same type of three-sided half-faced camp he'd built the previous evening for the use of the women, only this time it was slightly larger. Propriety was not to be considered; because of the the rain, the men would need shelter too. So the four travelers would share the only one available.

Quintana was past the point of caring. Without being told, she dragged the packs from the horses' backs and placed them near the shelter, then after she tethered the animals beneath the inadequate shelter of trees, she and Tilly stood anxiously by and watched Draper's attempt to kindle a fire in the downpour.

Sheltering the spot where he worked with his body, Draper coaxed a small blaze from the dried leaves and pine needles he'd stuffed into the saddlebags that morning, then slowly positioned pieces of dead wood, broad at the base and joined at the top to shelter the flames from the rain while fueling the fire. By the time the last of the light was gone, the blaze crackled gleefully near the entrance of their camp.

"Gae on an' get oot of them wet things," Absolute said, shooing the women into the structure. "I'll start the supper."

The Scot received no argument from Quintana. The velvet gown, once so lovely, had been reduced to little more than a tattered rag that clung to her cold wet skin. The hem of the voluminous skirt was torn in places, the velvet nap scarred from the brambles and muddied beyond reclaim.

She felt only a slight pang as she pulled the garment over her head and reached for the gray linsey-woolsey gown Tilly held out to her. "I can manage on my own, Tilly. Do get out of those wet things before you take a chill. Draper won't be pleased if either of us should succumb to the grippe and we're forced to delay."

Quintana finished hooking the simple garment, then glanced down at her feet. Her silk stockings and jaunty black riding boots were ruined. With a sigh of resignation, she stripped them away and tossed them onto the fire Draper had kindled in front of the open end of the structure.

The stockings the frontiersman had thoughtfully provided were made of a soft thick cotton and felt delightfully warm against her chilled skin. The shoes were sturdily made but surprisingly comfortable.

"Well, what say you? Do I look the part of a milkmaid?" Quintana spread her skirts with both hands and turned about with a spritely laugh that died upon her lips the moment she saw that she and Tilly were no longer alone.

Draper was crouched just inside the entrance of the shelter, his long rifle resting across his knees; he appeared every bit as cold and bedraggled as Quintana had felt a few moments ago.

Despite his obvious discomfort, he looked her up and down, from the crown of her still damp head to the tips of her leather shoes, with a gaze as warm as molten honey. "Your beauty needs no artifice, m'lady. I told you that in London long ago. Leave the velvets and laces, satins and powders and black silk patches to those less fortunate."

"You're out of your head with cold," Quintana said. "And you should get out of those wet things before you take a serious chill."

"A chill, m'lady? How so when my blood is boiling?"

"Hist, Captain! Tilly will hear you!"

"Tilly Bascombe knows I speak the truth, isn't that so, Tilly?"

"Indeed, Cap'n," Tilly said, "but I'd take it very kindly if you'd leave me out of this discussion."

Quintana faced him, hands on hips. "At the very least, remove your shirt and let me hang it up to dry."

"I'll surrender my shirt if it makes you happy, but it doesn't change the fact that even gotten up like a bloody milkmaid, you're enough to take a man's breath away."

"You are such a lying rogue at times," Quintana said not unkindly. "But charming. And I shall thank you for the pretty compliment." Dropping her gaze, she felt a soft blush creep up her throat to warm her cheeks. "And thank you for your thoughtfulness as well, albeit somewhat belatedly. The garments you purchased are not so difficult a cross to bear as I at first thought."

"You are indeed quite welcome, Quintana," he said. He laid the rifle aside and reached for the belt that kept his leather shirt closed in front. In less than an instant, he had removed the belt, and his shirt fell open.

The man beneath the leather garb was lean and hard, his muscles exceptionally well-defined, without an ounce of fat on his long-boned frame. His breadth of shoulder was impressive, his pectorals firm and compact.

Quintana's thoughts proved as ungovernable as her gaze. She could not bear to look at him, so lithe, so male, so tawny! But she could not look away for long.

It was difficult to countenance that just last night she'd been held so tightly to his savage breast, that she had reveled in his nearness, been so grateful for his strength, and been willing to accept him.

The thought of how close she'd come to lying unclothed with this man was strangely exhilarating, and more than a little frightening.

Feeling oddly and suddenly shy in his presence, Quintana moved near enough to accept the proffered garment from his hand, then turned abruptly away. It would not do for him to guess what she was thinking.

Her thoughts and feelings didn't matter in the greater scheme of things. She was promised to another, and Draper Boone, by his own admission, was not a man of whom Wolverine Wade would approve.

Smoothing the supple leather of his hunting shirt with reverent fingers, Quintana sighed and wondered what the future held in store for her.

Would Uriah Bell be anything like Draper? Or would she lie awake all the nights of the rest of her life, and dream about what might have been?

Sometime later, in the deepest part of night, Quintana wakened. She was unsure just what had disturbed her rest, and she lay for a long moment, listening to Absolute's low even breathing and Tilly's soft intermittent snores.

On the far side of the structure, Draper too was wide awake. He leaned forward slightly, bracing himself on one hand, and as she watched, took up the long rifle and crept soundlessly to the opening of the structure.

"What is it?"

He put a finger to his lips, cocking his head slightly to listen.

The sound came again, closer now and more distinct, a low and throaty rumble that caused the fine hairs on Quintana's nape and forearms to stand erect.

The horses, tethered in the bushes at the edge of the tiny clearing, whickered uneasily and strained against their tethers.

"Catamount," Draper said.

He would have slipped silently into the night had it not been for Quintana's urgent whisper, "You aren't going out there!"

Draper frowned. "There's a good seventy miles of rough goin' between us and the Raystown Path, and another hundred over the mountains to Pittsburgh. If that cat gets the horses, do you really want to walk it?"

Quintana shook her head. The day had been exhausting; she could not imagine crossing the mountains on foot. "Is there anything I can do to help?"

"There's wood in the shelter," he said, inclining his head toward a small pile of broken branches he'd collected the previous night and set inside to dry. "Fuel the fire slowly. And for Christ's sake, stay close to the camp."

Quintana's heart was thudding high in her throat as she crept closer to the fire and began adding the wood piece by piece.

Draper had gone, melting into the darkness as softly as a wraith, and there was nothing left to do but sit and worry for his welfare.

Somewhere beyond the perimeter of the camp, where the firelight didn't reach, the unearthly cry sounded again.

With a flash of tawny fur, the great mountain cat leaped from a stand of large boulders across the way, bounding toward the horses. At that same moment, Draper stepped from the stygian shadows into the light.

Quintana held her breath. The cat turned and, without warning, rushed toward this new threat, swiping with its huge forepaws. She heard the click of the lock of Draper's rifle as it fell, but no ensuing explosion, and in the sickening instant that followed the rifle's misfire, she knew that Draper was going to die.

All feeling drained from her then, replaced by a terrible numbing fear flooding up from the pit of her stomach, filling her chest and crowding her heart and lungs, until each breath came out a sob, each pulse of her normally steady heart felt as if it were her last.

Beyond conscious thought, beyond fear or logic, Quintana snatched a burning brand from the fire and, lifting her skirts with one hand, dashed toward the fray.

Back in camp, Absolute came awake with a growled imprecation; Tilly, exhausted by the day's exertions, snoozed on.

Draper was unaware of what was happening beyond the circle of golden firelight. All of his attention was focused on the cat that crouched a dozen feet away.

Time seemed to slow, distorting his perception and lending the scene an unreal sense.

Cold sweat trickled down Draper's neck. His heart felt sluggish in his breast, as heavy as lead. In his mind he emptied the flashpan and filled it again, but in reality there was no time.

The lion feinted slightly to the left, then almost before Draper realized what was occurring, pivoted back. Letting loose a bloodcurdling cry, it bared yellow-white fangs capable of tearing the flesh from a man's bones.

Draper brought back his rifle and, bracing himself, gave his undivided attention to the cat.

It flattened its ears against its sleek head and sprang forward low to the ground. It bounded at Draper, its movement startlingly swift. At the same instant, Draper raised the rifle high and brought the brass butt plate arcing down.

He hit the feline a solid blow; it leaped back and shook its head, then without warning streaked forward again. *Swat, swat, swat!*

The lion's claws were hooked and as sharp as razors. They sliced with ease through the buckskin leather of Draper's leggings, through the flesh of his upper thigh. With a vicious curse, he staggered back.

At first there was no pain, then feeling came back into his injured leg with a rush. His flesh felt as if it were on fire; the flames shot up to his hip, down to his knee . . . every bit as hot as the flaming brand Quintana carried.

Quintana.

He was suffering delusions. It simply wasn't possible that the colonel's only daughter, the pampered English beauty, was risking life and limb to save his ass.

"For Christ's sake, woman," he ground out. "Don't come any closer." But Quintana wasn't listening. She edged into his field of vision, waving the brand before her, her small taut face gone white with fear.

The distraction she provided, however unwelcome, gave Draper the precious seconds he needed to act. As the cat turned toward the terrified young woman, he tore the hatchet from his belt. Lunging forward, he sank the blade deep into the feline's skull.

Draper drew a ragged breath and slowly released it before turning to his charge. She stood at a little distance, dry-eyed and innocent-looking despite the fact that she had openly defied him a few moments ago. "That was a fool thing to do, Quintana," he said sternly. "You might have been killed just now."

She lifted her chin, but Draper swore he saw it quiver. "It was necessary," she said simply.

Draper stared at her. That the courageous young creature standing before him, golden and delectable in the flickering firelight, and the cool distant beauty he'd kidnapped in London were one and the same, was difficult indeed to countenance.

"This argument can wait, sir," Quintana said, slipping her arm around his ribs. "Your wounds can't. That leg needs stitching. You're bleeding profusely. Come over by the fire and let me see to your injury."

Draper grudgingly capitulated. The flesh of his leg was badly torn and would need to be drawn together so that it could heal properly. He glanced down at his leg and winced. His legging was bloody to the knee. "Do you know something of wounds, m'lady?"

Quintana smiled. He sounded concerned. "A little," she admitted. "Cook cut her hand in the kitchen once, and Tilly and Nigel were away. I had to tend the injury. Not worried, are you?"

He looked down at the leg, then at her. His glance was rueful. "I'll freely admit, there's nothing I'd like more at the moment than to have your soft white hands on me. I just wish it were in some other capacity."

"That's a bloody waste of damned good whiskey."

Quintana finished cleaning the blood away from the wounds and took up the needle and thread Absolute had provided. The sun had burned away the morning mist. "You may have what's left once I'm through. You'll need to rest if this is to heal properly."

Draper winced as she carefully caught the edges of the first slash scoring his thigh and pulled the thread through, drawing them neatly together. "Rest, hell. We'll leave right after breakfast." She took another stitch and he cursed softly. "Ouch! Goddamnit, woman! That's my leg you're working on, not a friggin' sampler!"

Quintana furrowed her brow and glared up at him through her tawny lashes. "Fie, Captain! You faced down death alone not an hour past, but quell at the thought of needle and thread? Where has your boundless courage gone to?"

"Boundless stupidity is more the like," Absolute quipped. He had stripped the hide from the catamount and was now busily working salt into the fleshy underside to cure it. "Ye're damned lucky the lass there had her wits aboot her, or I'd be saltin' you down for curin' right aboot noo."

Draper sent a pained grimace the Scot's way and gritted through his teeth, "Your confidence in my abilities is heartening."

"Absolute is right," Quintana said as calmly as she could. He'd stripped down to his breechclout and left legging, leaving the right side of his body bare from shoulder to ankle. With Draper in such a state of undress, and her working so closely on so intimate an area of his body, it was difficult indeed for Quintana to lift her gaze without the hot blood of embarrassment rising into her cheeks. "You are exceedingly lucky to have gotten off so handily."

She finished drawing the edges of the worst of his wounds together, and sat back to view her handiwork. "That should do nicely for now. Come," she said, standing. "I'll help you to the shelter."

But Draper wasn't listening. He drew on the right legging and fastened it to the belt that held his breechclout in place. "Ready the horses when you finish salting the hide. We'll leave when Quintana and I get back."

"Get back!" Quintana stared at him through narrowed eyes. "Where do you think we are going?"

"Not far, Quintana. Just along this path and past those trees. There's something I want you to see." He grasped her hand and started off along a narrow rock-strewn path.

"You should be resting, not moving about. You'll open your wounds and start bleeding all over again."

"I have to keep moving, Quintana. If I lie down now, I'll grow stiff and I won't walk again for several weeks. We can't afford to delay that long."

Quintana went with him reluctantly. She had serious doubts about the wisdom of his reasoning, but she knew the extent of his stubbornness. To argue with him would do no good. And he was likely to go off on his own. By staying close to him, she could at least keep his pace slow.

"Won't you at least tell me where we are going?" Quintana said after a few minutes.

"To the top of the world," he replied.

The path wound slowly upward to the summit of the mountain, where it abruptly ended. It was here, near an outcropping of great boulders, that Draper stopped, drawing Quintana in close against his side.

"I'm a man of humble means, m'lady. And this is as close as I can come to laying the world at your feet."

Quintana's heart seemed to swell in her breast, and for a long moment she could not trust herself to speak. Never in her life had she beheld such wild beauty . . . and Draper had not exaggerated, for surely this must be the very top of his own savage world.

Spread out below them, as far as the eye could see, were giant forested ridges, a veritable ocean of trees. The mountains in the fore were the vibrant green of spring, the deep cleftlike valleys separating the ridges shadowed and mysterious, the ridges marching ever westward a hazy shade of blue, the greatest of them concealed in the clouds . . .

Quintana continued to gaze at the vivid panorama. "They appear to go on forever."

The man at her side studied her small countenance with an attention that was equally as rapt. "Are you sorry you came?" he questioned at last.

She shook her head. "I never imagined it would be so breathtaking. Or that it would make me feel so small and insignificant."

"Small perhaps, but never insignificant." Draper smiled and turned to gaze out across the mottled blue-green ridges. "In the cities a man struggles to prosper; out here he must struggle to live."

Quintana turned to look at Draper. "You love it, don't you?" There was no need for him to answer, the truth showed plainly on his rugged face.

"It's home," Draper said simply.

"It's daunting," Quintana said, suppressing an involuntary shiver.

Yet far more daunting still was the future that awaited her beyond those primeval mountains . . . a future she greatly feared would in no way include the man called Draper Boone.

Chapter 11

On the afternoon of the day following Draper's encounter with the mountain cat, the small party of riders descended the final slope to the Valley of Virginia, and Quintana got her first glimpse of the land which had been Draper's boyhood home.

The "valley" was in truth a rolling plain. Twenty-five miles wide, it swept away westward, covered with verdant green woodlands the likes of which Quintana had never seen.

England had little forest left, and the woodlands it did possess were nothing like this.

Here, everything seemed to grow in profusion. Hickory and oak, sugar maple and pine, towered high above a sun-dappled forest floor. Vines hung snakelike from the trees, as thick in places as Draper's brawny forearm, and pink azalea bushes and white trillium lilies added a splash of bright color to the scene.

Riding pillion on the roan and holding tight to Draper's waist, Quintana was enchanted, and for a little while she set aside the dread with which she'd always looked upon this land.

They had progressed no more than a mile along the winding path when they came within hailing distance of a small homestead nestled close against the mountainside. It was nothing more than a windowless cabin made of rough logs situated in the center of a small clearing. The trees that had not been felled were stripped of bark in a narrow ring to kill the foliage and allow the sunlight to penetrate.

As the quartet of riders picked their way along the forest trail, a trio of towheaded children, barefoot and otherwise garbed in an odd assortment of clothing, ran to the edge of the clearing to peer after them with round blue eyes.

Draper hailed them but didn't slow the roan, and soon they were out of sight. It was a long while, however, before the image of the secluded forest home left Quintana, and she found herself looking back with a strange sense of longing.

The unmistakable fragrance of wood smoke lingered in the still afternoon air, teasing her senses—the smell of civilization.

With a pang, she thought that had they stopped, they might have slept the night indoors, that there might have been a soothing salve for Draper's wounds, a welcome distraction to deliver her from the deepseated feeling of loneliness that had found its way into her heart that morning when she stood gazing down at Draper's world and realized how limited was their time together.

An hour later they came upon an abandoned clearing near the banks of the Shenandoah River, where Draper drew rein. Tilly and Absolute were several minutes behind them, having taken a short break to gather some wild onions for dinner. The ruins of a log home stood far back in the trees. "This is as far as we go," Draper said.

It seemed an odd place to make camp for the night, Quintana thought. But she didn't argue as Draper took her arm and helped her down.

Anxiously, she watched him stand in the stirrups and then hastily lower himself into the saddle once more, cursing low and virulently. Beads of sweat broke out upon his ashen brow, and for a fraction of a second he hunched forward and laid his palm protectively on his injured thigh.

Seeing his obvious distress, Quintana rushed forward. "Here, let me help you," she said.

"It's not necessary, m'lady," he said stiffly. "I can manage on my own."

Quintana narrowed her eyes as she peered up at him. "If you are too proud to accept my help, then at least let me call Corporal Farquar—"

Draper clenched his teeth against the dull ache in his thigh and swung the injured leg over the roan's broad rump and down, determined not to give in to his pressing illness. But the wound simply would not cooperate.

The moment the sole of his moccasin touched the ground, his knee buckled, and he would have fallen beneath the roan's belly if not for Quintana, who was instantly there with a shoulder to lean on, a helping arm around his ribs.

It pained Draper's pride to accept her help, though he was forced privately to admit that he couldn't have managed without it. "My thanks, m'lady. But I c-could have managed . . . on my own."

"You would have managed to fall flat on your handsome face, Captain," Quintana said. "You're burning up with fever. Why didn't you stop before this?"

"Had to try and make time . . . " He groaned as he took a step, then looked at her with sudden interest. "Do you really think I'm handsome, m'lady?"

"You are incorrigible, sir," she replied. "Prideful, stubborn, and at times a very great fool." She averted her eyes, refusing to meet Draper's fevered gaze, but a telling blush burned high upon her pale cheek. "And yes, I find you quite handsome . . . in a wicked sort of way."

"Wicked . . ." Draper murmured thoughtfully. "Wicked, aye. I think I like that. Wicked can be fun, did you know that?"

She gave him a sidelong glance from beneath her tawny lashes, and her lips curved ever so slightly upward. "I think you've mentioned as much, Captain."

Draper's arm was resting on her slim shoulders. With little effort he turned his hand and brushed his knuckles along the long white column of her throat. "Your skin is so pale, so soft, like cream. I swear, I've never in my life seen the like . . ."

She made no reply, but Draper knew she'd heard, for the becoming rose that had touched her cheeks earlier deepened. "Does your injury hurt you badly?" she inquired.

"Aye, it hurts," Draper said. More than he was willing to acknowledge. His body felt as if it were aflame . . . Yet in his slightly befuddled state he wasn't quite sure how much of the heat was caused by the fever, and how much was a result of Quintana Wade's closeness.

Together they made their way to an ancient oak where, with Quintana's aid, Draper sank slowly beneath the spreading boughs, stretching the injured leg out before him.

He didn't look at all well, and Quintana was worried. His breathing seemed labored, and his eyes, when he gazed up at her, were unnaturally bright. "Quintana," he said. "Be a cant lass and fetch me the whiskey."

She turned away, but in a moment returned with a flask, which she handed to Draper. He accepted it with a grateful nod, but didn't drink. Instead he loosened the straps that secured his leggings to his belt, and carefully edged the leather casing down, baring his leg to the knee.

Quintana gasped. The leg was swollen to twice its normal size, and the angry purplish-red that surrounded the lacerations themselves extended far up his thigh. "Dear God! How long have you known about this?"

"Since early this morning." He uncorked the flask and slowly poured a small amount of the amber liquid onto the festering wounds.

Quintana saw him tense, and sweat ran in runnels down his face. After a moment he sighed and sat back against the sturdy bole of the towering oak, closing his eyes. "Find Absolute," he said quietly.

Quintana went off and returned with the Scot a few minutes later to find Draper dozing. Absolute crouched beside him and sniffed the wound. "I daen't like the looks o' this," he muttered.

"What can we do?" Quintana asked. "There must be something."

Absolute got to his feet and stood gazing down at the sleeping frontiersman. His expression beneath his bushy red beard was one of gruff concern. "That depends," he said.

"On what?"

"On how sick he b'cums," the Scot replied. When Quintana frowned at him, he elaborated. "I seen this kind o' thing b'fore, and it doesna bode well for the lad."

His evasive reply irritated her. She did not want evasions or hints about Draper's dire condition. She could see the precarious state of his health without having it pointed out to her. She wanted answers, a remedy, a cure. "Well, if you've seen it before, then you must know how best to treat it."

Absolute met her gaze levelly. "I can tell ye how they'd do back at the fort, m'lady. They'd bleed him till he didna gie no nevermind, then when the leg turned black, they'd lop it off."

Quintana felt the blood drain from her face. Her voice when she replied was chill and determined. "Then it's a very fortunate thing for Captain Boone that he is not at the fort, for I will be damned if anyone will take his leg. Now that we have eliminated that possibility, is there any other way to help him? Or must we simply wait this out?"

A glimmer of admiration shone in the Scot's obsidian gaze. "Ye might try the Injun way, if ye've a mind."

"And that is?"

"Plants and roots and sich."

"Find what's required and bring it to me," Quintana said emphatically. "I'll go help Tilly with the fire and set some water to boiling."

Quintana worked diligently, helping Tilly to lay and light the fire, washing and peeling the roots Absolute had dug for her, tearing up her only spare chemise to make a compress for the wounds . . . and the entire time, her thoughts trudged round the same worn track.

Draper, Draper, Draper . . .

Draper and his beguiling, wicked ways, his avowed predilection for soft white skin and amber whiskey . . . his silken hair, as black as midnight skies . . . his golden eyes and confident stride . . .

She'd been stirring the barberry root in boiling water, but had to close her eyes against the sudden sting of tears. She could not imagine him limping along with the aid of a crutch. Once again, she vowed that he would not have to choose between his leg and his life. She would see to that.

A short time later the preparations were complete, and the battle to save Draper's leg began.

Quintana knelt beside him, and with a gentle hand on his shoulder, shook him awake. Pressing a tin cup into his hands, she said, "Drink this."

He sniffed it suspiciously, wrinkling his nose in distaste. "What the devil is it?"

"Barberry root and willow bark tea. Absolute said the Indians use it to fight infection and fever." Quintana used a stick to lift a rag from a small pot of boiled comfrey leaves, and dropped it, steaming, onto Draper's leg.

She heard him draw a startled breath, but he didn't speak, and never once did he take his eyes from her.

The rag grew cool, and Quintana replaced it, repeating the procedure again and again, working tirelessly until the liquid in the pot had grown tepid and Draper had once again drifted off to sleep.

Darkness was almost upon them, and Draper dreaded its coming, for before the sun rose again death would come to claim his young brother, Hamlin Boone . . .

Crouched on the lonely forest path, Draper gathered Hamlin's tall form into his arms and held him, the lad's raven head pressed close to Draper's breast.

Hamlin was just a lad, and he was dying . . . Draper could hear with a sickening clarity each of his gurgling breaths, could see the bright crimson stain on the upper left breast of the new linsey shirt he wore, the shirt their mother had sewn for him before he left home a few months ago . . .

"Draper . . ." It was spoken so softly, Draper had to strain to hear.

"Aye, lad, I'm here. Save your strength. Don't try to talk."

Hamlin went softly on, as though he hadn't heard. "You ever been scared?"

"More times than I can count," Draper said.

"I'm scared now," Hamlin gasped out. His thin face was ghastly in the shadows, pale white . . . and the life was slowly draining out of his eyes . . .

"I'm here with you, Hamlin."

Hamlin didn't answer. The light had left his eyes. He'd gone on alone, leaving Draper behind to carry on.

The ache of an unspeakable grief welled up inside Draper, flooding his chest, crowding his lungs so that each breath he took was expelled as a ragged sob. Holding the lifeless body of his youngest brother tightly to him, he threw back his head and vented his grief. His hoarse cry echoed down the night, loud and long, but it didn't matter. There was no one left to hear.

With the coming of night, Draper's temperature rose to dangerous new heights, and he tossed restlessly upon the ground, as if caught in the throes of some unsettling dream.

Quintana, sitting close by his side, dipped a cloth in cool water, and after wringing out the excess moisture, sponged his fevered brow.

He turned his head, and an agonized expression came over his face. His chest heaved with silent, wrenching sobs. "Hamlin . . . Hamlin, no . . ."

"Shhh," Quintana murmured. "It's only a dream. You must rest now." She touched her fingertips to his brow, and then his cheek. The coolness of her touch seemed to penetrate the fever-induced haze in which he labored, for he came instantly awake.

"Hamlin." He dragged himself up to lean on one elbow. For an instant his eyes were wild. Then he saw Quintana, and he seemed to calm. "Quintana . . ." he said, falling back. " 'Tis you. I thought—oh God, I must have . . . been dreaming."

He was quivering violently, but whether from the lingering effects of the dream or from the fever, Quintana could not tell. She put an arm around his shoulders to steady him, and held the cup to his lips. "Drink," she said.

He drank the cool water and sighed. "So tired."

"It's the fever," she said. "Rest and try to get well."

"What of you? Have you slept?"

"I'm fine," Quintana said.

He caught her hand and brought it to his cheek. "Your skin is cool . . . Lie with me awhile."

His request startled and shocked her. "Oh, no. I couldn't possibly."

"I'll rest better with you here by my side."

Quintana shot a swift glance at Tilly and the Scot, who were rolled in their blankets on the opposite side of the fire.

Surely there was no harm in granting his small request. He was too ill to make improper advances, and she would have spent the night a foot apart from him in any case.

He lifted the blanket in silent invitation.

"All right," she said. "But just this once, so that you will rest." She lay down with her back turned toward him and drifted into her dreams as Draper put an arm about her waist and gathered her close.

Chapter 12

Quintana awoke next morning to a feeling of luxuriant warmth. It seemed to surround her, envelop her . . . She stretched, turning instinctively toward the source of her comfort, and opened her eyes to find Draper.

He was awake and gazing lucidly down at her.

At first, Quintana was taken aback by his nearness. She looked away, and then she remembered.

She'd fallen asleep here beside him, she'd shared his bed . . .

They were lying very close together still, her hand nestled in the thick black silk of his hair. The skin of his chest felt like sun-warmed satin, and the abnormal heat of the previous night was gone.

Quintana raised her gaze to his again, her eyes wide. "How are you feeling?"

He lifted his hand and brushed the tip of her nose with his fingertip, smiling down at her. "Hungry," he answered.

Quintana smiled in return and rolled away from him, sitting up. Tilly was making a great show of preparing breakfast. Absolute sat companionably near, smoking a long-stemmed clay pipe. He watched Quintana intently as she stood up, yet he said nothing.

Quintana felt her cheeks redden. Tilly and Absolute were both aware that she had spent the night in Draper's bed, yet her embarrassment was nothing compared to the relief she felt at the realization that Draper was going to recover. She was feeling strangely light at heart as she went to the fire and brought him back his breakfast.

During the two days that followed Draper made a rapid recovery. On the first day after his fever had broken, Quintana had managed with little effort to keep him abed and quiet, while she continued to apply the hot comfrey compresses to his wounds. But with the dawning of the second day, there was seemingly nothing she could say or do that would keep him still. He insisted on testing the injury by ambling around the campsite, and then as his leg limbered up, he once again took his rifle and ventured farther afield, exploring the valley.

On the evening of the third day, Quintana ventured along the banks of the Shenandoah River, which ambled through the valley, within sight of the camp.

An unhurried violet dusk was quickly descending, and with it the hush so typical of the wilderness fell upon the land. By slow degrees the darkness deepened and the stars emerged, one by one, until the black night sky was filled with glittering points of silver light.

"What say you, m'lady? Does the Virginia

night pale by comparison to your lofty English skies?"

A wave of pleasure rippled through Quintana at the sound of his voice. Somehow she'd half-expected to find him here. Perhaps some secret part of her had even deigned to hope. "I never knew such a profound silence existed," she replied with a candor that surprised her. "It reminds me of St. Paul's Cathedral. As a child, I always imagined that I could feel the presence of God, and so I was too humbled to raise my voice above a whisper. It's like that here, in this valley. One only has to look at the magnificence that's everywhere to know that God is nigh." Quintana frowned into the dark. She had spoken with such reverence about *his* wilderness. Yet she could not recant her observations. "It really is magnificent, isn't it?"

"They say that it's enchanted," Draper replied. "Once, before the whites crossed the Blue Wall into this valley, the Shawnee, Catawba, and Delaware peoples hunted here. They claimed that this valley was chosen by the Great Spirit as a place where the stars could gather to sing for joy. One night as the stars sang, the face of the mountain split open and a great fount of water sprang forth to form a virgin lake.

"The moon and the stars went away, and spoke with veneration of that night. A thousand years passed, and when the moon and stars again gathered in the valley to sing, they found it more breathtakingly beautiful than they had remembered.

"The Great Spirit had taken some of the water from the mountains and used it to form the Shenandoah River, henceforth known as the Daughter of the Stars."

Quintana risked a glance at Draper. He was gazing not at her, but at the night sky, and his strong features were silver in the light of the rising moon.

She was surprised at how full her heart felt at that moment, shocked that acknowledging the savage beauty of the wilderness night with this rugged, earthy man could seem so wondrous, so natural, so right.

As they stood upon the banks of the broad Shenandoah, close but not touching, a gentle breeze stirred the treetops, sighing softly. "Listen, Draper!" Quintana whispered, catching at his hand. "Can you hear them sing?"

"Every time I look at you I hear them sing." He pressed a brief but fervent kiss upon her hand, then slowly led her away from the river. "Come," he said. "There's something else I would like you to see."

They wound their way along a forest path, emerging near the ghostly shell of the abandoned dwelling. Quintana pulled against his hand, afraid of what might lurk in the midst of such decay. "You aren't going in there?"

Draper sent a swift smiling glance her way. "Not afraid now, are you?" He ducked through the sagging doorway, gently urging her to follow. "Trust me, lass. There's nothing here to harm you."

Quintana entered carefully, stepping around

the accumulated debris of seasons of exposure and neglect that littered the floor—branches and dead leaves, smelling of mold and slow decomposition, mouse droppings and broken shingles.

"What could you possibly wish to show me in this crumbling cabin? There is nothing of value here . . . only the long-neglected remains of some simple farmer's life."

Draper leaned upon the mantel, glancing around with a strange half-smile. "It never was as grand as your residence in London. Just a simple farmer's house, as you so aptly said. In a year or two the forest will reclaim it, and there will be nothing left to come home to."

Home . . . Quintana's stomach tightened. "You know this place?"

"You see this mantel?" he asked, not expecting her to answer. "I carved my initials into it with Garrick's barlow knife when I was ten years old. Mother wasn't angry, but Garrick thumped me soundly for taking his knife without asking his leave beforehand."

There was an air of sadness infecting the structure. Quintana closely watched him, and wondered if he felt it as keenly as she did. Or was he impervious to the melancholy, insulated from all unpleasantness by the warmth of his memories? "It is a shame it's fallen into such rampant disrepair," she said.

"There was no one left to make improvements after Garrick died. Hamlin's heart was elsewhere—he had wanderlust like me—and Mother wasn't able."

Draper paused, and a companionable silence stretched between them. He was in a rare fine mood, Quintana thought, expansive almost. It seemed an opportune time to satisfy her curiosity concerning him ... and she *was* curious. In all the time they'd been together she had learned very little about Draper and his life. His past, his origins remained shrouded in mystery.

"You never did explain about the others," she said. "Your mother and Hamlin."

Draper raised his gaze to hers, frowning slightly. "Why do you wish to talk of death on such a night as this?"

"Why do you wish to avoid it?" Quintana asked. "You told me of Garrick, and I felt somehow I knew him. I wish to know about your mother and Hamlin, for in knowing them I will also know you."

She smiled up at him, her face strangely radiant, and Draper felt his will crumble just the smallest bit. "My mother's death followed Hamlin's by one month. They say her heart gave out from grief. It happened last September."

"It must have been very difficult for you," Quintana said. "Were you with her when she died?"

Draper shook his head. "The news reached me just before I left for England."

"It was insensitive of Winston to send you so soon after—"

"Your father's blameless. He only did what he thought best at the time." Seeing her dubious expression, Draper laughed softly. "Oh, 'tis true enough. I did not wish to go to England. But it served the purpose he intended."

"What purpose, Draper?" Quintana asked.

"By sending me to find you he put an ocean between me and the good lieutenant. He sought to put time and distance between us until my temper had cooled."

Quintana felt uncertain. "What does Hamlin's death have to do with Lieutenant Bell, Draper?"

Draper's gaze turned flinty. "Hamlin was sacrificed to the incompetence and overweening vanity of your betrothed."

"Sacrificed?" His reply shocked Quintana. "Surely you don't mean that!"

"We were preparing for a foray against the Seneca towns to the north when Hamlin arrived in August of '77," Draper said. "There had been a number of alarming incidents with the opening of the spring campaign, and since the Six Nations had openly declared for the British, we had every reason to expect that the situation would only worsen as the year wore on."

"And so you prepared to take the war to the Indian towns?"

"Aye," Draper said. His voice had a hollow ring to it, as if his thoughts were far away. "The mission was ill-fated from the start. Lieutenant Bell was the highest ranking able-bodied officer at the garrison, and so he was given command of the expedition."

He paused and ran a callused hand through his raven locks. Free from the confines of the leather thong, the shining dark strands fell forward to frame his lean dark face.

"What happened then?" Quintana prompted. She was eager to know, not just for curiosity's sake, but for her own peace of mind. Winston expected her to wed Uriah Bell; it was her right to know what sort of man he was. She listened closely.

"We were ill-provisioned and ill-equipped from the onset. But your Lieutenant Bell was impatient to prove himself, thirsting for glory, and so he insisted that we march ahead and rendezvous with the supply train later. It never came. We later learned that one of the wagons lost an axle and decided to head back to the fort.

"On the third day out it started to rain, and for a week there was not the slightest relief from the incessant damp. What little meal we had for the troops molded. The men became sick and dispirited."

Quintana heard him grind his teeth. "I went to Bell on behalf of the enlisted men, requesting a brief layover so that the troops could rest and my men and I could try and scare up some game. He flatly refused to consider it, and issued the order for an enforced march to the Seneca towns in Venango.

"By the middle of the second week we lost six men to his blasted arrogance and the inclement weather . . . one of my small company of scouts among them. I openly confronted Bell. We exchanged some heated words in the presence of his men. He would have had me lashed, except that no one possessed the bloody strength to carry out the order. Instead he ordered me confined under guard to a wagon in the rear.

"Early next morning he marched the column directly into an ambush. Of one hundred and fifty men, seventy-eight were killed and thirty wounded, five were captured, and the rest routed."

Reaching out, he ran a hand over the initials cut deep into the blackened wood. "When I finally got free of the guard and caught up with the column, the men were in a panic. The road was strewn with dead and wounded, and those who could, ran as if the very devil was hot upon their heels. Your young lieutenant, so bent upon glory, shed his honor as easily as a black snake sheds its skin when he saw they were outnumbered. He left the dead and the dying lying on the forest path and he ran for his worthless life."

"What became of Hamlin?"

A ragged sigh, a subtle tensing of his jaw. "I found him among the wounded. He'd taken a ball through the lung—his death was slow in coming. Seventeen years old," he said slowly. "He died in my arms . . . and there was not a goddamned thing that I could do to save him."

Quintana looked at him, her heart in her eyes. "What will come of all of this, once you return and face my father?"

He shrugged. The subtle movement of his broad shoulders set the fringe adorning his breast to swaying. "If I'm fortunate, the colonel will have persuaded Bell to reconsider the complaints he's leveled."

"And if not?" Quintana asked.

"Then I will have to take my chances," came Draper's soft reply. "I did assault an officer, and there were witnesses. For that alone, I could be lashed." As he spoke, he lifted his hand and ran his fingertips across her velvety cheek. "Let us speak of something else, Quintana . . . like the way your eyes capture the moonbeams." He bent and kissed her lowered lids. "I love your eyes, sweetheart, their limpid softness when you smile, their flash like quicksilver when you're angry . . ."

Quintana laughed uneasily. "For an unschooled backwoodsman, you have a pretty turn of phrase."

Draper smiled and gave her a look of practiced indolence. "I never claimed to be unschooled. In fact, I can think of many things that I could teach you. Things I'll wager staunch and staid Lieutenant Bell does not know."

"Wicked," she said with a cluck of her tongue. "Ever wicked."

She turned and walked to the opposite end of the hearth, putting a little distance between them, then glanced at him over her shoulder. "What will you do when this matter concerning Lieutenant Bell and his charges is at last resolved?"

His answer was simple, yet it chilled her. "The war continues, Quintana."

"It cannot go on forever," Quintana insisted. "One day the contest will be decided. What will you do then?"

A slow smile curved Draper's hard mouth, turning devilish by degrees, causing his eyes to crinkle at the outer corners. "Is this genuine concern? Or simple curiosity?".

"Concern implies that I care about you," Quintana quipped. "And *that* I will not admit! So I shall claim curiosity. The question, sir!"

"Either way, I'm heartened," Draper said. "I haven't given much thought to the future, beyond the mess I'm in. But I doubt that even after the war has ended, I would consider coming back here." He turned his hands over, palms up. "These hands weren't made to guide a plow. And I'm content to let the forest reclaim the land, the house. There's nothing here for me."

Quintana was surprised, and on some level strangely disappointed, though not at all sure why she should be. "Somehow I imagined you'd feel otherwise," she admitted. "I thought perhaps you'd want to settle here, to someday start a family."

But Draper only shook his head. "I've precious little to offer a woman besides a heated tumble and a name that's somewhat tarnished."

"What of love, Captain?" Quintana asked.

While she awaited his reaction, he slowly came toward her, closing the little distance she'd put between them. "Love is elusive," he proclaimed.

"Perhaps. But nevertheless love is all important," Quintana countered. "Passion, without deep abiding love, is worthless."

"How can you be certain?" Draper's dark head dipped, and he would have claimed her lips, but guessing his intent, Quintana hurried to place her slim fingers over his mouth.

"I will not be your paramour, Draper Boone, if that's what you have in mind!" she said.

He nibbled at her fingers. "Your sweet face haunts my dreams at night, Quintana. Thoughts of your delicious body drive me mad with wanting." He removed her hand and brought her close to nuzzle her fragrant hair. "Come, sweetheart. You've kept me at arm's length long enough. 'Tis time we had this out between us."

But Quintana remained implacable and pushed away, out of his arms. "Marriage may not play a part in your future, but it seems destined to play a part in mine."

Draper laughed scornfully. "You can't consider what you contemplate a marriage, or the good lieutenant a fitting husband!"

Quintana felt as if an icy hand closed over her heart. "Who are you to judge, sir? A man who scoffs at the concept of love, and wants no part of marriage? What you promote, I want no part of! I've suffered enough shame in my life because of the precipitous actions of others. I will not bring more degradation down upon my head for the sake of a 'heated tumble'!"

Draper frowned into the half-light. Damn her for using his own stupid utterances against him! "There is more than that between us, and you well know it!"

She spun around to face him, her silver eyes flashing. "Indeed? Then why don't you explain to me, sir, precisely what is between us?"

"How can I explain what I myself can't fathom?" he demanded harshly. Then with obvious effort he softened his tone. "I've known a lot of women in my lifetime, Quintana, but never has a woman had the effect upon me that you do. You're in my blood . . . and I can no more quench this burning need I feel to make you mine than I could will the moon from the night sky, or curse the stars from the heavens . . ."

Quintana shook her head, not wanting to believe him, or what was in her heart. "The night, this enchanted valley, has you in its grip. In the bold revealing light of day you would never say such things."

Draper came slowly forward; Quintana backed away. "Not the night, Quintana," he murmured, voice husky with emotion. "And not the Shenandoah. 'Tis you, and only you."

He touched her, and she weakened. He brought her soft and yielding self against his lean hard length, and their hearts thundered in unison . . .

"Trust me," he said. "Just this once. I swear to you, you won't regret it." Against her lips he coaxed convincingly, "Trust me . . ."

Draper kissed her then . . . and in his kiss there was no tenderness, no gentle consideration; that had all been swept away before a raging tide of desire too long held in check.

Quintana's will to resist, never strong enough where Draper was concerned, gave way with the sound of a softly uttered sigh.

Draper thought it the sweetest, most welcome sound he'd ever heard. Bending slightly, he gathered her into his arms and strode swiftly from the ruined house.

The copse was just as Draper remembered: secluded, and a little distance from the house. Here the moss grew thick and fragrant to make the perfect bed.

Draper sank down, taking his lady with him. The lacings at the back of her gown were easily managed. With studied care, he slipped the garment down, baring the soft curve of her slim shoulders, the uppermost contour of her breasts.

She was lovely.

Her skin was smooth, a pure and flawless alabaster in the light of the incandescent moon. Her breasts were high and full, veined with fragile blue.

Regarding the delicate beauty of her feminine form, Draper smiled to himself. Not long ago he'd wondered . . . and now he knew with certainty.

Her nipples were a soft, delicious shade of pink, just as he'd imagined they would be ...

Still smiling, he lowered his head, worshipping her with his mouth.

Quintana, watching Draper breathlessly, saw his dark head descend and knew that this was real. The seeds they'd sown so long ago in London were about to come to fruition. Draper Catworth Boone, frontier scamp and ne'er-do-well, Indian fighter and womanizing rake, was about to become her lover.

He captured her nipple, wringing a startled gasp from Quintana. His mouth was shockingly hot, his tongue exquisitely rough, teasing and abrading her sensitive flesh.

Quintana felt her stomach flutter, and in that instant something lower down and deep echoed a dim and restless reply. Her response to him was unsettling. Had she erred in giving in so easily?

Sensing her doubts, Draper hastened to reassure her. Tonight she was warm and almost willing and he was consumed by the burning need to have her; this was not the time for second thoughts. "You are so delectable, so soft and utterly desirable," he said, gazing deep into her silver-colored eyes.

She wet her lips, nervously, Draper thought. "I am ... uncertain that this is right. Perhaps we shouldn't—"

"Shouldn't what, sweetheart?" he deftly countered, slipping his hand beneath her linsey-woolsey skirts. He placed a gentle questing hand upon her derriere. Her flesh was smooth and silky, so warm, so wondrously soft. "Shouldn't touch when that is what we ache to do?"

He kissed her brow and shuttered lid, nuzzled his full lower lip over her starry lashes. "What shouldn't we do, lass? Hmmm? This perhaps?" Kissing her lips, he drew her even closer, urging her hips to meld with his, allowing her to feel his passion, hot, and hard and waiting for her . . . only for her.

Drawing in a startled breath, Quintana trembled, but she did not attempt to pull away. Instead she raised her eyes to his, which were large and luminous, which mirrored her doubts, her indecision.

Draper took her lips again, kissing her deeply, languidly, until she relaxed once more. "Place your trust in me for a little while, Quintana. I swear to you, I'll bring you no pain, and no regrets. In a way, you've been asleep. Let me be the one to awaken you, to show you how varied and how miraculous the ways of love can be."

Draper's words were persuasive, but his touch was the deciding factor, for while he'd spoken, his questing hand had slid across her hip to the downy curls that crowned her womanhood, to the source of the restless fluttering Quintana had noticed before. With deft care, he urged it once again to trembling life.

Sighing her sweet surrender, Quintana let

go of her doubts and inhibitions and gave herself up to Draper's tender ministrations.

In that first instant when his skilled fingers met her virgin's flesh, Quintana felt strangely shy, hesitant. Her reaction, however, was fleeting as she warmed to Draper's sexual play. She grew bolder, touching Draper in return, tangling her fingers in his thick black hair.

It was astonishingly soft, like cool silk against her palms. She kissed the shining strands, straining against him, slipping her small hands inside his belted shirt, reveling in the satiny texture of his skin stretched taut over rippling muscle.

Groaning against Quintana's ear, Draper loosened his knotted sash so that his shirt fell open and she could explore his rock-hard frame.

Emboldened by a desire she couldn't comprehend, Quintana ran her hands across his chest.

Dear God. His body was smooth and tawny, even in the moonlight, wonderful to touch.

Splaying her fingers, she slid her palms across his tautly drawn pectorals, feeling them flex involuntarily though her touch was feather-light, lingering there.

Yet Draper grew impatient with her innocent play, for he covered her hand with his and groaned against her ear. "Touch me, sweetness. *Touch me.*"

Guiding her fingers down, across his corded ribs and flat stomach, he urged her to a slow and thorough exploration of his magnificent body.

Quintana felt the shallow indentation of his navel and, just below, the thin line of coarse hair that knifed downward to the base of his pelvis, where his manhood stood erect.

Her fingers brushed the turgid flesh. He was fully aroused, and radiated a fevered heat.

Feeling startled and unsure, she started to withdraw, but Draper would not permit it. Whispering endearments close at her ear, he took her small hand, molding it firmly around his swollen shaft.

"Don't be afraid," he said, kissing her lips, touching her intimately. "Don't *ever* be afraid of me."

Draper's touch became insistent; Quintana sighed and closed her eyes, caressing him. But he would not permit her to escape him in any way. "Look at me, Quintana."

At his soft but urgent command, she opened her eyes, lifting her gaze to his dark face.

He was so handsome. It pained her to look upon him, knowing they would soon be parted, possibly forever, yet because he bade her, she could not look away.

He brought his left hand up to cup her cheek. "Don't close your eyes when you're with me like this. Hide from your betrothed if it pleases you to do so, Quintana, but don't ever seek to hide from me. Selfish bastard that I am, I want all of you. I want to know that I'm the one who's in your thoughts this moment."

Quintana's throat felt strangely tight, so full she couldn't speak. When his fingers moved against her cheek, she nodded weakly, too prideful, too frightened of losing him in that moment to tell him that for her there could be no other man . . . in her thoughts . . . in her heart.

He drew her closer, gazing deeply into her eyes as he worked his magic on her senses, not allowing her to look away, to conceal from him the naked emotion she knew must plainly show upon her face.

It was cruel of him to demand every scrap, every morsel of herself, leaving nothing to her but her empty virtue. Yet even in his selfishness, Quintana found she loved him, loved the throbbing sensation of heat that he coaxed from her secret places, loved the yearning, so deep, so exquisite, that filled her woman's flesh.

Draper teased and he tormented, and all the while the feeling of sweet anticipation mounted within Quintana, bursting all at once in an explosion of ecstatic frenzy, and she was helpless to stem the soft cry of bliss that escaped her lips.

Wondrous sensation washed over her; she gripped him, released, then gripped again.

And then he was dragging her to him, kissing her hard . . . melting against her . . .

For long moments Quintana and Draper lay touching, the warm wet evidence of a passion shared lying unnoticed between them.

Holding Quintana tightly, Draper nuzzled her soft fragrant tresses. She smelled faintly of roses, English roses . . . Her small face was pressed against his breast, and he could feel her breath soft and sighing on his skin.

How sweet she was, how virginal and untried . . . and he was the worst kind of fool for taking it upon himself to awaken her sexually.

Uriah Bell would not thank him, despite the great pains he'd taken to preserve her sainted virginity . . . And then there was Winston, who would doubtless be livid if he were to discover the liberties a mere captain of the scouts had taken with his only daughter.

There would be hell to pay for this night, Draper thought with a sigh. Yet as he recalled Quintana's willingness, her lusty response to so simple an act, Draper knew that whatever the price he must pay in the end to possess her, Quintana Wade was worth it.

Chapter 13

In the days that followed, the quartet of travelers left the Virginia Road behind, heading west along the Raystown Path, into the very heart of the Allegheny Mountains.

Because of Draper's injured leg their pace at first was slow, but as the days ticked by and his wounds began to heal, they once again resumed their relentless push to breach the mountain barrier that stood between them and the Monongahela Country.

Land-hungry settlers had begun crossing the Blue and Tuscarora mountains as early as 1740, carving farms and fields out of the trackless forest, yet for the most part, the complexion of the land itself was little changed.

Miles of nearly impenetrable woodlands separated cabin from lonely cabin; the land between was dark and brooding, a mysterious realm of deep green gloom and endless shadows for which Quintana felt not only horror, but an unshakable fascination.

Ancient trees, too great in circumference for Tilly and Quintana joining hands to reach around, soared a hundred feet and more above the forest floor. The heavy foliage combined with the tangled vines of wild grapes to form a dense canopy through which the strongest sunlight could not completely penetrate.

But the strangest aspect of the wilderness, and the one Quintana found the most unnerving, was the profound and eerie silence through which they made their laborious way.

There was no birdsong, no noise to break the unearthly quiet, and the same deathly stillness that ruled the deepest part of night held an unchallenged sway at noon.

It was a frightening place, Quintana thought, as harsh and primitive as Draper's Shenandoah was enchanted, yet it possessed a haunting beauty that seemed to cast a spell upon the heart and soul, and even she was not left unaffected.

Just past the Burnt Cabins on Little Aughwick Creek they came upon an isolated cabin. An elderly man sat in the dooryard, carving on a length of wood. He raised a gnarled hand as they rode by. Draper called his name, but didn't slow the roan.

"Is he living out here all alone?" Quintana asked.

"Not alone, precisely," Draper replied. "There's a small settlement a few miles ahead called Fuller's Gap. If it pleases you, we'll stay the night with a friend and continue on tomorrow."

"If it pleases me!" Quintana laughed, a trifle wryly. "After all this time in the wilderness, the idea of spending the night beneath a real rooftree pleases me very much indeed! But how do you know we'll be welcome? Your friend can't possibly know we're coming."

"Maeve is always glad for company," Draper said matter-of-factly.

"Maeve?" Quintana said, striving hard to keep the disappointment she felt from creeping into her voice.

"She was Maeve Gordon until she married Farley MacDivitt a few years back. Farley died two years ago."

Quintana digested this information, saying nothing.

They were approaching another cabin, this one slightly larger than the last, a two-room dwelling constructed of squared logs and chinked with wattle and daub, a mortar made of mud and deer hair that helped seal out the chill winds that swept down the valley in winter.

The building itself was windowless. Glass, Draper explained, was a luxury that most families west of the mountains could ill-afford. Twin portals, however, had been fashioned on either side of the door, and the heavy shutters that normally sealed them in times of strife had been thrown wide to catch the balmy breeze.

In the dooryard, at a little distance from the house, a woman of middle years was busily stirring a smoking kettle. She was short in stature and shaped like a dumpling, with hair the color of straw. When she heard the horses approach she straightened, shading her eyes with her work-worn hand.

Quintana held her breath and hoped that this was Maeve MacDivitt. But as Draper drew rein and leaped lightly to the ground, her hopes were dashed.

"Have those eagle eyes of yours grown so dim with age, Anna, that you don't recognize me?" he demanded.

"Not so terribly dim, young man, that I can't tell a rascal when I see one!" the woman called Anna quipped. She came forward to grasp Draper's hand. "Truth to tell, I'm shocked to see you. We'd heard that you were missing and figured that some Mingo buck had claimed those shaggy locks to decorate his lodgepole."

Draper grinned and bussed Anna's cheek. "Are you set for guests, Anna? Or should we move along?"

"Why, Draper Boone!" Anna said. "Of course, there's room. I'm surprised that you would even ask such a thing." She pushed him brusquely away, but Quintana noted the rosy blush of pleasure shining high upon her apple cheeks. "You always were a sinful young man, swift to tease, and it's easy to see you haven't changed. Now, mind the manners your ma taught you, and tell me who this is."

Draper took Quintana by the waist and swung her down. "Anna Lawson, this is Mistress Quintana Wade, Colonel Winston Wade's daughter, newly arrived from England,

and this is Tilly Bascombe. I believe you know Absolute." Then to Quintana, "Anna is Maeve's aunt. She's lived with Maeve since Farley's death."

There was no time for further explanation, for at that moment a voluptuous dark-haired woman appeared at the far end of the cabin. For the space of a heartbeat she stood stockstill, and then with a squeal of delight she lifted her skirts and ran to Draper, flinging herself into his arms.

Laughing and crying at once, she kissed his smiling face. "I knew you'd come back! I told James so just yesterday, didn't I, Anna?"

Draper smiled down at the raven-haired beauty, seemingly oblivious to the fact that they were not alone.

Quintana watched from where he'd left her. It was not an easy scene to witness, and she had to struggle hard to fight down her rising jealousy. That the two had once been very close was blatantly obvious. And she could only speculate as to whether their relationship had ended.

Not that it truly mattered, she told herself. She herself had no real claim upon Draper. One night of intimacies shared did not forge a commitment, and that night ten days ago when they'd stood in the ruins of his boyhood home, Draper had made it exceedingly clear that he wanted no woman, *nothing* to tie him down, to curtail his precious freedom.

Where Draper was concerned, Quintana had no illusions. So why would this cold, burning ache seated deep within her vitals not simply go away?

"We heard about Hamlin," Maeve was saying. "I'm sorry, truly I am." She hugged him tightly, then stepped back. "How are you, Draper, really?"

"Hungry," he said evasively, his golden glance unreadable as it shifted from Maeve's rapt face to Quintana, who immediately looked away.

"How long can you stay?"

"Just the night. I have to get back—"

"A single night!" Maeve cried, then, planting her balled fists on her hips, she bent a hard stare upon him. "Draper Catworth Boone, I'll hear no talk of your going off so soon! You only just arrived, and knowing you as I do, I've little doubt you've pushed your poor companions relentlessly. Besides, James and I are getting married two days hence. You can give the bride away."

Draper snorted. "As full of piss and vinegar as you are, I'm surprised you've found a man who'll marry you."

"James Reed knows a good thing when he sees it!" With a saucy look and a toss of her dark head, Maeve turned on her heel and proceeded to take her guests in hand.

"My dear Miss Wade, Miss Bascombe," Draper heard her say. "How difficult your journey must have been, how trying!" Maeve threw him a dark look over her shoulder. "Being at the mercy of that arrogant, impossible, pigheaded man!"

For a long moment, Draper stood staring after the retreating women, a thoughtful frown upon his face.

"Draper tells me you're from England," Maeve said, smiling at Quintana. She was placing wooden trenchers on the rough plank table as she spoke. "What brings you to America, if you don't mind my asking?"

"And if she does mind, will it stay your naturally nosy bent?" Draper put in.

"Oh, do be silent!" Maeve said. "I'm trying to have a civilized discourse with Miss Wade."

"It's quite simple, really," Quintana answered. "My father sent for me. As you may already know, he commands the garrison at Fort Pitt, west of the mountains."

"Simple! I should think the passage alone would be a harrowing experience in these troubled times. Why, with British men-of-war prowling the Atlantic, I'm surprised you were able to find a captain willing to run the risk of losing his ship."

Quintana sent a teasing glance in Draper's direction. "One might think so, but Draper has proven himself a very resourceful man. Not only was he able to find a ship to transport us to America, he was also able to convince me that I should come to his homeland when I was quite adamant about wanting to remain in England."

Maeve's startled glance flew to Draper's face. "*You* went to England?"

"He did indeed," Quintana replied. It was wicked of her to bait him intentionally, but he himself had told her once that wickedness could at times be highly entertaining. Watching as his face flushed dark, she smiled, twisting the blade the smallest bit. "In fact, he quite took us by storm, throwing the household into a tizzy. And I daresay, nothing has been the same since his arrival on my doorstep."

Maeve was still gaping at Draper. Shifting in his chair, he cleared his throat and asked if she had any liquid refreshment. She brought him a gourd full of fresh spring water, which he eyed suspiciously. "This isn't exactly what I had in mind."

"I know very well what you have in mind," Maeve said. "And it won't kill you to abstain until the wedding."

"Oh, aye, *the wedding*. When's Jamie comin' back?" Draper drained the gourd and pulled a face.

"He's been home two weeks, but will be returning to Fort Pitt soon. His furlough is up at month's end." She ladled a rich chicken stew into Draper's trencher, then moved on to Absolute. "You'll consent to stay for the wedding, won't you?"

Draper glanced up. The room had fallen suddenly silent, and every pair of eyes were trained upon him. "The stew's delicious, Anna," he said. "My compliments."

Maeve drew down her dark winged brows and glared at him. He sensed a storm coming.

"Draper!" she said. "It's two days hence, and you know what fun it will be. These good people are tired, and so are you, if only you'd admit it."

Absolute stroked his beard with one knotted brown hand. "We could all o' us use the rest, lad."

Tilly said nothing, but the gaze she'd fixed upon him was hopeful.

Draper clenched his teeth.

Such a lengthy delay had not been part of his plans . . . yet two days with little to do but woo Quintana was a highly tempting prospect, difficult indeed to resist.

Maeve sidled close to his chair. Her voice was soft and persuasive. "Quintana has never witnessed a frolic the likes of which we're planning. Surely you haven't the heart to deny her a few days of innocent, much-deserved fun."

Draper's gaze slid to Quintana. Her lovely face was alight with interest and anticipation, and though she didn't say a word, he knew that she, like Tilly and Absolute, Maeve, and even Anna, was hoping that he would capitulate.

Shifting his gaze back to his hostess, Draper decided to try and strike a bargain. "If I consent to stay, will you not badger me about staying a minute more than three days and find me some whiskey?"

Without a word, Maeve went into the adjoining room and returned with a crockery jug which she placed within easy reach—yet did not relinquish. "Your solemn word," she said.

Draper nodded. "Three days we'll stay, no longer. We leave for Fort Pitt the morning following the nuptials."

Maeve pushed the jug into his hands. "Agreed. Now take that jug and Absolute and go on over to James's place. He'll be glad for the company, but mind! If you get him drunk before the wedding, you won't have to worry about the Mingo. I'll have your scalp myself."

As Draper rose to go, he met Quintana's glance. "I'll be back long before dark."

"Don't bother," Maeve told him. "James has ample room to put you up. You can stay with him until the wedding."

Draper frowned down at Maeve, seeing the slow disintegration of his plans mirrored in the black eyes of his former mistress. "What about Quintana? Her father placed her in my care. I'd be remiss in my duty if I left her unprotected."

Placing her hands against his chest, Maeve backed him toward the door. "It's Quintana I'm thinking of," she insisted. "She's the colonel's daughter, Draper. And there's little privacy in this cabin. Do you truly want to run the risk of ruining her reputation?"

His answering scowl was ominous, but Maeve was not impressed. "If you're worried for her safety, then don't. Anna and I can make use of a rifle and an ax, the same as you. And we have old Scratch to keep watch and warn us." Upon hearing his name mentioned, the

huge hound lying near the hearth thumped
his tail against the puncheons.

"I still don't like it."

Maeve shoved him out the door after Absolute. "And I know why you don't like it," she
said in a voice too soft to carry. "We'll discuss
it later, of that you may be sure."

With a final burning look directed at
Quintana, Draper tucked the jug securely
beneath his arm and turned reluctantly away.
"I can think of nothing worse than a meddle-
some matron with time on her hands."

Maeve closed the door and leaned against
it. "Now we can talk freely," she said. "But
first come with me. There's something you
must see."

Quintana left her seat at table and followed
Maeve into the adjoining room.

The log house built by Farley MacDivitt was
sparsely furnished; it contained only the sim-
plest necessities of life: the rough plank table
and hard wooden benches, a spinning wheel
and low stool residing in a corner by the great
stone hearth, a three-legged bed built against
the corner wall in the adjoining room, and
placed near the foot of the bed, a brass hip
bath very like the one Quintana had owned
in London.

"My first husband, Farley, spoiled me
shamelessly," Maeve explained. "We met and
married in Virginia, and spent the first two
months of our marriage in Richmond. Farley
knew how I loved a hot bath, and so he bought
me the tub for a wedding gift. When we came

north, he hired a man who owned a pack train to carry that tub over the mountains, knowing in his heart how I hated the thought of leaving it behind."

"It must have cost him a small fortune," Quintana said.

"It did," Maeve answered. "But Farley didn't care. He told me not long before he died that it had been worth every cent and then some because it had brought me such delight." She touched the high backrest with loving fingers, smiling softly at Quintana. "There's water warming on the hearth. If you'd like, we could fill it for you."

"Oh, but I couldn't impose," Quintana said, then bit her lip, looking at the tub. She had been dreaming of a bath since England.

"Don't be silly," Maeve told her. "Your journey has been a long one, and a good long soak in a steaming tub is precisely what you need."

A half-hour later Quintana stepped over the rim and sank down into the steaming bath. The soap Maeve provided did not smell of English roses. Made by Anna's clever hands, it was strong and smelled slightly acidic.

Quintana didn't care. She vigorously scrubbed every inch of skin and washed her hair, not emerging from the bath until her feet and hands were pale and wrinkled.

She'd finished wrapping the length of linen that served as a towel about her just as Maeve entered the room. "This should fit you well enough, I think." She spread a gown of creamy yellow linen upon the quilted counterpane, along with stockings and chemise. "Anna's set your things to soak. We'll wash them out properly tomorrow and they'll be fresh for your departure."

"I don't know how to thank you," Quintana said. "Your kindness to a stranger, and an Englishwoman at that, is overwhelming."

"Nonsense! I'm very glad that Draper brought you here to me. It's a real treat to talk with someone near to my own age. Not that I don't value Anna's company, for I do."

Quintana understood, having had no one to turn to but Tilly throughout the years of her girlhood and adolescence. And while she'd always been very fond of the older woman, there had been certain matters they'd never broached . . . matters of the heart. And the strength of her feelings for Draper had taken her quite by surprise.

"I recognize that look, Quintana," Maeve said. There was empathy in her voice as well as a deep underlying thread of concern. "I daresay I've worn it a time or two myself, for all the good it did me."

Quintana sat down on the edge of the bed, busying herself with rolling one of the borrowed stockings so that she wouldn't need to meet Maeve's eyes. "I'm not sure I know what you mean."

"I saw the way you look at Draper, and though I know it is none of my business, I feel compelled to warn you." Maeve sighed and, gathering her skirts, sat down on the mattress near the foot of the bed. "You may not know it yet, but Draper is not the sort of man a woman marries."

I've precious little to offer a woman besides a heated tumble . . .

Those words had been burned into Quintana's thoughts, underscoring the hopelessness of her romance with Draper.

Promised to one man, desperately in love with another . . .

Quintana took a deep breath, forced a smile, and lied through her teeth. "You needn't worry, Maeve," she said. "I'm not looking for a husband. Indeed, my betrothed awaits my arrival at Fort Pitt. I expect we shall be married soon."

It was a wonder that she hadn't choked on the words. After learning from Draper the part Uriah Bell had played in the death of his brother Hamlin Boone, Quintana had been able to summon nothing but scorn for the lieutenant.

"As for Draper," Quintana went on, "he is my father's envoy, assigned to escort me to the fort and to Uriah, and once we arrive, I honestly doubt I will be seeing him again."

"What a terrible liar you are," Maeve said. "But I can take a hint. It's easy to see you don't wish to discuss it, and I won't press the point."

Feeling somewhat relieved, Quintana glanced at Maeve. "Have you known Draper long?"

"Since I was six years old," Maeve replied.

Quintana wet her lips. She had no right to ask. Indeed, she was making herself out to be the liar that Maeve had accused her of being just by displaying an interest in a man she pretended meant nothing to her. Yet she had to ask, had to know everything about Draper there was to know. "What was he like as a boy?"

"Wild." Maeve smiled softly. "He hasn't changed at all in that respect."

"You loved him, didn't you?"

"Since the first day I laid eyes on him."

"But you wed another man."

Maeve nodded. "Yes. But Draper and I were always at cross purposes. I wanted a home and babies. He wanted his freedom. For a time we were lovers. I was sixteen and he was twenty. But he was always going off somewhere, and as the years went by, I grew tired of waiting. And then Farley came along, and he was the very opposite of Draper. I never regretted my decision."

Maeve sighed and wiped her eyes with the back of her hand. "And in two days hence I will marry again. James is every woman's dream. Strong, steady, reliable, and he loves me to distraction. He'll be a good provider, and once the war is over, he won't go off adventuring again. He'll stay here with me, and we'll grow old together."

"You make it sound so idyllic," Quintana said.

"It is *my* idyll, Quintana," Maeve said, taking Quintana's hand. "Oh, I know that James isn't Draper. He's plain of feature and inclined to stoutness. But he's mine, and I can go to sleep knowing that he'll be there when I wake up." With that, she rose from the bed. "I didn't mean to prattle on. But I do hope you'll think about what I've said . . . and guard your heart well where Draper is concerned."

Quintana watched Maeve quit the room. She didn't have the courage to admit to Draper's former mistress and her newfound friend that her warning came too late.

Chapter 14

Life on the fringe of civilization was insular; the cycle of hardship and toil, the struggle just to keep body and soul and family together, unending. It was a harsh environment, where only the strong or the canny survived and prospered, and where opportunities to cast one's cares aside seldom rose.

Maeve Gordon MacDivitt's marriage to James Reed was just such an occasion, and word had spread like wildfire on a hot August wind that there was to be a wedding frolic on Little Aughwick Creek.

Folks from up and down the valley would attend, and from as far away as Tussey Mountain, where James's sister and her family resided.

It would be a time of merriment, Draper knew, and he was greatly looking forward to spending some long anticipated time alone with Quintana.

His thoughts were full of the colonel's flaxen-haired daughter and a night of uninterrupted carnal bliss, and Draper had no more than touched the razor to his soapy chin when he saw the apparition appear in

212

the cracked and faded glass above his right shoulder.

Startled, he flinched, cutting his chin and letting go with a string of muffled curses as he turned to glare at the dark-haired young woman whose sudden unannounced presence had precipitated the mishap. "Damn it, woman! You know better than to sneak up on a man like that. I might have cut my throat!"

"It would save Colonel Wade considerable trouble," Maeve said, meeting his gaze in the glass.

"Precisely what is that supposed to mean?"

"Wolverine Wade's daughter, Draper! What are you thinking?" She threw a hand in the air and made a noise of disgust. "Never mind. I *know* from experience *exactly* what you are thinking!"

Draper deliberately delayed his reply. It was bad enough he must answer to Quintana's father; he didn't welcome the interference of this dark-haired harridan in his life. "Has it occurred to you, madam, that you are overstepping the bounds of our friendship by sticking your nose where it does not belong?"

Maeve crossed her arms beneath her breasts and glared at him. "Precisely what are your intentions toward Quintana?"

"Has she sent you here?" Draper demanded coldly.

Maeve stamped her foot in irritation. "You know that she has not! I've come of my own accord because I cannot abide the thought of you harming that innocent girl."

"Innocent!" Draper laughed harshly. "She's not the wilting lily you make her out to be. She damned near shot me in London, and would have, I might add, had she not had such pitiful aim. Your concern is misplaced and unwanted, madam. I highly suggest you limit it to your husband, where it rightly belongs, and leave Quintana to me."

"You'd like that, wouldn't you?" Maeve shot back. "Nothing would please you more than to have me stand aside and sing your praises while you steal both her heart and her virtue and trample them merrily into the dust. The grand and imposing Draper Catworth Boone, bloody risk-taking unthinking fool!"

"You've got James, damn it! Why in bloody hell must you nag at me?" Draper started to turn his back on her, to simply walk away, but she was determined to have it out, and grabbed his arm, bringing him back to face her.

"Quintana is a sweet girl, Draper. And she does not deserve what you have in mind for her."

The look he bent upon her would have chilled a lesser woman to the very marrow, but Maeve stood toe to toe with him, completely undaunted by his black expression. "I can see now that I made a grave mistake in coming here. But I had no way of knowing how shrewish you've become in my absence."

His insulting tone didn't seem to faze Maeve, who narrowed her dark eyes. "You're sticking out your neck by playing fast and loose with the daughter of Wolverine Wade."

Draper snorted derisively. "It's my neck, now isn't it?"

She pursed her lips and stared thoughtfully at him for a long moment. "If you are so bent upon having her, then why not court her properly?"

Draper knew the wild urge to laugh, but he could see she was deadly serious. "What the devil are you suggesting?"

"Marry the girl," Maeve said with a casual air Draper found maddening. "You're twenty-nine, and that's not young by any standard. Why not take the girl to wife, settle down, and raise a family? It seems to me you could do far worse than to marry the colonel's daughter."

"What have I to offer her?" he demanded, wondering how she could even make such a suggestion. "I have no fortune, no family, and damned few prospects."

"Offer her the one thing of value that you are at liberty to give. The only thing she wants. Your heart, your love, your all," Maeve said, unperturbed. "From the little I have seen of her, I would wager all that I own that she would accept with alacrity."

Draper raked a hand through his tousled dark hair. "For Christ's sake, Maeve! The girl was reared in England! She could never adjust to this!"

"Then you *have* thought of it," Maeve said, eyes bright with female cunning.

"Enough to realize that it would never work." He sighed. "This discussion is a foolish waste of time," he said abruptly. "It doesn't matter what I want, or what Quintana will or won't accept. She's promised to Lieutenant Uriah Bell."

Maeve shrugged lightly. "I've heard it said that engagements are made to be broken." Tapping her cheek with one long and elegant forefinger, she frowned. "Uriah Bell . . . Why is that name so familiar?" A moment passed and a look of dawning suspicion came over her lovely features. "Dear God. Uriah Bell. James mentioned him. He was the one commanding the expedition that cost your brother Hamlin's life!" Suspicion turned to horror. "Oh, Draper . . . you wouldn't think of taking Quintana's virginity to gain revenge upon Lieutenant Bell?"

He was no longer sure of his motives. Indeed, he couldn't seem to think beyond their next encounter, beyond her haunting beauty, beyond her cool, enchanting spirit . . .

Maeve's query was met with stubborn silence.

She came forward, laying a hand upon his forearm while gazing intently, worriedly, up into his handsome dark visage. "Are you truly so embittered that you would abuse an innocent to get back at Uriah Bell?"

"Uriah Bell can sup with Satan for all I care," Draper said in a low voice. "As for your obvious distress, Mrs. MacDivitt, it's unwarranted where Quintana is concerned. She's as virginal today as she was when I first laid eyes on her in England. Her virtue, I assure you, is not being threatened. Least of all by me. Now, if you don't mind, I'd like to finish shaving."

Maeve gave him a last suspicious glance, then turning on her heel, stalked into James's cabin.

When the cabin door clicked softly shut, Draper brought the blade along his throat, scraping away the last remaining bit of soap that clung to his skin.

Maeve was far from satisfied with his evasive replies, but he felt sure she'd hold her tongue in Quintana's presence and save the brunt of her displeasure for him.

That knowledge alone should have eased his mind considerably, yet he felt restless, unsettled, a feeling that was heightened by the realization that it was becoming increasingly difficult to think of Quintana as the lieutenant's woman, the colonel's chit, and far easier to imagine claiming her as his own . . .

The danger of this way of thinking was not totally lost on Draper, but somewhere along the way, it had ceased to matter quite as much as once it had.

Preparations for the wedding began in earnest that same day. Maeve was busy making pumpkin pies while Anna Lawson boiled cabbage; Tilly pared apples brought from the cave behind the hill for tarts. The cabin was filled with a variety of wonderful aromas, and there was not an idle hand among the four women.

Having no experience in culinary arts, Quintana took the split broom and swept the bedroom and the common room clean, then turned her hand to polishing the two pewter candlesticks that once had belonged to Maeve's grandmother in Sheffield, England.

Maeve took the last pie from the hearth and placed it on the great plank board to cool, then sank down upon the bench and fanned her flushed face with her apron. "You needn't do that, Quintana. You're a guest here, and you shouldn't be working."

"I don't mind, really," Quintana replied simply, then smiled to herself. Once, not so very long ago, she would have considered such tasks beneath her. Yet as strange as it seemed, she derived a certain solace in performing the simple chores, in knowing that in some small way she was contributing to the celebration of Maeve's and James's newfound happiness, and for a little while she could be included in the tightly knit frontier community, a part of Draper's world.

Hoofbeats sounded outside the cabin, swiftly approaching. Wiping her hands on her apron, Anna hurried to the doorway. "Looks like we've got our work cut out for us. Maeve, dear, if you and Quintana can finish up here on your own, Tilly and I will supervise the roasting of the meat. It appears our young Mr. Boone has put his talent with a rifle to good use."

Just the mention of Draper's name made Quintana's blood pulse a little faster through her veins. Every cell of her being urged her to rise and go to the door, where she might catch a glimpse of him, yet she resisted, forcing herself instead to concentrate on the task at hand.

Maeve rose and wandered to the door. "I'll just go out and see that the menfolk have some refreshment."

Alone at last, Quintana paused in her labors and closed her eyes, straining hard to hear the rich baritone of Draper's voice, the warm stirring sound of his laughter . . .

When she heard his voice, it was not outside the cabin, but very close to her ear. "What are you dreaming of, m'lady?"

Of you . . . her yearning heart replied.

She raised her shuttered lids and gazed into his beloved amber eyes. How clear they were, their sparkling depths brimming with some deep and undefined emotion.

If only she could read his thoughts . . .

"I didn't expect to see you." Quintana's statement sounded lame, even to her own ears.

Draper took her hands, pulling her to her feet and into his arms. "Upon my life, sweetheart, I could not stay away."

One swift kiss and then Maeve's voice came to Draper's ears, ever closer. He lifted his head and looked toward the open door. "Flaming, harping shrew!" he muttered, breaking away just long enough to close and bolt the door.

"Draper!" Quintana said, shocked. "What on earth do you think you are doing?"

"Managing a few moments alone with you," he replied, closing the shutters and securing the latches.

"You are wicked," Quintana said.

"I am desperate," he returned. He closed the distance between them in three swift strides. "Now, where were we?"

"Here," Quintana answered, lifting her hand and touching a finger to his sensuous lips.

Draper gave it a nip, then took its tip into his mouth, chuckling when he heard her startled gasp. "You taste like ashes."

"I was helping Maeve," she said.

"Help me instead. I've missed you." Draper's dark head dipped and his lips brushed Quintana's tentatively.

Instinctively Quintana opened to him, savoring him, drawing his tongue into her mouth and gently sucking, until she heard his low and anguished groan and felt the pulse of his maleness press against the softness of her belly.

"Draper? Draper! Are you in there?" Maeve's voice filtered through the plank door, full of ire. She rattled first the door, and then in turn the shuttered windows, but to no avail, for Draper paid her little heed. "Why, of all the nerve! Barring me from my own house!"

"See to the wedding feast," Draper suggested. " 'Twill keep you busy!"

"Busy! I'll show you 'busy'! Open this door at once!"

Quintana bit her lip. "Draper, it is her house. And it's terribly rude of you to lock her out."

"Quintana? Quintana, are you all right? He hasn't harmed you, has he?"

Draper put a finger to her lips and urged her toward the bedchamber, but Quintana dug in her heels. "Heartless wretch! Tomorrow is her wedding day!"

"So it is. What has that to do with us?"

He attempted to steal a kiss, but Quintana eluded his advances, ducking beneath his arm and backing cautiously away while he slowly stalked her.

"Tomorrow is her wedding day, Draper! A day every woman dreams of. A day she'll remember the rest of her life. It *must* be special . . . and I won't stand by and help you to spoil things for her."

Draper frowned at Quintana. There was something in her tone he didn't like. He touched her face with wistful fingers and sought to turn her thoughts from Maeve. "Every woman, you say. But what of you? Do you dream of your wedding day, Quintana? Do you wish for it? Will you carry it in your heart the rest of your days?"

Draper saw her lovely features tense, and her pale gray eyes took on a hunted look. "If my father has his say, then my life is planned for me. What I want cannot be realized in this lifetime, and so I dare not dream at all."

Draper watched in thoughtful silence as she lifted the bar and slipped outside. He knew from experience that life without dreams was impossibly empty and dull. He had never dreamed beyond what lay west of the next spiny ridge, beyond the close of each dawning day, until this small slip of English femininity had entered his life and turned it upside down . . .

Yet Draper was keenly aware that having dreams, and seeing them to fruition, were two entirely different things.

Chapter 15

Because it originated high in the mountains, the creek that flowed behind James Reed's cabin was icy, even on the hottest days in summer. The chill did not deter Draper. It had been a while since he'd indulged in a thorough dunking, and he wished to look his best for the nuptials and for Quintana.

Stripping to the skin, he dived into the frigid depths and swam beneath the surface . . . and when he finally came up for air he saw that he was no longer alone.

Thirteen in number and mounted to a man, the groom's procession was an unruly band, full of ribald talk and raucous laughter. But one man stood out from the rest. Mounted upon a pot-bellied mare, he towered head and shoulders above his companions, his feet nearly dragging the ground. Yancey Claus was ugly, with large ungainly limbs and huge slablike muscles; his face was pockmarked, framed by lank sable hair; his features were as sharp as a hatchet.

He looked at Draper a long moment before speaking, his black eyes glittering with ill-concealed malevolence. "Well, I'll be dipped," the big man sneered. Then to his companions, "Look you here, boys, who's come to spoil the weddin'! You here ta give the bride away, Boone? Or did you have in mind a final toss for old time's sake before Cousin James claims her?"

With icy water swirling around his hips, Draper ignored the other man's crudity. He was of no mind to fight Yancey Claus, unclothed as he was, and in the frigid depths of the river. "Yancey," he said. "I haven't seen you since '76 . . . Let's see, Hagerstown, wasn't it? The widow Jones tried her best to split your skull that night, as I recall, for bustin' up her house."

"You had no call to interfere, Boone. An' that old whore Shelly Jones got what she had comin' to her for refusin' me her house. I didn't hurt that li'l' gal o' hers none, only roughed her up a bit. 'Sides, it weren't your business, no ways, and I ain't forgot how you left me in that hog wallow."

"You looked right at home, Yancey," Draper said. "Hell, it was damned hard to tell you from those razorbacks."

A ripple of uneasy laughter ran through the assembled riders, but it died away as Yancey Claus's angry gaze shifted to his fellows. "You al'as was a smart-mouthed bastard," he said. "Come on outta there and we'll see if you kin do more'n talk."

Yancey made to step down from his mount, but the soft double-click of a rifle hammer being brought back into full cock made him freeze. "Who's there?" he called out warily.

Absolute stepped out from the cover of the trees, Draper's long-barreled Pennsylvania rifle in hand, his own musket slung across his shoulder. "Ye left this in the barn," the Scot said to Draper. "I know as how ye feel nekked withoot it, so I thought I'd fetch it for ye." He smirked at his choice of words, then tossed the firearm to Draper, who deftly caught it. "What's gaein' on here?"

"Yancey and I were just reminiscing."

Absolute gave the big man a look of pure disdain. "Mayhap ye oughta pick yer friends more careful-like," he told Draper.

Yancey eased back in the saddle. "You best sleep with that squirrel gun tucked beneath your pillow, Boone. This ain't over yet."

Fred Biggs, Yancey Claus's partner, sat a slender bay mare with white socks a few feet away. The two men owned a packstring— fifteen horses with which they carried freight over the mountains.

Biggs looked worried. "You think you oughta mess with Draper Boone? Last time you had it out with him, he busted you up bad. You spent nigh a month just tryin' to mend them busted ribs. We gotta be headed East by Friday, Yancey, and we can't afford no lay up whilst you heal."

Yancey Claus hawked and spat. "Lay up, my ass!" he growled in an aside. "I'll snap him like a twig, but before I do, I'm gonna take a hellish pleasure in messin' up that purty face of his!" His smile was evil. "They won't be a

woman willin' to give him a second look when
I'm through."

The guests began trickling in shortly after
sunrise. Tom Vassal and his wife, Sarah, both
short in stature and given to roundness, were
the first to arrive. Tom had a pronounced stutter when he talked and because of it was rather
shy, a trait for which Sarah did her level best to
compensate by her incessant talk and bubbling
laughter.

There was Madelaine Poltz, a pretty woman
in her middle thirties, red-haired and dark-
eyed, a friend of Anna Lawson. Also Jules Fitch
and Bentley Bowes, and a number of others,
each of whom was presented to Quintana in
turn, but the one who was last to arrive was the
one that touched the young Englishwoman's
heart.

Her name was Betty Edgar, and she was
newly widowed, with a babe at her breast and
another to arrive by summer's end. Betty was
small and thin, with soft brown hair and great
brown eyes, and an expression that was per-
petually sad.

Quintana's glance kept straying to Betty, a
fact that was not lost upon Maeve. "Quintana,"
Maeve said after a time. "I've made Betty a nice
cup of catnip tea. Would you mind taking it to
her? I promised Sarah a look at the cuttings
James's mother sent to us."

Because it was put in such a way, Quintana
could hardly refuse. But the last thing she
wanted to do was speak with a young woman

whose husband had been killed by British-led Indians a few miles up the Allegheny River from Fort Pitt.

Until this moment, she hadn't given more than a fleeting thought to the families who lived beyond the bounds of civilization, or to the devastation being visited upon their world by her own countrymen. Now, quite suddenly, she felt keenly ashamed. "Quintana?" Maeve said. "Are you quite all right?"

"What? Yes! Yes, I'm fine." Quintana took the cup from Maeve's hand. There was no tactful way to avoid this, and she could only hope that Betty would not scorn her as she had once scorned Draper and his kind.

The girl looked up as Quintana approached, a glance full of surprise and perhaps question, not unlike that of a startled doe. Quintana smiled and hoped her unease did not show. "Maeve thought you might like a cup of catnip tea."

Betty smiled, but the gentle curve of her lips did little to banish the sorrow in her eyes. "How thoughtful of Mrs. MacDivitt to think of me. I'd take it from you, but I'm afraid I've got my hands full."

The girl knew by now that Quintana was English, yet her smile never wavered, and there was not the slightest trace of bitterness apparent in her wide brown eyes.

Quintana hesitated, then plunged bravely onward. "If you'd like, I could hold her for you." If Betty intended to denounce her for her English origins, then she would do so now.

Instead, Betty looked relieved. "Are you certain you don't mind?"

Quintana placed the cup on the long wooden table beneath the trees and sat down close to Betty, who placed the blanketed baby in her arms.

The babe yawned widely, blinking at Quintana, then jammed a tiny fist into its rosebud mouth and settled down to sleep again. "So lovely. What do you call the child?"

"My Henry named her Miranda," Betty replied. "He always favored the name." She raised the cup and sipped. "Mrs. MacDivitt said your home's in England."

Quintana nodded, smoothing the dark fuzz that capped the baby's head. She'd never considered children. There had been no reason to consider the possibility, with no man in her life, but now she couldn't help but dream of black-haired babes with Draper's amber eyes.

But Draper didn't want a wife. And her dream was nothing more than a foolish fancy.

Aloud, she said, "It was. My father is the commandant of Fort Pitt. I'm en route to join him there."

Betty smiled. "My Henry was with the militia at Ligonier, but he often spoke of Colonel Wade. He said that he's a great man."

Quintana was saved from forming a reply, for at that moment a triumphant savage cry broke over the gathering, accompanied by the thunder of hoofbeats and answered by the cheers of the wedding guests.

Quintana turned just as the groom's party burst into the clearing, a familiar raffish figure at their lead. Reining in the roan, he leaped from the saddle and was immediately surrounded by the jubilant throng.

Draper had ridden the five miles from James's place to Maeve's as if a horde of Iroquois were hot upon his heels, the memory of Quintana's eyes, her smile, her soft white breasts spurring him to recklessness . . .

He glanced around. Most of the faces he saw among the crowd of well-wishers were familiar ones, but there was no sign of Quintana.

Now where the devil was she?

He quickly spied Tilly Bascombe, who was standing with Absolute beneath the boughs of a spreading white oak. "Good morning, Cap'n," she said as he brushed past them. "Nice day for a wedding, isn't it?"

"It'll do, Tilly Bascombe," Draper replied, scanning the crowd in hopes of catching a glimpse of a certain shining flaxen head.

"Are you looking for Miss Quintana?" Tilly inquired with a slight smile.

"Aye," Draper replied. "Have you seen her?"

"Not in the last hour or so. She was helping with the food earlier. You might check the kitchen . . . or perhaps she's gone with the children to gather the eggs. She did so take to the little ones."

Draper started off again, going first to the henhouse, which sat near the barn at the rear of the house. He scattered a bevy of children along the way, who shrieked and tumbled about underfoot, yet there was still no sign of Quintana.

On the way back to the cabin he met Bentley Bowes and Jules Fitch. Both were glassy-eyed and well into their cups. Bentley thumped Draper's back. "We heard that you'd returned, and think it mighty sportin' of you, Boone, to give the bride away to James."

"James is welcome to her," Draper informed them. "I've no interest in the bride." He was growing irritated with the constant reminders that he and Maeve had once been lovers. All of that was past; 'twas the immediate future and the fire in his vitals that concerned him at present, a fire only Quintana's sweet charms could ease. "Listen," he said to Jules, "have you seen a young woman still fresh on the vine, with hair like pale winter sunlight and eyes of silver-gray?"

Bentley Bowes thoughtfully scratched his bristled chin. "I surely woulda noticed such a fetching creature. Are you sure she's here, Boone?"

"He's talkin' about that Englis'woman," Jules said. "We seen her a bit ago, but I can't quite recall where it was."

His friends were of little help, and Draper's patience was wearing precariously thin. He had brought Quintana here to Fuller's Gap for the sole purpose of spending some much deserved time alone with her, but things had

somehow gotten horribly out of hand—a circumstance that he meant to remedy just as
soon as he could find her.

To that end, he turned to go, but Bentley
stopped him. "We got a jug of old man
Hardwick's rye whiskey over by them trees
yonder. Come on with us and have a lick, and
you'll soon forget that Englishwoman."

Forget Quintana? It wasn't bloody likely.

His attempt to protest, however, fell upon
deaf ears. "Come on, Boone! Where's your
sense of fun?" Bowes said. He took Draper's
arm and fairly dragged him off to join the
others gathered around the jug.

Reverend Greets and the bridegroom, James
Reed, were among the company. James looked
a little bleary and his cheeks were flushed, but
he listened intently as the reverend extolled at
length upon the joys of wedded bliss.

"Glad you came to join us, Draper," James
said, passing the jug to the newcomer. "We're
just here to partake of a bit o' fornication before
the ceremony begins . . ."

"*Fortification*, friend," the cleric corrected
with a tight-lipped smile. "I have found that
a dram now and then aids the digestion."

"Oh, aye. Of course." James flushed in truth.

Draper hooked an index finger through the
narrow handle and, resting the weight on his
forearm, tipped up the jug for a long and satisfying pull.

The whiskey tore down his throat, singeing
his belly, fueling his impatience. He lowered
the jug and passed it to the man on his right.

"Listen, James, have you seen Quintana? I can't seem to find her anywhere, and I'm beginning to think Maeve has locked her in the root cellar, just to keep us apart."

James furrowed his brow, and a look of great concentration came over his blunt features. "I didn't know Maeve had a root cellar," he said.

The jug came around again and Draper shook his head.

He was seriously considering employing Scratch, Maeve's bluetick hound, to ferret out his quarry when, glancing around, he caught sight of her sitting beneath the shade of a tall elm tree by the far corner of the cabin.

She was dressed in the light yellow linen and soft doeskin moccasins Maeve had provided; with her pale gold tresses coaxed into a neat chignon at her nape and Betty Edgar's babe asleep in her arms, she resembled more a wild wood flower than his sainted English rose.

She made a lovely picture, yet Draper found the sight of Quintana with babe in arms vastly unsettling, and for one irrational moment he imagined himself sitting by her side, staring down in open wonder at the product of their love . . .

She smiled up at him when he came over to her, lost in thoughts of their impossible future. "Are you gathering wool, Captain? Or did your wild ride have some lingering effect upon you?"

"Must have been the whiskey," Draper said, shaking his head in hopes of clearing it. Yet despite his best efforts, the disturbing glimpse of a life that for him was unattainable, simply would not go away.

James Reed was everything Maeve had proclaimed him to be. Short and thickset, with hair the shade of meal and a serious demeanor, he was as different from Draper as a cloudless day from darkest night.

There was no mystery to James; he was open-faced and bland, singularly unexciting, and it was clearly evident from the moment Quintana saw them together that Maeve adored him.

The sun was high when the minister called the assemblage together in the cool shade of the dooryard. "Friends and neighbors, we are gathered here today to witness the joining of Maeve Gordon MacDivitt and James Lincoln Reed in holy matrimony . . ."

The ceremony was simple and brief. James finished making his declaration and the Reverend Greets turned to the bride.

"Maeve Gordon MacDivitt, do you take James Lincoln Reed as your lawful wedded husband, to have and to hold, for better, for worse, in sickness and in health, so long as you both shall live?"

Maeve looked at James and her face shone.

It was easy to see that she was happy—happier by far, Quintana thought, living here on the fringe of the civilized world, with danger and deprivation always near, than she herself had been living in relative splendor in

London, surrounded by silks and satins and servants to do her bidding.

Unbidden, Quintana's gaze slid from Maeve's bright and shining face to Draper's, which was dark and impassive as he watched his former mistress pledge her life and love to another man.

James is every woman's dream, Maeve had said not long ago. *Strong, steady, reliable, and he loves me to distraction. He'll be a good provider, and once the war is over, he won't go off adventuring again. He'll stay here with me, and we'll grow old together . . .*

Recalling Maeve's words, Quintana felt a keen and unaccustomed twinge of envy, for in that instant, as Draper's eyes met hers, she would have gladly given the London house and all its grand appointments for a simple cabin and the bare necessities of life, as long as she could be as certain of Draper as Maeve seemed sure of James.

Draper's unwavering gaze warmed as it slowly traveled over her, lingering for a breathless instant on her parted lips before rising again.

Quintana's stomach fluttered as she looked away.

The crucial moment had arrived. The minister cleared his throat and demanded in his sonorous voice, "If there is any man here with reason why this man and woman should not be joined together, speak now, or forever hold your peace."

All eyes turned as one to Draper.

He flushed beneath his tan; Quintana giggled.

"Hell, don't look at me," he said. "I'm as anxious to get on with the frolic as the next man."

Satisfied that all was as it should be, Reverend Greets bade the newlyweds to turn and face the company. "Then without further adieu, I present to you Mr. and Mrs. James Lincoln Reed!"

The guests cheered, while somewhere nearby the fiddler struck up a lively tune.

Draper took Quintana's hands. She could smell the faint pungent scent of whiskey on his breath as he pulled her close against him, could feel the body beneath the supple leather garb, so hard, so muscular, so wonderfully, mysteriously, powerfully male . . .

Quintana shivered.

It seemed an eternity ago that they had lain together beneath a starry sky, touching yet not joined—two hearts rebelling against capricious fate, sharing stolen kisses and unbearable intimacies that even now had the power to render her weak and trembling in every limb.

The tempo of the music changed. The poignant strains of an Irish ballad quivered through the still afternoon air, stirring and bittersweet, plucking at the heartstrings.

"Dance with me, Quintana," Draper said. "Sway in my arms until the darkness gathers and we can slip away unnoticed."

"But I've never danced a country dance!" Quintana protested.

Draper only pivoted on a moccasined heel and started off toward the revelers, fairly dragging Quintana along. "Then it's high time you learned!" he said, laughing.

Chapter 16

Draper led Quintana through the steps of a cut-out Irish jig. The lively quickstep, the stamp and sway in triple time, left her laughing and breathless and begging a reprieve that did not come, for just as Draper took her hand and made to quit the crowded dooryard, James Reed stepped up to claim her.

Quintana glanced at Draper, but he was already surrounded by his fellow frontiersmen, and there was much laughter and good-natured back thumping as they pressed the jug upon him.

The Highland reel was a test of Quintana's forbearance. Draper possessed an agility and grace that in James Reed was sorely lacking.

James swung her off her feet, circled back, and trod upon her toes, then seized her hands, and together they barreled down the aisle created by two lines of dancers, separated to circle back to the head of the double line and clap as the next couple entered the fore and the lines fell back to give them room.

Quintana tried to sneak away, but James caught her elbow, swung her around, and trod upon her poor beleaguered toes again.

She closed her eyes, held her breath, and prayed for the reel to end.

Mercifully, Quintana's prayers were answered. A few moments more and the reel slid to a quavering close.

With a pained smile, she thanked James for the dance and, turning to look for Draper, collided with a veritable wall of human flesh.

Quintana's disbelieving gaze moved up across the linsey shirt and bearskin vest the man wore, dark with sweat and grease, to his evil, leering face.

He reeked of some unidentifiable animal smell, cloying and sickeningly sweet. The strange odor enveloped Quintana; instinctively, she brought a hand up to her face and tried to back away.

The giant would not permit her escape. Clamping a massive hand over her shoulder, he grinned down at her, calling out in a voice as rumbling and ominous as distant thunder, "Fiddler! Strike up a lively tune! I've a notion to tread me a measure with this fine English lady!"

Quintana recoiled. His touch made her flesh crawl, and she had to strive very hard to achieve a level of politeness. "I thank you for your offer, sir. But I'm afraid I can't accept. There's something I must see to."

The big man snarled down at her, a look of stupid suspicion coming into his eyes. "High-flown Lobsterback bitch. You danced with Boone. You'll dance with me. They ain't a woman alive refuses Yancey Clau—"

Draper's fist seemed to come out of nowhere, smashing into Yancey's mouth with a force that would have felled a lesser man. The blow rocked him back upon his heels, and before he could recover, Draper stepped in close and hit him two more times, hard swift jabs that bloodied his nose and mouth.

Yet Yancey merely grinned at Draper, a slow bloody grin that caused a prickle of dread to crawl along Quintana's spine. "Are you mad?" she cried at Draper. "You can't fight him!"

"Stay out of this, Quintana," Draper said. He advanced on the big man, who spread his knotted arms wide in a brutish gesture of welcome.

"Would appear you'll have to wait your turn, Tory. Boone here wants the first dance, an' I'm inclined to oblige 'im. But that ain't no cause to fret. There's plenty of old Yancey to go 'round."

Draper's expression was hard. "You lay a hand on her again and I swear to Christ I'll tear it off and feed it to you piece by bloody piece."

"You al'as did talk big," Yancey sneered. "Let's see if you got the stones to back it up."

With a thunderous whoop, Yancey leaped forward, crashing into Draper and sending him sprawling. The two men went down in a tangle of limbs and rolled on the grass while the crowd fell back to give them room.

This was a frontier fight, with no rules and no restraint, and bound to be a fine entertainment, a subject of enthusiastic discussion for many weeks to come by those witnessing it.

Quintana, terrified for Draper, ran to Absolute. "Oh, Absolute! You must stop him!"

The Scot looked at her as if she'd lost her senses. "Why the divil would I stop him?" he said, incredulous. "The laddie's winnin'!"

But it didn't look to Quintana as if the laddie was winning.

She turned anxious eyes back to the combatants just as Yancey Claus brought back his massive fist and caught Draper squarely on the chin.

Draper staggered—almost fell. A vicious right split his lip and drove him to his knees. He tasted blood, warm and metallic. He shook his head. There was a strange distant buzzing in his ears. Yancey's wheezing laughter seemed to come from far away.

"I'm gonna make you howl for mercy 'fore I'm through with you," the big man promised. "Then me and that pretty little Tory bitch are gonna stomp all over what's left o' you."

"You'll have to kill me first." Draper heard the words—his own voice—yet he wasn't quite sure where they had come from. Everything seemed unreal, disjointed, and nothing was the way it should have been.

Yancey's massive square-toed boot came arcing up; somewhere in the crowd a woman screamed.

But the movement was too slow.

Draper tried to concentrate; that was the key to victory over Yancey, but damned if Quintana's soft gray eyes, so luminous, so fearful, didn't keep getting in the way . . .

For weeks the tension had been mounting inside him, with little hope of release. He hadn't been looking for trouble, but there had been something about seeing Yancey put his hands on Quintana's soft white shoulder that had driven out every ounce of self-restraint he'd possessed.

In that moment, when he'd pulled back his fist and hit the big ungainly ape, it hadn't seemed to matter that Yancey outweighed him by nearly six stone.

All he had been able to think of, could think of still with the boot arcing toward his chin, was that Yancey showed no compunction whatsoever about fondling a woman to whom Draper had been so long denied.

The mental image of Yancey's filthy hand on Quintana's soft white flesh stuck with him, compounding Draper's frustration, churning it into a swirling, black, all-consuming rage.

He didn't have to think. He reacted instinctively, grasping the heel of Yancey's boot, heaving with all his might, forcing the big man's leg up and up and up . . . until he toppled, landing like a turtle on its back, and Draper was on him.

Locking his hands around Yancey's throat, he began to squeeze.

Yancey heaped a string of strangled curses upon Draper's head and tried to throw him off. Jamming a massive hand beneath Draper's chin, he levered up and back, his blunt fingers splayed and reaching. They slid along

Draper's cheek to his eye, edging toward the socket, while his vulnerable thumb brushed Draper's mouth.

Draper caught Yancey's thumb and bit down hard.

Yancey howled, as did several of those watching. Standing on the inside perimeter of the circle, Bentley Bowes roared, slapping Jules on the back. Jules shoved Bentley off, calling out to Maeve, "Fetch the stew pot, Mrs. Reed, looks like Draper's found his dinner!"

Draper barely heard them. He continued to squeeze the big man's throat. Nothing seemed to penetrate the thick red mist swirling all around him.

Yancey represented everything that had gone wrong in his life—the unfairness of Hamlin's death, the colonel's sending him away without giving him the chance to defend himself, his hatred of Uriah Bell, and his own misplaced passion.

"Draper, lad. *Draper!*" Absolute's face loomed up before him. The Scot shook him hard, breaking through the crimson haze. Draper blinked, shook his head to clear it. "Let him go, lad," Absolute said. He pried Draper's hands from Yancey's throat and helped him to his feet. " 'Tis over noo. 'Tis over."

A short distance away, Quintana stood watching, her heart in her throat. His face, so heartrendingly handsome, was awash in blood, and it was impossible for her to tell if the blood belonged to him or to his opponent.

Their eyes met as he moved forward, silver melding with gold, and the crowd, which had gathered near to watch the contest, drifted away one by one, leaving her alone to face him.

"That was the most barbarous thing I have ever witnessed," Quintana said flatly, "and without a doubt the most insane!" She stood glaring down at Draper, who sat on a low stool in the barn behind Maeve's cabin, patient beneath her ministrations.

"Ill-advised perhaps. Risky, but I'd hardly call it 'insane,' " Draper said, wincing.

A cut had opened beneath his left eye and his lip was split, but he wasn't seriously injured. The fight was over, the danger past, and Quintana's fear had turned to righteous anger.

Her narrowed eyes glittered. " 'Ill-advised.' How nicely put. You can seek to brush this off if it pleases you, but it won't alter the facts. Fighting that man was foolish."

"And defying me and entering the fray when I faced that cat on the mountain was an example of wisdom?" Draper shot back.

"The two situations have no parallel! You faced a definite threat; Mr. Claus's attentions, however undesirable, were a mere annoyance."

Draper gave a derisive snort. "That's a matter of opinion."

"He would have grown tired of his game eventually and left me alone."

"Eventually! And what was I to do in the meantime? Stand meekly by with a smile on my face while he mauled you at his bloody leisure?"

"Yes!" Quintana cried. "If it saved you from being killed!" She threw the rag with which she'd cleansed his wounds into the brimming bucket at her feet and made a noise of irritation and disgust. "Why must you be so damnably mulish?"

But Draper had had enough of stress and strife. He caught her hand, drawing her into the shaft of golden sunlight that fell through the chinks in the clapboard roof. "Quintana," he said, his voice soft and drawling. "Our time together is swiftly fleeting. Must we squander it with mindless argument?"

Quintana touched his battered face with gentle loving fingers, the anger she felt dissolving. "I was so afraid for you."

Draper pulled her slowly in against him, enfolding her in his embrace. For a long moment he held her close, sighing deeply, saying nothing . . . and when at last he spoke, his voice was rough with emotion barely held in check. "He had no right to touch your sweet pale flesh, to put his hands on you, to claim in any way what to me is forbidden."

His words, so bittersweet and so revealing, brought the painful subject of their eventual parting suddenly close.

The future loomed for both him and Quintana, no longer distant, but immediate.

Quintana felt the prick of tears and closed her eyes, pressing her cheek against his naked breast. "If I had one wish to come true, then I would wish tomorrow away. You cannot imagine how deeply I dread its coming."

Draper's lean fingers found and cupped her chin, forcing her to meet his gaze. "Damn tomorrow," he said with soft ferocity. "We have the night, Quintana. One night, in which nothing and no one can come between us. One night . . . when you belong to only me."

Quintana didn't speak. There were no words to tell him what was in her heart. Oh, she could tell him that she loved him, but the simple sentiment was inadequate—too oft used, too soft and gentle and caring.

Quintana's feelings for Draper were neither soft nor gentle. The terrible emptiness at the thought of being separated from him, the savage longing unfulfilled, the churning caldron of tempestuous emotion that was her heart went far beyond simple caring, simple sentiment, simple worn-out words.

Yet they, who had little chance of a tomorrow, *did* have the night . . . one night in which to share the joys of an ill-starred love.

In that moment as she stood gazing up at him, her gray eyes filled with the light of longing, Draper's dark head dipped, and his carnal mouth slanted over hers, drawing forth, accentuating, echoing her need.

His kiss was scorching.

Quintana needed little urging, but opened to him eagerly, thrusting her tongue as he thrust his, warming to his play, wanting all of him . . . everything her dashing young adventurer had to give.

He was bold, and he was brash, practiced in the ways of erotic love, yet exceptionally patient when confronted with her innocence.

He encouraged her to explore his body, to tease, to kiss, to caress. Her palms pressed flat against his ribs, Quintana slid her questing hands upward, to his tautly drawn pectorals. His skin was satin smooth, his body sleek; his reaction to her play was involuntary, immediate. The small brown nipples capping the masculine swell came erect, pushing insistently against her palms.

Quintana paused long enough to abrade the sensitive buds lightly with her nails before moving on, hearing in her heart of hearts his pleasurable gasp, sliding her hands up across his deep chest, around his neck, threading her fingers into his lustrous mane.

Draper's answering groan rumbled low in his throat. Quintana was so wonderfully warm, so seemingly eager to learn, and he was more than willing to accommodate her virgin's curiosity.

Her simple gown of yellow linen was all that stood in his way. But it presented no challenge. With ease he found and parted the laces at the back, drawing the garment down, exposing his lady's softly rounded shoulders, the pale upper curves of her succulent breasts.

Her skin shone a gilded ivory in the softly diffused sunlight, flawless, untouched, and pure, calling him to worship. Yet he gave no pause, continuing to draw the garment down, unveiling the beauty that was Quintana Wade inch by lovely inch, until she stood before him, Venus rising from the saffron linen pooling around her trim ankles.

Eyes downcast beneath her tawny lashes, and a dull rose blooming high upon her cheeks, Quintana slowly walked toward him. "You said you wanted nothing between us, and yet you stand before me clothed . . ."

Quintana's cool fingertips brushed Draper's belly, an infinitesimal touch, the soft caress of butterfly wings against his heated skin. When confronted by the belt securing his buckskin leggings and the plain dun-colored breechclout that girded his loins, she paused.

Draper's heart picked up its pace; his blood raced through his veins. A moment of those sweet fingers searching and the belt was free, the breechclout floated to the floor, forgotten, and his leggings slipped down to his knees.

He kicked free of the simple garments, and in one swift fluid movement, lifted Quintana, carrying her up the ladder to the loft where he laid her down and kissed her long and languidly before moving further down.

At her breasts he lingered, teasing, touching, tantalizing with his lips, his teeth, his practiced tongue . . . worrying one of her sensitive nipples to exquisite hardness before giving his attention to the other.

Quintana sighed, reveling in their closeness, their intimacy, the luxurious feel of skin on warm and vibrant skin. Draper left her breast, moving downward, over her ribs and across her taut belly.

Quintana watched him intently, but she spoke not a single syllable.

He paused at her navel, encircling the shallow declivity with his tongue, plunging in briefly to tickle and tease. Quintana's breath caught in her throat. Draper ignored her startled gasp and continued to blaze a trail of languorous kisses downward, ever downward, to the golden curls that crowned her womanhood . . .

Still Quintana did not speak. Instead she tangled her fingers into the thick midnight silk of Draper's hair and silently willed him to come to her.

Draper did not heed her silent plea. Instead he baptized her yearning flesh with fiery kisses while Quintana writhed beneath his tender ministrations and burned . . .

Draper was an experienced lover; with seemingly no effort he teased her woman's flesh to startling awareness while holding the world at bay.

For Quintana, time and the certainty of tomorrow ceased to be, leaving only Draper and the wondrously wicked sensations he was evoking within her flesh.

Fire leaped along her veins, creating in her a keen physical hunger that only Draper could satisfy. The feeling gradually intensified, the conflagration growing hotter, its white-hot tendrils unfurling, fiery fingers strumming along her heart.

Quintana tossed naked upon their bed of hay and moaned, restless and yearning, and in that crucial moment when her need seemed greatest he came to her, gathering her quaking form close against him, covering her face with kisses, showing her quite clearly that what she'd thought was nearing an end, in reality had only just begun.

The folds of her woman's body, still damp and dewy from his loving, parted slowly before the insistent press of his maleness until inch by wondrous inch he filled her, pausing only when confronted by the proof of her virginity.

Gazing down into Quintana's face, his features taut with longing, Draper withdrew slightly, then with one swift downward plunge, he pierced her maidenhead.

Quintana uttered not a sound, certain in her aching heart that the pain of their first joining would be as nothing to the agonies she'd come to know at the moment of their final parting.

After a long and breathless moment in which they clung to each other, Draper began to move, subtly at first, then with a slow rocking rhythm that took him nearer, ever nearer to Quintana's soul.

Sliding her hands down his back to the firm lean swell of his buttocks, Quintana urged him even deeper, lifting her hips to greet him on his inward push, welcoming him in.

Tension mounted swiftly inside her, climbing to unbearable heights. She writhed beneath him, a silent sob caught in her throat, wanting an end to this exquisite torment, wanting it to go on forever.

Just when she imagined she would be driven to madness by this wild unquenchable desire, the rapture overtook her—wave after thunderous wave of unbearable physical delight that was every bit as slow to die away as it had been slow in coming . . .

Draper felt the deep contractions of her woman's flesh, felt her tension melt away, and knew the time to shed his rigid self-control had come. He pushed deep, burying himself within her silken sheath, and filled her with his seed, the only promise of tomorrow that was his to offer.

The light filtering through the chinks in the clapboard roof was dirty gray and unwelcome. Tomorrow was nigh, and Draper's heart was strangely heavy.

Last evening he had damned this day, begging one night of love from the woman who lay curled beside him. She'd responded sweetly, giving more generously of herself than he had ever dreamed was possible, and bringing him to realize fully what a fool he had been to imagine that a single night with her would ever be enough.

They made love again and again throughout the long evening hours while the sounds of revelry echoed all around them.

And then at last Quintana had drifted off, her head pillowed upon his breast, hand curled innocently against his heart.

Draper hadn't slept. Instead he'd lain awake to watch over her as she dreamed.

She was an innocent no longer. He'd taken especial care to initiate her in the various ways of love. He'd listened to her enraptured cries, her soft sweet sighs, he'd heard her cry his name, and now that the dawn he'd damned so feverishly was near and she was his in truth, he wondered how on earth he'd ever let her go.

Chapter 17

Fort Pitt
The Monongahela Country
June 10, 1778

T he letter had arrived in London long ago,
one of the last Winston had written to
Rowena, shortly after his arrival in the wilderness outpost, Fort Pitt.

My dearest Rowena,

*At last I have arrived in the western country.
We reached Fort Pitt on Thursday last, and
found the place in a state of disrepair . . . but
I feel with a little effort we can set things to
rights once more.*

*Aside from the needed repairs, I was relieved
to see that we are in good circumstance. The fort
itself sits upon a triangular spit of land at the
confluence of three great rivers that command
the gateway to the Ohio country.*

*The Allegheny, so named by the savage
inhabitants of this country for its comely dark
complexion, flows down from the mountainous
northeast, converging with the Monongahela*

*beneath the very walls of the fort to form
the Ohio . . . life's blood of the vast uncharted
wilderness that lies to our west . . .*

Quintana had consigned the passage to
memory, but Winston's narrative had done
little to prepare her for the stark reality of
Pittsburgh and Fort Pitt.

He'd spoken of the rivers and the wilderness, the advantageous location of the fort, yet
he'd failed to mention the squalid town that
crowded close about the walls of a partially
dismantled Fort Pitt.

Two hundred rude log structures flanking
the muddy streets and a number of ramshack-
le traders' huts in various degrees of disrepair
squatting on the banks of the Monongahela
River comprised the town of Pittsburgh.

So this was to be her home, Quintana
thought, frowning at her surroundings. By
comparison, the settlement of Fuller's Gap
seemed a woodland paradise.

A fortnight had passed since they'd left the
settlement and the newlyweds behind, and set
out for the West.

Their leavetaking had been especially difficult for Quintana. She'd found a friend in
Maeve Gordon MacDivitt Reed, and she had
hated to leave her. Tears had sprung to
Quintana's eyes as she and Maeve had embraced. "Remember what I told you," Maeve
had whispered fiercely. "Guard your heart!"

Quintana had nodded and watched as
Maeve stepped up to Draper. "Take care of

her," she'd softly scolded. "And of yourself."
She'd sniffed, looking up at him. "Stay out of
trouble."

Draper had smiled and chucked her chin.
"I'll do my level best."

Maeve had hugged him close for an instant,
kissed his weathered cheek, then turned back
to the cabin dooryard where James Reed was
waiting.

With a will, Quintana roused herself from
her musings. They left Grant's Hill behind and
proceeded up Water Street, a muddy thorough-
fare teeming with all manner of humanity.
Gentlemen in dark cloth coats and bonneted
ladies mingled with mechanics, rough-looking
traders, and a smattering of Indians.

These last were not at all as Quintana had
imagined they would be. Slight of build, with
straight spines and dusky skins, they did not
seem particularly savage. In fact, the few she
glimpsed seemed to her much less so than
the tall frontiersman who rode so effortlessly
before her.

The big roan picked its way past a two-
story log building at the corner of Ferry and
Water Streets. Above the door hung a sign
proclaiming: Ormsby's Tavern.

A barrel-chested man of middling years was
lounging in the shadows of the doorway, a
pewter tankard in his hand. He hailed them
loudly and waved as they rode past, and
seemingly without regard for his boots, waded
out into the mire, falling in step beside them.
"Draper Boone! I see you've made it back!"

"You sound surprised, John."

The big man laughed. "I suppose I am. There's been some open speculation as to whether you might opt to stay in England to avoid this mess you find yourself in. Why, some o' the boys over to the fort have gone so far as to wager on the outcome. 'Course my money was on you comin' home, but given the temperament of that young lieutenant, a practical man does have to wonder if it might not have been best if you'd just stayed away."

Draper smiled. "I've been accused of a lot of things in my life, but practicality isn't one of them. Good to be back, John."

Near the old redoubt, John Ormsby halted. "Listen! If you and Corporal Farquar are free this evenin', stop by and join me in a pint!"

Draper spoke to the roan and they cantered on toward the fort, with Absolute and Tilly following along behind.

Quintana held tight to Draper's lean middle. The big man didn't know Draper very well to think that he'd have stayed in England.

Before them loomed the fort, a frowning pentagonal bastion with tall earthen ramparts, secured by brick and stone. They entered the fortification by way of the land bridge connecting the triangular earthwork, the East Ravelin, to the lower town road, not pausing until challenged at the gate.

The sentry was a young man, dressed in faded uniform coat and ragged breeches. He wore no hat or wig, and his thin face had been burned a deep nut-brown by the relentless summer sun. "Cap'n, sir." His salute was laconic, halfhearted. "Colonel Wade's been expecting you this fortnight past."

"The voyage took longer than I'd anticipated, and we had some minor difficulties along the way," Draper said.

"Nothing serious, I hope, sir?"

"Nothing I couldn't manage." Draper booted up the roan, cantering across the land bridge to the parade ground and to the neat brick residence that was the commandant's house. It was situated near the Monongahela Curtain, and a pair of gaunt militiamen stood at ease outside the door.

Draper halted the roan and dropped lightly to the ground. The pair of militiamen came to attention. "Hawser," Draper said to the taller of the two, "be so good as to inform Colonel Wade that I've arrived."

"Captain, sir," Hawser replied, "Colonel Wade is in a meeting, and I have explicit orders that he's not to be disturbed."

"Those orders do not pertain to his daughter, Miss Quintana Wade," Draper said emphatically. "Miss Wade's journey has been long and difficult, and I can't imagine Colonel Wade will be pleased that you've prolonged her discomfort by forcing her to cool her heels in the street." Then, when Hawser still stood hesitating, "Damn it, man. I said *move!*"

Draper took a menacing step forward and Hawser spun on his heel and ran for the door.

Draper helped Quintana to alight. His hands were warm and hard at her waist, his touch oddly reassuring. "Just remember who you are," he said softly.

Quintana searched his face, hoping perhaps for some deep underlying meaning to those few words of reassurance. She found none. His face was curiously impassive, unreadable, and despite the lean hand that continued to linger at her waist, she felt suddenly, terribly alone.

"What the devil is it?" Terse and cold and bearing only the slightest inflection of his native Britain, Winston's voice filtered through the open doorway to Quintana.

The private's reply was low, his tone apologetic.

Winston's came more clearly. "Boone? Why didn't you say so immediately? Show them in without delay, and then you may inform Mrs. Mimms that her services will be required."

The footsteps retreated and a red-faced Private Hawser appeared in the doorway. "Colonel Wade says you're to go on in—" Hawser began, but Draper was already striding past him into the house, his rifle in one hand, the other still riding Quintana's trim waist.

The interior of the brick house was cool and dim after the heat of the day and the harsh summer sunlight, and smelled pleasantly of beeswax and tobacco.

Quintana glanced around. The furnishings were sparse and worn; there were no rugs to warm the rough puncheon floors, no curtains at the windows.

She thought of the comparative luxury
of the London house and wondered how
Winston, the younger son of a great and
powerful family, could be content with this
Spartan existence.

And then, unbidden, her thoughts turned
to Fuller's Gap, to the simple life of Maeve
Gordon MacDivitt Reed, which she herself had
envied, and for the briefest instant she wondered if perhaps she and Winston didn't share
some common bond, however obscure. They
both had come to revere the untamed land and
the hardy souls who dared to dwell within its
bounds.

The parallel, once drawn, would not retreat
from Quintana's thoughts. But it made her ill-
at-ease to think that she shared anything with
Winston Halcourt Wade, beyond the bond of
blood, and that particular bond, Winston had
proven, meant little.

They reached an open doorway, where Draper paused. "After you, m'lady," he said.

Looking up into his face, Quintana wished
desperately for something more. But he merely gave a slight motion of his hand to indicate
that she should precede him, calmly waiting
for her to enter.

Quintana drew a shuddering breath, while
images of a single glorious night in the stable
loft flashed before her eyes. She glanced at
Draper's impassive face one last time, then
looked reluctantly away.

The moment she had dreaded for months
had at long last arrived. Her time with Draper

was at an end, and there were to be no heart-felt emotional farewells, no whispered endearments, no promises. She was left with nothing except the memories of a passion shared, nothing beyond the golden moment when she'd belonged to him and only him . . .

That night, that moment, was behind her now, and her future, her reality, lay waiting beyond the bright rectangle of the door.

It was a chilling thought.

Quintana drew herself up, then, shoulders squared and head held regally high, she walked into the room, unaware of the unmistakable glint of pride that entered the golden eyes of her escort as he followed her into Wolverine's lair.

Two of Winston's subordinates had been seated companionably near their commander's desk, but as she entered the room they abruptly stood. Quintana barely noticed them. All of her attention was given to her reason for being in this strange and forbidding place.

It had taken a long ocean voyage and an arduous journey through the wilderness for Quintana to realize that she'd been preparing for this moment all her life, yet now that it had arrived and she was facing down the infamous Wolverine Wade, traitor to the Crown, she didn't know quite what to say.

Like the town itself, he was not at all as she had anticipated. Tall and spare, he stood behind his desk, a mortal man of middle years, with hair more silver now than gold, and with features very like her own.

Quintana stared at him, but there was no visible trace of villainy lurking in his face or form. Indeed, he hardly seemed capable of throwing her world completely off its axis, yet by issuing the fateful order that had sent Draper Catworth Boone halfway around the world in search of her, that was precisely what he'd done.

Coming forward, he took her hand. "My dear," he said, "I trust your journey was not too taxing."

Quintana met his gaze levelly, praying that none of her inner turmoil showed on her face. "Captain Boone did his utmost to see that Tilly and I were made comfortable."

Draper made no reply. He simply continued to watch her with a curious half-smile.

Winston cleared his throat, and his cold gray gaze shifted to Draper. "As well he should have. Well done, Captain. You may go."

"If it's all the same to you, sir, I'll stay," Draper replied.

Quintana saw the young officer standing slightly to her father's left stiffen. He was several inches shorter than Draper and lacked the frontiersman's breadth of shoulder. Indeed, he was a narrow young man, narrow of face and form, and judging by the air of staunch, unbending pride that surrounded him, narrow of mind as well.

Introductions weren't necessary. Quintana knew without being told that *this* was Lieutenant Uriah Bell.

Bell had yet to meet her gaze, but he readily met and clashed with Draper's. Quintana saw his face flush dark at Draper's insolent grin.

"Sir," Uriah said, drawing himself up. "I must protest this intrusion. Boone has no interest whatsoever here—"

"I beg to differ," Draper said. "Since my future rides on the outcome, I've more right here than you."

"Captain!" Winston's voice sliced through the air. *"You may go."*

Quintana, well-acquainted with Draper's temper, held her breath. But the explosion she anticipated was not forthcoming. Draper merely glared at his nemesis a moment longer, then turned to her and chucked her chin, a gesture that was all his own, and therefore very dear. "I'll see you later," he said softly. Taking up his rifle, he stalked from the room.

With Draper gone, the tension leveled off. Winston turned his attention once more to Quintana. "I apologize, my dear. Now, where were we? Ah yes, I was just about to present my staff. This is Major Abrams, our field surgeon."

Major Abrams bowed. He was pleasant-looking, with a full florid face and bright blue eyes that twinkled as he bent over her hand. "My pleasure, Miss Wade," he said. "I regret I cannot stay and chat, but I'm sure you're weary after so long a trip, and regretfully my services are needed elsewhere." Leaning close, he confided behind his hand, "Sergeant Fulmer

has a pernicious boil on his backside to which I
must attend."

"You will come for dinner this evening,
Major," Winston said. It was an order, not an
invitation. "And be sure to bring Mrs. Abrams.
I am certain she and Quintana will get along
quite well."

A slight frown creased Quintana's brow.
He'd brought her here against her will,
had chosen Uriah for her husband. Now
it seemed he would choose her friends as
well.

"Sir, if you please," Uriah said, stepping forward.

"Ah, yes," Winston said. "I'd nearly for-
gotten. Quintana, this is Lieutenant Uriah
Hampstead Bell. Lieutenant, my daughter,
Quintana."

"My dear Mistress Wade," Uriah said.
"You'll never know the sweet anticipation
with which I awaited this moment." He
seized her hand and brought it to his lips.
His kiss was chaste, unlike the slow seduction Draper had ruthlessly practiced upon all
of her senses from the first. Quintana was
unaffected.

Withdrawing her hand from the lieutenant's grasp, she turned her cool implacable
gaze upon Winston. "If you don't mind, I
should like to find Tilly and retire. The
day has been a long and trying one for us
both."

If Winston was disappointed by her tone, he

did not show it. "Of course," he said quietly.
"Just let me see what's keeping Mrs. Mimms,
my housekeeper and the wife of our quarter-
master. Lieutenant Bell will be joining us for
dinner this evening; the two of you can get
acquainted then."

Quintana wandered to the window behind
her father's desk. The small panes were thick
and wavy, distorting the images beyond, yet it
didn't prevent her from searching for a familiar buckskin-clad form.

Uriah moved to stand beside her. "It may
not look like much compared to London, but
it's a good place for advancement. A man with
ambition can move up through the ranks rather
quickly in a small outpost such as this."

"And you are an ambitious man, I take
it?" There was a note of scorn underlying
her words.

Uriah didn't notice. He nodded, a swift jerk
of his dark head. His hair was brown and lack-
luster, his eyes dark and their expression shallow as he assessed her. "Ambition in certain
situations is a highly prized attribute. Without
it, a man drifts aimlessly through life, much
like your hallowed guide."

"I beg your pardon?"

"The backwoodsman," Uriah said with obvious distaste, "your guide. A shiftless, quarrel-
some individual, yet typical of his kind." He
had gained her full attention now, but he
blissfully ignored the bright glitter of her
silver eyes and went on to elaborate. "I

must say I was appalled that your father should trust that lowborn, untrustworthy wretch with your life, and with your, ahem, *virtue*. 'Tis only by the grace of God that both are still intact."

Quintana smiled up into his thin face, a knowing secretive smile, and watched his color rise. *Let him think whatever he damned well pleased.* "You were appalled, you say?" she said. "That's something I can well understand, for I myself am much appalled at the prospect of this marriage."

Uriah flinched visibly, but recovered quickly. "A little time and you will change your mind," he said with utter confidence.

Quintana's silver glance slid to his face, and her smile turned chill, a fine imitation of Winston's. "I would not stake my life upon it, were I you."

At six o'clock that same evening Quintana sat on a faded divan in the shabby downstairs parlor, wishing fervently that she were elsewhere. Seated in a chair to her right, and looking every bit as tense and uncomfortable as she felt, was Winston Halcourt Wade.

The moments ticked by and there was no lessening of the tension that filled the air. Quintana felt it keenly, indeed, she reveled in his discomfiture. She watched mercilessly as he sighed, shifting in his chair, then drummed his elegant fingers on the padded arm. "You do not look at all like the Chamberlains," he said.

"Indeed?" Quintana said, her tone snappish. "Precisely what were you expecting?"

Winston frowned, and something flickered behind his eyes. "Call it an old man's fancy, but somehow I thought perhaps—"

"That I would be more like Rowena," Quintana supplied with an icy smile. "If you expected me to be like Mother, then you must be gravely disappointed. I've none of her softness and gullibility. In fact, you'll find when you come to know me better that my nature is a great deal less forgiving."

"I can see that you are intent upon making this transition difficult."

"Difficult?" Quintana questioned scathingly. "You cannot know the meaning of the word."

His expression hardened. "I understand that you must be upset with me, and given the unusual circumstances of our reunion, I am not unwilling to make certain allowances—"

"How very generous of you to do so."

"I am even willing to admit," he went on, "that ours has not been the ideal relationship. My absence in your life has obviously created some feelings of bitterness—"

Quintana stared at him, amazed at his ability to twist a hard and ugly truth into an innocent oversight. "What lies between us, *Father*, could hardly be termed a 'relationship'!"

"You have every right to be angry with me—" Winston began.

"I have every right to detest you!" Quintana cried, coming abruptly to her feet. All restraint abandoned her, just as he had abandoned her all of those years ago. "You are a faithless, heartless rogue with little regard for anyone besides yourself. You betrayed your homeland even as you betrayed my mother! And while the one sin I might in time be able to understand and even forgive, the other I never shall!"

"I never betrayed your mother," Winston said sharply. He pushed out of his chair and stood. "I was faithful to her until the day she died."

"You abandoned her! Knowing that she was not as strong as you! You left her to care for a three-year-old child!"

"I loved Rowena," Winston said, his features taut with the strain of containing his own emotions. "But I found out too late that love was not sufficient to overcome our differences. There was nothing for me in England, Quintana. And Rowena refused to accompany me to my post in Ligonier. I wanted her with me; I wanted both of you with me!"

"Liar!" Quintana cried, her voice quivering high on the air. "She waited for you to send for her! We both waited!"

Winston took her by the arms. "Quintana, please, you must listen to me."

But Quintana didn't listen. No excuse he offered could erase the hurt of his rejection all those years ago. Wrenching herself from his grasp, she hugged her arms where he'd sought to hold her. "Why?" she said, her voice breaking. "Why did you send for me now? After so many empty years?"

"Because you are my daughter. My flesh and blood. I want to see you settled, I need to know that you are well cared for when I am gone."

"I do not need your interference in my life!"

"Not interference, daughter. Caring. Fatherly concern."

She gave a weak and watery laugh. "Where was your fatherly concern all those years ago when I was struggling to assume the responsibilities foisted upon me by an ailing fragile mother? Where were you when I needed you?"

Winston raked an agitated hand through his hair. "I cannot change the past, Quintana, but if we try we can find our way to a better future."

Quintana only shook her head, and the blur that was her father grew brighter through the veil of her unshed tears. "Therein, sir, lies your folly. You cannot mend fifteen years of hurt in a day or a month . . . and perhaps not in a lifetime."

"But you are here," Winston countered. He held out his hand, palm up, beseeching. "Surely that accounts for something."

"You have Draper Boone to thank for my presence in your wilderness. If not for his resourcefulness and determination, his unyielding nature, I would be in London still."

Winston's head snapped up; his eyes were chill and penetrating; his outstretched hand curled in upon itself, forming a fist, dropping to his side. "Determination? He did not harm you?"

He'd changed her. Made her think and made her feel. He'd been the direct cause of the slow metamorphosis she'd undergone since his arrival in London, turning a selfish, spoiled, bitter child into a caring, capable woman, worthy of his affections.

Aloud, she said, "No. He didn't harm me. In fact, he has been the only good thing to come of this entire episode, and the one thing I shall never regret."

Winston frowned. "It would not be wise to become too familiar with Captain Boone."

Quintana bristled. She liked neither his tone nor the idea that he felt free to dictate to her with whom she could or could not associate. "I'm a grown woman, and perfectly capable of making my own decisions as to whom I wish to become 'familiar' with!"

"You are a woman betrothed," he ground out. "And if you care at all for Captain Boone, you will strive to keep a respectful distance between you. He has a number of personal difficulties pending at this point and can ill afford entanglements of a personal nature."

"If you are referring to the charges your Lieutenant Bell has leveled against him, then you surely must know that they are false!"

Winston's manner became at once implacable; it was clear that Draper's predicament was a subject he was unwilling to discuss. "The guilt or innocence of Captain Boone will be decided at his court-martial by a jury of his peers. The matter is out of my hands."

An uneasy silence settled shroudlike over the room, and in the interim a discreet cough sounded from just beyond the open parlor door.

Uriah Bell stood in the doorway, his color high and his eyes carefully averted. And Quintana knew from his expression that he'd witnessed all that had transpired.

Somehow it did not matter. The only thing that mattered in that moment was the awful crushing need she felt to be free of the stilted confines of the parlor, away from her father's house. And so she swept up her skirts and ran from the room, down the short corridor, and into the tranquil evening.

Winston cursed beneath his breath, while Uriah assumed a look of concern. "Shall I go and persuade her to come back, sir?" the lieutenant asked.

Winston shook his head and sighed. "This difficulty is my own doing; I must be the one to make her see the wisdom of my decision."

Chapter 18

⌒⌒◯◯⌒⌒

The anger and frustration occasioned by her confrontation with Winston still rode Quintana hard when she reached the gate curtain and was halted by the sentry. "Sorry, miss, but I can't let you pass. The sunset gun's about to sound, and it's nearly time to close the gates."

He was only doing his job, but Quintana did not care. She was possessed by a violent urge to walk beyond the close confines of the fort, and this beardless boy, this *underling* of Winston's, was not going to stand in her way. "Do you know who I am, Private?" she asked with cold hauteur.

"Yes, miss."

"Then you'll be more than happy to make an exception and allow me to pass."

"Beg pardon, miss, but the colonel's orders say—"

"Damn the colonel's orders," Quintana said with quiet wrath. "You have a choice, Private. You can either step aside or spend the rest of the evening trying to explain away my hysterics to my father, your commander, for I will make such a scene as to bring the entire

270

garrison down upon your hapless head unless you stand aside!"

The young militiaman swallowed twice and started to stutter a reply when Draper stepped into the fore. "Is there a problem here, Private?"

"Would you tell this dolt to step aside?" Quintana snapped. "He will not listen to a thing I say!"

"Cap'n, I was just trying to explain the colonel's orders to Miss Wade—"

"Miss Wade does not take orders well, I'm afraid," Draper allowed. "It's part of her undeniable charm."

Draper smiled down at Quintana while she continued to seethe. "Would you get me out of here?"

"As m'lady wishes." Draper tucked her hand in the curve of his arm and started for the gate. "You needn't worry, Private. I'll be happy to assume full responsibility for the colonel's daughter."

They made their way in silence across the land bridge to the East Ravelin and past the King's Gardens. By the time they reached the banks of the Monongahela River, the sun was setting and a pale golden glow radiated above the low black line of the western hills.

On the grassy slope leading down to the water's edge, Draper paused, surveying Quintana's tear-ravaged face. "Things did not go well between you and Winston, I take it."

Her silver-colored eyes clashed with his,

then just as swiftly slid away. There was a breeze drifting off the dark surface of the river; it smelled of wet wool and dampness, fresh and faintly fishy. She turned her face into the wind and would not look at him again. "I *loathe* him, Draper, nearly as much as that pompous ass he would have me marry."

Draper sighed. "They say there exists but a fine line between love and hate," he said. "Given a little time, perhaps you'll find some common ground."

She shook her head. "Time will only serve to widen the chasm that separates us." She paused, and a tremor passed through her slight frame.

Draper felt it and hastened to gather her in against him, rocking her slightly as if she were a child he were comforting, stroking and kissing her soft flaxen hair. "You needn't speak of it at all if it troubles you to do so."

But Quintana went on as if she hadn't heard him. "As a girl, I worshipped him. I used to lock my door at night and lie awake, reading and rereading the letters he had written to Mother. Oh, yes," she said. "He wrote her often. And when I discovered that she'd discarded the letters, I scavenged them from the trash, and wrinkled and tearstained and torn though they were, I painstakingly pieced them back together, secreting them away, because I was so desperate for anything, the smallest scrap of Winston Halcourt Wade."

A small forlorn sob escaped her, and Draper held her more tightly still. "Did your mother know?"

Quintana shook her head. "Mother was too consumed by her own bitterness and heartbreak to notice an eight-year-old girl." She sniffed. "Do you know that in those days I would have given anything to have him notice me. I would have gladly come to America had he thought to send for me."

Draper could only listen, saying nothing, while he fervently wished for some way to ease her plight. It tore at his vitals to witness her anguish, to know he was helpless to soothe the hurt little lass inside her.

"All of my life I waited for him to love me. But he could not. Now, years later, he has reentered my life, seemingly for the sole purpose of arranging my marriage, a union carefully planned, absent of the smallest bit of warmth and affection.

"I can only ask myself what I have done that makes me so undeserving. What is there about me that sparks such cold contempt?" She was crying in earnest now, the tears tumbling over one another in their haste to dampen her cheeks. "Why, Draper? Why must I live without love in my life?"

The lash of her anguish cut Draper to the quick. Cursing softly, he took her small face in his hands, forcing her to look at him. When he spoke, his voice was hoarse with emotion. "You are not undeserving, and don't have to live without love in your life! It's yours for the taking. All you have to do is open your eyes and look at me."

She pushed back just far enough to gaze up

at him. Her eyes were streaming and her nose was mottled red, but Draper thought that he had never seen her look as lovely or as desirable as she appeared in that moment.

"What are you saying?" she said.

"I am saying that I've little to offer a woman, besides a heated tumble . . . and my heart. But it's yours if you want it." He smoothed the tears from her cheeks with gentle fingers. "It's virginal, I'm afraid, untutored, and so I beg you to be gentle with me."

There was a look of open wonder on her face. "Draper Boone, are you saying that you love me?"

"I am saying that I love you," Draper said. "And hoping to Christ that for now it will sustain us through this time."

Wordlessly, Quintana slid her arms around his neck, pulling his dark head down to meet hers and kissing him deeply, blissfully unaware that Wolverine Wade observed them from the parapet, a look of dark displeasure on his face.

Snatches of conversation drifted from the open door of the officers' barracks and were carried away on the cool evening breeze.

Seated on a rough plank bench outside the long frame building, Draper passed the oily rag over the browned barrel and the curly maple stock of his long rifle, allowing his thoughts to drift, down to the river's edge, where the last of the evening's golden light still glimmered faintly through the rents in the gathering violet clouds.

There was rain on the wind. He felt its chill damp breath upon his cheek, felt it in his bones.

Maeve had been right. He wasn't getting any younger, and it was more than time he started to think of settling down.

A month ago it had been the farthest thing from his mind, yet a month ago he hadn't suspected that the strange symptoms he'd been suffering since London—the ever-present irritability, the insatiable desires that kept him from sleep, the maddening need to possess the colonel's flaxen-haired daughter body and soul—were but indications of a hidden malady that had taken him completely by surprise.

Love.

It had all the subtlety of a sneak thief abroad in the night, stealing up behind a man, catching him unawares and defenseless, altering his thoughts and his desires until he but little resembled the man he'd been before its coming.

Draper shook his head, barely able to countenance the fact that he'd at last been caught, or credit that it had been a haughty young slip of an Englishwoman who'd stolen his heart.

He turned his attention to the hammer and the lock of his rifle. The scene at the river had taken on a dreamlike quality, yet he had only to glance at the man just then emerging from the gathering dusk to know how very real it had been.

"I've been expectin' you, Colonel," Draper said, without pausing in his labors.

Winston's expressionless face was so hard it might have been carved from granite. "Leave that for later and come with me. I'd like a word with you in private."

Draper threw down the rag, hefted his rifle in one hand, and fell into step beside Colonel Wade.

They made their way past the officers' barracks to the Monongahela Bastion, and with every step they took, the tension grew more palpable. On the bastion, overlooking the great earthen ramparts and the river beyond, Winston halted. "How long have you been attached to Fort Pitt, Captain?" he asked without preamble.

"Three years, sir," Draper replied. "I joined up just after the fighting broke out in Massachusetts."

"Time passes quickly. It seems only yesterday that I left my wife and infant daughter in Philadelphia to come West. And now my wife is dead and my daughter grown, and I am filled with regrets."

Draper stared out across the low black line of the western hills. He said nothing by way of reply, but no reply was expected of him.

Winston went on, "In the past I have been remiss in my duties as Quintana's father—but no more. She has suffered enough, needlessly, and I shall not stand idly by and see her hurt again."

"Am I to assume this has something to do with me?" Draper bluntly asked.

"It has everything to do with you, Captain,"

Winston said, his tone as clipped and as cool as the damp night breeze drifting in off the river. "I came looking for Quintana earlier this evening. The guard at the gate informed me that she had passed that way sometime earlier, in your company, and so I came in search of her. I can tell you that what I witnessed distressed me."

"Am I to be given the chance to explain?"

"I assure you that no explanations are necessary. I am not a fool, Captain, no matter what you may think. I know what I saw." He paused to collect himself, then continued more calmly. "I can also fully comprehend the hardship and peril incurred in a journey the magnitude of the one you have just undertaken; nor am I insensible to the temptations a girl as young and as beautiful as Quintana presents."

Draper stiffened slightly. There was something in Winston's tone that raised his hackles, and the civility in his own voice was strained. "Precisely what is it you are saying, sir?"

"I am saying that your assignment has been completed, Captain Boone. And as of this moment, your association with my daughter is at an end. You are not to see her again. Is that understood?"

"What about Quintana?" Draper demanded.

"What about her?"

"Have you informed her of your decision?"

The eyes Winston turned on Draper were totally devoid of warmth. "Quintana is my daughter. She will abide by my dictates. I know what is best for her."

Draper snorted. "Somehow I doubt she'll see it your way. The lass has a mind of her own, as I suspect you've already discovered. She'll do as she damned well pleases."

"You misunderstand me, Captain," Winston said icily. "She isn't being given a choice in the matter, and neither are you. Thus far, I have been lenient toward you, willing because of your talents to make certain allowances, despite the blatant contempt you ofttimes display for authority. However, it would not be wise to test the limits of my restraint where my daughter is concerned.

"Since you seem to have forgotten," Winston continued, "I shall take it upon myself to remind you that the charges leveled by Lieutenant Bell are still pending, and you continue to enjoy your freedom at my sufferance. I am all that is standing between you and the guardhouse, Captain, and if I hear of any impropriety, so much as a single glance my daughter's way that can be misread and so jeopardize her relationship with Uriah Bell, I shall revoke your parole so fast your ruddy head will spin."

Winston straightened his uniform coat with a jerk and turned away, melting once again into the shadows.

His parting thrust came clearly back to the tall frontiersman, who stood on the bastion, watching him go. "Stay the hell away from my daughter, Captain. And that's an order."

A moment passed, and Draper took up the rifle for the walk back to the officers' barracks.

He knew in his heart that it was one order he was destined to disobey.

As the week wore on, the atmosphere of the Wade residence became increasingly stilted. Quintana, still angry and hurt, did her level best to avoid Winston, taking her meals and whiling away the daylight hours in the company of Tilly and the opinionated Mrs. Mimms, or strolling the parade ground in hopes of seeing Draper.

During the daylight hours her stratagem worked admirably; the evening meal, however, simply could not be avoided. The burdens of Winston's command were prodigious, Quintana knew. And at the end of a long and trying day he expected to enjoy a civilized meal with the daughter he barely knew.

Quintana, however, was not inclined to comply with Winston's wishes. She was no longer the three-year-old toddler he'd left so long ago in Philadelphia, but a woman fully grown. And as she had pointed out during their first interview, there was very little of Rowena Chamberlain Wade's softness in her.

Indeed, Winston saw himself in Quintana's cool gray stare and was discomfited by their very likeness.

Seated on Winston's left and directly across the board from Lieutenant Bell, Quintana was unaware of her father's growing sense of disquiet. She only knew that Winston, with his usual cold detachment and disregard for feelings not his own, was doing his best to ruin her life.

"It was my hope that the two of you might enjoy a prolonged period of engagement," Winston was saying, "and in that way you could come to know each other; however, these are extraordinary times in which we live, and my original plans are proving unfeasible."

Quintana's mouth curved slightly, but the smile held no warmth. "I'm glad to see you've come to your senses, Father. This match was doomed from the start."

Across the board, Uriah flushed, and looked hopefully to Winston, who sighed.

"A gentlemen's agreement cannot be so cavalierly put aside, Quintana," Winston said.

A triumphant Uriah fairly beamed, much to Quintana's disgust. "Any man who would give his daughter into an uncertain future on a damnable handshake, sir, is no gentleman!"

"Your language, Quintana!"

"My language, like my life, is *my* concern!" Quintana threw down her napkin and stalked from the room without a word to her betrothed.

Winston caught her before she reached the staircase. "Where do you think you are going?"

"I am going to my room."

"Not while the lieutenant remains," Winston said. "Uriah is a guest in this house, and as such he is owed a certain degree of courtesy and respect. I will not allow you to insult him in the futile hope that he will reconsider the wisdom of this match and break the betrothal."

Quintana's glance was stormy. "And I will not marry that man and be miserable, simply to please you!"

"I am your father, and despite the animosity you bear me, you will do as I say."

Quintana's bloodless lips tightened. "Is that why you brought me here? So that you could play at being my father? If so, then you are fifteen years too late!"

Winston stiffened at the derision in her voice. "I want to be involved in my daughter's life."

"You want," Quintana said. "It always comes down to you, doesn't it, Father? Well, it may surprise you, but I stopped caring about your wants a long time ago. It is *my* life you seek to ruin with your petty machinations. And I simply will not have it!"

"You are young and willful, Quintana. You can't be expected to know what's best for you. You need a wiser, cooler head to help you make the right decisions—"

"Help me?" Her tone was incredulous. "Help me into a loveless marriage with that pompous ass you've chosen? I think I have had enough of your brand of help, Father. As for not knowing what is best: I know my heart, and if you force this union it will wither and die, just as my mother's did. Is that truly what you want for me?"

Winston remained unmoved by her impassioned speech. "That young reprobate Boone has no place in your future. No, he hasn't told me," he said when she glanced up, startled. "But neither am I blind."

"If you know, then perhaps you can understand why I will not accept this marriage," Quintana said.

"I understand more than you know," Winston replied. "I understand that warm feelings are not enough to sustain a marriage. Time tempers emotion, Quintana. The fire dies away too quickly, and all you are left with are the ashes of a deep and lasting discontent. Boone has nothing to offer; he's a penniless roamer and unlikely to change; unprincipled, reckless, and wild. Men like him are unreliable, and because of that they make poor mates. Uriah, on the other hand—"

"Uriah is staunch and staid and priggish and I will have none of him!"

"Uriah," Winston said again, "is as prosperous as he is reliable. He can give you the stability and comfort in life you so richly deserve."

"Stability and comfort," she said flatly. "What of love, Father? Does love have no part in your grand and glorious scheme? Or am I to be expected to exist without love in my future as I have in the past?"

Winston looked as though she had struck him. He had to struggle for his answer. "Love is elusive, Quintana."

Quintana smiled sadly then. "How very ironic that you should share that opinion with the man you named a penniless roamer a moment ago; unprincipled, reckless, and wild. Truth to tell, you do not want me involved with Draper Boone because you see in him too many of your own shortcomings. But know this: I would rather have a year of bliss with that penniless roamer than a thousand uneventful lifetimes with your safe and stable alternative!"

Winston released her, watching as Quintana turned and mounted the stairs. His voice rang out behind her, implacable, unyielding. "I have arranged for the wedding to take place in the chapel one week from today."

Chapter 19

At half past ten that same evening, Quintana stood alone in her bedchamber, gazing through the wavy glass of the window at the newly risen moon. Huge and white, it rode the night sky, flaunting its freedom as it sped in and out of the fast-moving clouds.

Quintana was envious. Her own freedom had been greatly curtailed since her arrival at the fort, much to her annoyance. Why, she couldn't so much as walk out of the house during the daylight hours without arousing Mrs. Mimms's curiosity, or beyond the walls of the fortification without having her right to do so challenged.

Her father's men were everywhere, and they all seemed to live in fear of his displeasure, a circumstance that left Quintana without allies except for Draper, Tilly, and Absolute.

Outside, the moon momentarily broke free of the clouds, shining full upon a cloaked figure scurrying across the parade ground.

Quintana pressed close to the glass, watching until the figure plunged into the deep shadows at the side of her residence, disappearing from sight.

A moment passed; she held her breath, then the door edged noiselessly open and the cloaked figure slipped into the room.

"Did you deliver the message?" Quintana immediately demanded.

There was a brief pause, during which a pair of bony hands came up to fumble with the deep hood of the cloak. Tilly's aging worried face emerged from the folds. "Against my better judgment."

Quintana ignored the note of disapproval in the older woman's voice and questioned her again. "Did he say that he would come?"

Tilly snorted. "He waits your coming in the lee of the building, where the shadows are deepest. And I might add that I've seldom seen a man so eager to march to his own ruin!"

Quintana donned the cloak, jerking the ribbons tight beneath her chin. The knowledge that Draper was waiting caused her heart to beat a little faster, and it was with a great deal of difficulty that she concentrated on Tilly's cryptic comment. "What is that supposed to mean?"

"Only that it won't go well for Cap'n Boone if he's found dallyin' with the colonel's daughter. He'll pay handily, if Mr. Farquar can be believed, and mayhap with his head!"

Quintana knew that Tilly spoke the truth, yet she simply could not stay away. She *had* to take the chance, had to speak with Draper, had to warn him of Winston's plans.

If anyone could help her to thwart her father and Uriah and cheat them of their nuptials, then surely Draper could. "What would you have me do?" Quintana whispered urgently. "While away the days until my wedding hoping that Winston will have a change of heart? He's given me a week! I don't have time for miracles!"

"There are times when I wonder if that old fool has a heart," Tilly grumbled under her breath. She sighed, a sound of pure disgust, and thrust her worries aside. "Go then! Go to the cap'n. I suppose 'tis better to boldly steal a little joy than to spend your life counting your regrets as Winston has. Just be careful you're not seen!"

Quintana moved to the door, where she paused to glance back at Tilly. "Douse the light, and do not keep watch for my return. If Father comes, pretend you are sleeping."

"God go with you, miss," Tilly said, but Quintana had gone.

Silent as a wraith, Quintana made her way down the servants' stair and through the kitchen door into the moonlit night. She skirted the rear of the building, approaching the easternmost end where the light of the moon could not reach, and without preamble, threw herself into Draper's outstretched arms.

"Thank God, you've come!" Quintana softly exclaimed.

She was trembling. Draper held her tightly to him, seeking to calm her, breathing in her sweet fragrance, willing himself to remember the feel of her soft body straining against him, the sound of her voice. "Come," he said quietly. "We need to talk, but not here . . ."

Taking her hand, he guided her from the shadows, and in silence they made their way to the Monongahela Bastion.

In the shadow of the great frowning cannon, Draper halted. "What is it? What's happened?"

"He's given me a week," she replied shakily. "In seven days I'm to wed."

Draper cursed, low and with a half-strangled vehemence. When he'd calmed sufficiently, a rueful smile twisted his mouth. "What impeccable timing," he said. "Your father summoned me to his office late this evening. He said there'd been recent reports of trouble on Beaver Creek. He's sending a party of scouts out to reconnoiter, and I'm to lead them."

Quintana's head came up, and there was a look of alarm in the depths of her clear gray eyes. "How long will you be gone?"

He clenched his teeth and a muscle jumped in his jaw. "Ten days, maybe more. I don't know."

"Refuse to go!" She clutched his shirt in her fists. "There must be someone he can send in your place!"

"I can't refuse a direct order. No matter how much I want to."

A small moan escaped her; her fists slackened and she leaned against him. "If you leave now it will all be over. He'll have his way, and by the time you return I'll be married to another."

Draper pulled back and held her at arm's length. "There cannot be a wedding if there's no bloody bridegroom, now can there?"

Quintana caught his hands as a thrill of horror crept through her. "If you harm Uriah you'll only make things worse! Winston would see you hanged!"

"What would you have me do? Stand quietly among the well-wishers as you repeat your bloody vows?"

"There is another way," Quintana said. "We can leave this place—now, tonight! We can go back to Fuller's Gap, back to the Shenandoah. Anywhere! So long as it's far from here—far from Winston's reach!"

Draper stubbornly shook his head. "I won't run from this, Quintana. My name is all that I have left to me, the only thing of worth. If I leave now, it will be blackened beyond reclaim for all time, and Uriah will have won. Do you understand what I'm saying?"

Quintana nodded. Her eyes were dry, but filled with sorrow. "I understand," she said, "but I'm afraid, Draper. I shudder to think how all of this will end."

"I swear to you, I'll make it right. Believe in me, sweetheart. Trust me."

He pulled her to him and held her tightly, as if he'd never let her go. Somehow it was not enough. Quintana wanted more. She needed to be close to Draper, needed to feel his strength, to revel in the ruthlessness of his possession. "You are my strength," she said with soft fervency. "My only hope. Take me,

Draper. Make me forget. Make me yours."

Draper brought Quintana to him, raising her soft linen skirts, kissing her with a fevered urgency, lifting her upon him, impaling her, flesh with heated flesh . . .

Braced against the cannon, with her arms wrapped around his corded neck, Quintana strained as he strained, closer, ever closer, two shadow beings melding, mating in the shifting, fleeting, ghostly light of the incandescent moon.

This time there was no tenderness between them. Their coupling was savage and urgent and swift, unlike the slow and leisurely seduction he'd practiced upon her virgin's flesh on the mossy floor of the Valley of Virginia, unlike the night of sweet surrender in the loft at Fuller's Gap, unlike anything Quintana had ever imagined.

Draper had complete control of the depth of his penetration, the rhythm and movement, and his powerful thrusts ruthlessly swept Quintana toward a shuddering climax that she was helpless to control. She could do nothing but cling to him and bite back the cry of joy that welled up in her throat as the rapture took her, carrying her off to a place of shimmering silver light . . . and Draper joined her there.

The ethereal peace that settled over them was slow to fade, and the lovers were loath to part. For long moments they remained locked in love's rapt embrace, neither one aware of a third presence close by.

Standing quietly a dozen yards away, his pipe in hand and a stunned expression on his angular countenance, was Lieutenant Uriah Hampstead Bell.

It was nearing midnight when Draper and Quintana returned to the brick residence near the Monongahela Curtain. The garrison was dark, but lamplight flooded from the windows of the commandant's house, pooling pale and yellow upon the trampled grass.

Before the steps Draper paused, pulling Quintana in for one last bittersweet embrace, a final parting kiss. "Come, I'll walk you around the back. Go directly to your room, and wait."

Quintana glanced worriedly up at him. "What do you intend to do?"

Draper's amber eyes glinted in his shadowed visage. "I think it's time I talked to Winston."

"We can face him together," Quintana said. "This concerns me as much as you, and I have a right to know what is said."

Smiling, Draper stroked her tumbled flaxen tresses. "I'd rather you waited upstairs, sweetheart. Winston is not going to be pleased with what I have to say. I don't want you exposed to any unpleasantness."

The door to the brick residence swung open. Winston stood stiffly in the portal, a straight, unyielding figure, starkly silhouetted against the bright glare of the candlelight. "How very good of you to try and shield my daughter from any undue unpleasantness, Captain. More's the pity this chivalrous bent of yours didn't strike you sooner. You could have saved yourself a great deal of inconvenience."

Quintana stepped forward. "This night was none of Draper's doing. I specifically asked him to meet me here—"

"You will go into the house this instant, young lady, and await me in the study. I will join you the moment my business with Captain Boone is concluded. It won't take long, I assure you."

Quintana squared her shoulders, and the light of battle entered her eyes. "I will not be ordered off to await chastisement like some recalcitrant child. Whatever concerns Draper Boone concerns me."

Winston regarded her, his stern expression unwavering. "Very well, then," he said. "Just remember that I attempted to spare you this." He turned his frigid stare upon Draper. "Captain, your blatant contempt for authority has proven your downfall, and it is only out of consideration for my daughter's feelings that I forgo the pleasure of seeing you shot. Instead, I'm ordering you remanded to the guardhouse, where you will remain until such time as a court-martial hearing can be arranged."

"Father, no, you can't arrest him!" Quintana cried.

But Winston wasn't listening. "Sergeant!" Winston barked. "Take him from my sight!"

The sergeant, a burly fair-haired man with a bluff square face, who'd been hanging back in the shadows, stepped forward, producing a pistol, which he waved at Draper's chest. "Set aside that squirrel gun, Boone, and don't get no fool ideas. I wouldn't want to have to hurt you."

Draper let go of the rifle and it clattered to the ground. "You can lock me away, Colonel, but it won't change a bloody thing." He offered his wrists to be manacled. "I'm in love with your daughter, and I have every intention of making her mine."

"Not in this lifetime, Captain. And not my daughter," Winston snarled. "I'll bury you so damnably deep, you'll be exceedingly lucky to ever again see the light of day."

Six days passed without the slightest indication that the impasse between Quintana and her father would end soon.

Winston's stance was rigid. Quintana tried to discuss Draper's situation with him, but he adamantly refused, and he even went so far as to forbid her to visit the guardhouse.

The turmoil within the household was felt by all. And it was with the greatest difficulty that Winston managed to maintain the brittle veneer of civility in the presence of his officers.

Colonel Wade's impetuous daughter did not care a fig for appearances. Her every thought, every concern, centered around the brash young adventurer currently languishing in the confines of the guardhouse. And in the face of Draper's difficulties, nothing else seemed to matter.

She worried for him constantly, lying awake until dawn touched the sky, and when at last exhaustion overtook her and she slept, she dreamed of Draper.

Tilly's scratching on her chamber door roused Quintana from her musings, and she called out for the maid to enter, sitting up in bed.

"I've brought you some gruel," Tilly said. " 'Tis all Mrs. Mimms will prepare for you until you show your face at table. She says it's easy on the stomach, and the only thing that's fitting for an invalid who's taken to her bed."

Quintana made a face, dismissing the thought of sustenance altogether in light of more important matters. "Is there any news? Has Absolute seen him?"

"Nay," Tilly replied. "But you mustn't worry. They can't keep him locked away forever, no matter what the colonel says."

Quintana's head came up and she looked hard at Tilly. "You *have* heard something."

Tilly sniffed. "I should have told you before, but I was hopin' this would all blow over soon. I can see now that it's not likely to."

"Tilly," Quintana said, narrowing her eyes.

The older woman hastened to comply. " 'Twas the night they arrested the cap'n— shortly before you both returned. I was passin' by the study on me way to the kitchen for a late-night bite, and I heard voices."

"Voices?"

Tilly nodded. "Your father and that bantam cock's. I only stopped to listen because I heard the cap'n's name mentioned. That young lieutenant was all fussed up and fumin.' Said as how he'd seen the cap'n takin' advantage of your innocence on one of the bastions—"

"*What?*"

"That's not all. He said he'd still be willin' to wed you, provided justice was swift and the cap'n got his just deserts. Winston wasn't happy to hear it, I can tell you. He ordered the lieutenant back to his quarters, and said he'd have Bell's head on a platter if he spoke of this incident to anyone."

The color had drained from Quintana's face while she listened, but now it came back in a rush. "So that's how he knew. Draper was right, Tilly. Uriah Bell is truly a weasel."

"I couldn't agree more. What will you do now, miss? You aren't thinkin' of marryin' Lieutenant Bell just to please your father, are you?"

Quintana did not reply immediately. "Where is my father this morning?"

"He's with yon bantam cock, at breakfast. There's a staff meeting at ten. Mrs. Mimms can talk of little else. It seems her husband's come down with the grippe, and she's worried that she'll not have time to tend him."

"Indeed?" Quintana said.

"Indeed, yes." Tilly drew her brows down and a suspicious look crossed her features. "I've seen that look in your eyes before, and

I'm not sure I like it. Precisely whose demise are you contemplating?"

Quintana rose from the bed and walked to the window, her soft white night rail trailing behind. She spoke without turning, her words heated and desperate. "I don't care what Winston says. I'm going to the guardhouse. I need to see for myself how he's faring. I need to reassure him that I'll be strong no matter how long it takes, that I won't give up until they set him free."

"That's all well and good. But how can you manage to see the cap'n if Winston won't allow it?"

"Absolute will help me," Quintana said quickly. "He'll escort me there, for Draper's sake. The greatest difficulty lies with Mrs. Mimms. The woman has a nose like a hound, and can sniff out a plot before its making! It's little wonder Winston values her services. Her vigilance and loyalty have doubtless kept him safe from many an insurrection within the ranks."

"She's loyal to a fault, it's true," Tilly concurred. "And you may be glad that her loyalty extends to her husband. I'll just go and have a chat with her, express my sympathies that her poor mister is ailing. While I'm at it, I think I might offer to do her a kindness by assuming the household duties this morning. That way, if you should happen to slip out while my back is turned, Mrs. Mimms will be none the wiser."

Quintana flew to the older woman and hugged her. "Thank you, Tilly. You've been so unfailingly good to me. I don't know how I could have gotten along without you."

Tilly sniffed. "Well. That's why I'm here, now isn't it? To help you?" She walked to the door, where she paused and looked back over her thin shoulder. "And, miss?"

"Yes, Tilly?"

"You will be sure to tell the cap'n that he's remembered in me prayers?"

Quintana's eyes were suspiciously bright as she replied, "I'll tell him."

The East Ravelin jutted out beyond the thick walls of the fort, an arrow-shaped earthwork that not only provided an unsurpassed view of the wooded hills beyond the King's Gardens, but also served as the primary entrance to Fort Pitt.

The narrow bridge that crossed the epaulement and outer moat cut directly through the center of the triangular earthwork, so that all traffic, pedestrian or otherwise, passed this point when entering and leaving the garrison.

At a little distance from the well-traveled road, a steep flight of steps led downward into the earth, to the guardhouse where Draper Catworth Boone was housed.

It was a lightless, airless place, where the odors of damp black earth and moldering straw hung heavy in the stagnant air. With earthen walls and a low-beamed ceiling, and still more earth above, little sound could penetrate the long, narrow subterranean room.

That which did was muted and indistinct, a dim echo of daily life in a dank and dreary tomb.

On a pallet of musty straw in the farthest corner of this noisome hell, the man who had the unwelcome distinction of being the sole prisoner at Fort Pitt groaned and came slowly awake.

He'd been dreaming again, of the world outside the earthen boundaries of the hated cell, of flowing pale golden hair and silver eyes alight with passion, and as always, he was left with a feeling of deep disappointment when confronted anew with his own bleak reality.

Draper sat up, brushing the hair from his eyes, and as he did his restlessness stirred to life inside him, gnawing at his vitals.

He didn't bear up well under the strictures of confinement, and he wondered for the thousandth time just how long Winston intended to keep him there.

Doubtless just long enough to assure that he was repentant. To make him fully regret his lack of wisdom in trifling with the daughter of Wolverine Wade, to make amends if not restitution.

He smiled at that thought, knowing that he was likely to be there a very long time, for he couldn't restore Quintana's lost innocence, and they couldn't force him to regret a single instant spent in her sweet company.

"The hell with both of them," Draper muttered into the dark. "Bloody, manipulative bastards . . ."

His voice died away as another sound intruded, the sound of a light swift tread on the stair. Draper froze, listening. The footsteps continued, and he heard quite distinctly the soft swish of a feminine skirt.

The sound drew him off the pallet, beckoned him to the door. The slit he had to peer through was small and at a level with his chin. The creeping damp brought discomfort, aches and pains he hadn't known existed, but Draper forgot all that the moment Quintana came into view.

She was so fresh, so lovely, it hurt Draper to look at her. Yet he was powerless to look away. Time was dwindling. If Uriah married her, he would take her away. The thought of Uriah Bell taking her to his bed was more than Draper could stand. It made him silent and morose.

Quintana paused on the landing and peered at the slit, but it was virtually impossible to discern anything beyond the door. "Draper? Are you there?"

"Quintana, you shouldn't have come." His voice sounded hollow, melancholy, reinforcing her fears.

Quintana frowned. "Are you well?" she asked quickly. "Have they mistreated you in any way?"

He moved slightly, and the ominous rattle and clank of metal against metal came to her ears. *Damn them, damn them all . . . He still wore the irons . . .*

"No one's laid a hand on me since they threw me in this stink hole. Indeed," he said, and here he laughed a little, a haunting mirthless sound. "Winston's method of punishment is extremely civilized. But I'd expect no less from an Englishman. He'll not order me whipped, or hanged, or shot. He has something more genteel in mind. He intends to bore me to death."

He laughed again, but broke off abruptly, and from the bowels of the cell came the sound of swift movement, the rattle of the chains, a fleshy thump and sharp piercing squeal that made Quintana's flesh crawl.

In a moment Draper came back to the door. "As you can see, I'm bloody well occupied. What of you? How are things at the house? Have matters worsened between you and Winston?"

Quintana's heart was leaden. "We've talked but once since your arrest. Or I should say that we argued. I have tried to reason with him. He simply will not listen."

"It's no more than I expected. I knew he'd be furious if he found that I'd seduced you. But for the life of me, I'd do it all again."

Quintana sighed. "I shouldn't have asked you to meet me that night, but I was so upset. I never imagined that Lieutenant Bell would see us together and fly to Winston."

"Bell told Winston?"

Quintana nodded. "He saw us by the cannon. Tilly heard them talking."

Draper cursed and kicked the door. "That frigging little weasel. I swear to Christ, when I get out of here I'll make Lieutenant Bell rue the day that he set eyes on me. He's made depriving me of those I love a bloody habit, and one he's bound to pay for—with his precious hide, if not his life."

"Please," Quintana said. "The guard may hear you. Don't spoil the few moments we have left by bringing Uriah between us. He'll be coming between us soon enough if Winston has his way."

Quintana saw his head come up behind the slit. By straining hard, she could just make out his eyes, glowing dimly, like points of fire in the deep gloom of the cell. "What of the wedding? Has Bell relented now that he knows your innocence has been stolen?"

Quintana grimaced. Those had been Winston's exact words the last time they had argued. "Lieutenant Bell has generously agreed to overlook my lack of purity in light of the familial alliance with his commanding officer he stands to gain through our union. Winston seems impressed by his magnanimous gesture and is pressing ahead with his plans."

"It's tomorrow, then?"

Quintana's reply stuck in her throat. She could do no more than nod.

"Damn, damn, damn." His manner changed abruptly. He left the door and paced the width

of the room and back again, and all the while
Quintana could hear him muttering beneath
his breath.

He was like a caged beast, pacing, pacing,
restless and wild at the thought that there was
no escape from his abhorrent circumstances.
Quintana listened to his quiet rantings, listened
as he hit the door again, this time with his fist,
and felt her heart begin to break.

Perhaps Winston was right. Love was not
enough to sustain a man like Draper. He
needed his freedom. And she was the only
one who could give it to him. "Draper, please,
come back to the door," she said, her voice
tight with unshed tears. "I need to know that
you've heard me. Please, Draper . . ."

Her pleading somehow reached him, cutting through his fury, if not his desperation
to be free. He returned to the door, and with
a rattle of the chain, slipped his hands through
to grip the lower edge of the slit. "Quintana—"
he said.

"No," she cried. "Don't speak. I need to say
this quickly, before I lose sight of what's truly
important and succumb to selfishness. I'll get
you out of here. I know of a way."

"There is no way. They haven't even set a
date for the court-martial—"

Absolute appeared at the top of the stairs.
"A moment more. The guard's cum back, lass.
We'd best be goin'."

Quintana nodded once, then turned again to
the door, forcing a smile upon her lips. "I'll do
it, you'll see. I'll see that you're set free, very

soon, and everything will be as it was meant
to be."

As Quintana watched, his hands tightened
over the edge of the door. His fingers were
dusky from the filth of the cell, but the knuckles
still showed white. "I don't like the sound
of this," he said. "Don't do something foolish,
Quintana."

Her voice was steady, but her chin quivered
slightly as she replied. "Giving you your
freedom isn't foolish. Uriah wants the daughter
of Wolverine Wade for his wife, and he
shall have his wish. But know this, Draper
Catworth Boone; he will never touch my heart
as you have done, and I will never love any
man but you."

"Quintana, don't do this! For Christ's sake!
Quintana!" He gave the door of the cell a thunderous
shake and called out to her again, but
by now Quintana was fleeing, up the stairs to
where Absolute waited, half-blinded by her
tears.

Draper's eerie cry drifted out of the slit and
filled the stairwell; the startled guard came
running.

The sound, half growl, half warrior's wail,
was magnified by the thick earthen walls of
the dungeon, echoing eerily, never dying away
completely before beginning again.

With the buck and rattle of the heavy oaken
door, it sounded as if all of Satan's imps had
crept into the darkened corners of the dreary
enclosure to take up their comrade's cry . . .

Chapter 20

It had taken Quintana an hour to calm herself sufficiently, to bathe her face and change her gown, but at last she stood outside the door to her father's study.

Summoning every ounce of courage she possessed, she raised her hand and rapped firmly on the door. Winston's reply was instantaneous. Quintana took a deep fortifying breath and pushed the door open.

He was alone, seated behind his oversized desk, the pages of a half-finished letter spread across his desk. "Yes, what is it?" he demanded without glancing up.

Seeing him thus made Quintana think back to the letters she had saved as a child, the letters he had written that she'd kept until this day. She hardened her heart to the image and spoke. "I would like a word with you, Father. It concerns Draper."

He glanced sharply up at the sound of her voice and his features hardened. "You are very well aware of my position concerning this matter, Quintana. There is nothing for us to discuss—"

"Then I was mistaken, and you no longer

303

desire a reconciliation of sorts between us."
She turned to go, praying that he would call
her back.

A beat of her heart and her prayers were
answered.

"You know there is nothing I desire more
than to bridge this chasm that lies between
us."

"Then we do have something to discuss."

"What, may I ask, has occasioned this change
of heart?"

"I have been to the guardhouse," Quintana
said flatly, regarding him steadily from eyes
very like his own.

"After I forbade you to go?"

"Yes." Calmly.

Winston pressed a hand to his brow, but
before he could speak, Quintana continued on
with her plan. "I have come to ask for terms,"
she said in an emotionless voice. "You wish to
be a father to me; Uriah wants a wife."

"What precisely are you saying?" Winston
asked.

"That you both shall have what you most
desire," Quintana replied. "That I will wed
Uriah, and be a dutiful, if not loving, wife
to him. That I will make an effort to mend
what's wrong between us . . ."

Winston's expression changed—softened—
and he moved around the desk. He was going
to embrace her. But Quintana would not have
it. Not yet. Not until her own needs were fully met.

She put up a hand to stay him. "There are

conditions to my surrender, Father. That's something I am sure you can understand."

"Go on."

"They involve Draper. As I said, I've been to the guardhouse, and I was appalled at the squalor in which I found him."

"He is a prisoner, Quintana, and as such he can expect no leniency."

"You did not revoke his parole because of the charges Uriah has leveled against him! You jailed him because he had the temerity to love me! And only the most heartless of men would consider that a crime."

Her thrust had hit home. Winston paled beneath his tan. "What exactly do you want from me?"

"I want his freedom guaranteed. And I want his good name restored."

"What you ask is impossible—"

"*Nothing* is impossible," Quintana insisted. "Uriah Bell filed the charges, and Uriah Bell can dismiss them."

Winston sighed. "He will not agree."

"If he wants me for his wife, he will indeed agree," Quintana said.

"There is more, is there not?"

"Yes, there is more. I am bargaining for Draper's freedom with my own. The cost to me is dear; I would know beforehand that I receive in return more than empty promises." She went to the sideboard and splashed a bit of sherry into a glass. "You'll forgive me," she said. "This is not easy for me."

Winston watched her, saying nothing.

Quintana sipped the cordial before continuing. "I want the papers drawn up immediately, and I want them signed by Uriah and witnessed by an impartial party. The documents are then to be given to Corporal Farquar for safekeeping."

"Down to the smallest detail," Winston said. "Is there no one you trust?"

"The one man I would entrust with my life is languishing in the dungeon you call the guardhouse," Quintana said emphatically.

"I see."

"No, I don't think you do see, but your understanding is of no consequence to me. The only thing that matters to me in this moment is Draper Boone." Quintana replaced the glass on the sideboard. "There is one thing more."

"I figured as much."

"There will be no wedding tomorrow."

Winston's mouth hardened, but Quintana pressed on. "I will not wed Uriah Bell within the walls of this fort. To do so would be the worst sort of cruelty to Draper, and to myself. To put it bluntly, sir: I do not trust you. If all of the terms are carried out forthwith, then I will bid you goodbye on the morrow and travel with my intended husband to his home, where we shall be married."

Winston's look was level. "You are shrewd, Quintana, I'll give you that."

"I am your daughter in more ways than one," Quintana replied.

At last he smiled, though the expression was slightly grudging. "I shall send for Uriah and present your terms to him. You shall have his reply within the hour. If he agrees, I will draw up his transfer to Ft. Forty."

Quintana had gauged Uriah Bell correctly in surmising that his lust for power and privilege far exceeded his hatred for Draper Boone.

He agreed to her every condition with little more than a disgruntled whimper, then promptly settled down to preparing for their imminent departure as though it had been his doing all along, instead of his willful bride-to-be's.

The following dawn found a small contingent of a half-dozen men, mounted and prepared to depart the fort for Uriah Bell's home in the Wyoming Valley, two hundred miles Northeast of Fort Pitt.

Uriah stood stiffly off to one side, watching as Tilly and Quintana embraced.

"I don't feel right about your goin' off alone," Tilly said. "I should be goin' with you." She sniffed and wiped at her tears with a workworn hand.

Quintana tried to smile, but couldn't quite pull it off. "Absolute is here," she said. "And I will not hear of your leaving him. One of us deserves to be happy."

Tilly's tears were flowing freely. "Whatever will the cap'n do without you?"

"He'll live his life," Quintana replied. "He'll revel at the sunshine on his face. He'll gaze at the night skies, filled with glittering stars, and perhaps, just perhaps, he'll think of me . . ."

Her voice trailed off, and Quintana did smile, though a trifle sadly. "It's for the best, Tilly. And I would rather sacrifice my own freedom than have Draper cruelly deprived of his. You understand what I am saying, don't you?"

Tilly nodded.

"And now I must be going." Quintana pressed cool lips to Tilly's wrinkled cheek, then turned to Winston.

He took her hands in both of his and cleared his throat, seemingly at a loss for words. Quintana, recalling her pledge, stood on tiptoe to kiss his cheek. "Farewell, Father," she said simply.

In that moment, Winston's cool facade crumbled and fell away. With a curse, he pulled her to him and held her tightly, the daughter he had never had the chance to know and likely never would. "Take care of her, Lieutenant," he said. "She means the world to me."

Quintana mounted the dun-colored mare, arranging more comfortably around her legs the skirts of the gray linsey-woolsey gown that had caused such strife between her and Draper in Williamsburg.

She had made the ultimate sacrifice, yet as she rode across the land bridge and past the steps leading to guardhouse and Draper, she had no regrets.

Chapter 21

Winston himself had come to the guard-house the morning of Quintana's departure to inform Draper that Lieutenant Bell had formally dismissed the charges, and that Bell and Quintana were on their way to wed at the lieutenant's home.

Draper had listened, silent and morose, to Winston's explanation. "Have you nothing to say, Captain?" Wade said once he'd finished. "I should think you'd be grateful to my future son-in-law for his generosity. Your release, after all, is entirely his doing."

Winston's words were salt in a festering wound. Uriah Bell was indeed giving him his freedom, giving him back his good name, dispelling the pall that had overshadowed his future, but at what cost?

Without Quintana, Draper had no future. Without Quintana, he had nothing.

His reply was far from gracious. "The good lieutenant can take his frigging generosity and shove it up his pompous ass for all I bloody care."

Winston smiled dryly. "Your sentiment comes as no surprise. Indeed, I rather thought

you'd feel this way. That's why I'm post-
poning your release until such time as I
am certain my daughter has reached her
destination and embarked upon her new
life with her husband. Call it a preventive
measure, if you will. It simply wouldn't
do for you to follow and disrupt her life
again."

Draper had cursed him roundly then,
cursed him each time he thought of the incident, though a week had already passed, cursed
Uriah Bell.

Between them, Winston and the lieutenant
had conspired to steal his reason for living,
and he didn't give a damn what happened to
him now.

Stretched out on the straw pallet in the corner of the cell, Draper stared into the darkness,
but saw instead Quintana's face.

The image was dear to him, and Draper was
so reluctant to let it go that Absolute had to
speak to him twice to gain his notice.

"Hist! Laddie! Are ye awake in there?"

Draper came slowly off the pallet and with
a rattle of chains made his way to the door.
"What brings you here so late?"

"Unsettling news," Absolute said. "A run-
ner arrived not an hour ago, bound from Fort
Bedford. Seems Bentley Bowes showed up in
Carlisle two days ago. Said he and Jules Fitch
had been near their hunting camp on Miller's
Creek when they spied a large flotilla. Looks
like Butler and his Rangers have their sights
on the Wyoming settlements."

Draper's head came up. "How large was the flotilla?"

"Upwards of a thousand men." Absolute's stare was fierce. "Butler and his Rangers, Tories and Injuns."

A cold dread settled in the pit of Draper's stomach. Major John Butler was a rabid king's man, and he was headed for the largest and most isolated settlement in Virginia, Pennsylvania, and Maryland combined, a prime target for attack, and Quintana was bound to be in the middle of it. "What's Winston got to say about this?"

"He's called his officers together. I dinna know what he intends to do, if anything. He canna spare a large force, and they canna march withoot provisions. It could take days to organize an expedition, and two to three weeks to get 'em there."

"Aye, damn it, and Butler isn't likely to wait around for help to arrive. He'll strike hard and be headed back up the valley before Winston can move."

Draper thought of Uriah, who had left his men to die along the woodland trail, his young brother Hamlin among them . . . He did not trust the lieutenant to put Quintana's life ahead of his own. She might as well be alone. "Absolute, can you get me out of here? Now? Tonight?"

There was the sound of scraping and the turn of metal tumblers, music to Draper's ears, and then the door pushed open. "The sergeant an' me had a bit of a chat a while ago, an' he thought it prudent to gie me these here keys, so ye may want to thank him as ye pass by."

Absolute jerked his head at the figure oddly hunched against the wall at the top of the stairs. There was little light in the shadowed stairwell, but Draper could see the man was securely bound and gagged. "Hold out yer hands and I'll get the manacles off ye," Absolute said. "Tilly's waitin' by the sally port. If we go that way we won't be seen. She's gathered together a week's worth of provisions from the colonel's kitchen, and she has yer rifle and shot pouch."

The shackles fell away; Draper was free.

Draper and Absolute struck out immediately, skirting the walls of Fort Pitt and the upper town, heading northeast along the Allegheny River.

The half-moon provided little light, and so for the first few hours, their progress was slow. Still, Draper refused to wait until sunrise. Every mile covered brought him one mile closer to Quintana, and he was determined not to waste a single moment that could be better spent in the pursuit of his objective.

He had been relentless in his push to breach the mountain barrier during their journey to Fort Pitt, now he was a man possessed, unable to think of anything but the two hundred miles of rough country that lay between him and the Wyoming Valley.

Daylight came on quickly, and with it a cottony mist rose off the river and hung heavy and damp above the valley floor. The two men traveled at a dogtrot until they tired, then slowed to a walk and kept on. Yet the moment Draper regained his wind, he set off at a lope once again.

By the time the harsh afternoon sun had softened into the muted golden light that preceded twilight, the runners were entering Kittanning.

For three decades, one of the largest Delaware Indian villages in the East and the base of operations for the devastating raids that had terrorized the settlements in Pennsylvania, Maryland, and Virginia during the French and Indian War had been located here. And then in 1756 Colonel John Armstrong had marched over the mountains with a body of troops and put the town of Kittanning to the torch.

Now nothing remained of the once thriving Indian village. Indeed, there were no signs of human habitation in the valley; the countryside was hauntingly still. The large, low-lying field that sloped down to the edge of the river had grown thick with vegetation. Saplings had taken root where wigwams and log houses had once stood.

Draper and Absolute paused at the river's edge to drink and fill their canteens before turning their backs on the dark winding river, and striking out along the Great Shamokin Path.

They traveled until darkness overtook them, then stopped to sleep until the rising of the moon.

Fort Forty
Wyoming Valley, Pennsylvania
July 3, 1778

Winston's intentions had been noble, despite their disastrous outcome, Quintana could see that now. By arranging this match, he had truly believed that he was doing her a service, securing her future so that she would be marginally content.

He'd also believed Uriah to be a suitable mate for his only daughter, steady and strong, a safe alternative to the wild young rakehell with whom Quintana had fallen in love.

Yet looks were ofttimes deceiving; Uriah Bell was not at all what he appeared to be, and Quintana's present situation was far from secure.

Looking back upon the events of the past two days, Quintana could not suppress the wry twist that curved her lips. If not for Major John Butler's arrival in the valley shortly before their coming to Wyoming, she might at this moment be Mrs. Uriah Hampstead Bell, bitter beneficiary of Uriah's legacy of lies.

Yet "Indian" Butler, so called because of his close affiliation with the Six Nations, *had* come to the valley, arriving late in June with an indeterminate number of Rangers and Indians. The presence of the enemy in the valley sparked a frantic attempt to shore up deteriorating fortifications in anticipation of a siege. Every able-bodied man present was pressed into service, without exception, and so the hasty exchange of vows Uriah had planned was postponed.

The postponement had worked in Quintana's favor, giving her time to discover the extent of his perfidy, a discovery that was unwittingly aided by Blanda Bell, Uriah's mother.

When Quintana and Bell arrived at Fort Forty, a woman came rushing forward out of the crowd to clutch at Uriah's boot. She was old and withered, her diminutive emaciated form all but lost in the tattered linsey gown she wore. Her expression as she gazed up at Uriah was one of elation. "Uriah, son! Amos and me are so terrible glad ye've come home, and with yer blushing bride in tow! Ain't that so, Amos?"

The rheumy-eyed man seated on an upturned keg at a little distance turned his head and spat. The set of his features clearly showed his disdain for the young officer.

"Uriah," the woman said. "Ye know there's trouble afoot in the valley? The savages have come to take our blessed home, yer own inheritance. Ye won't let them take it, now will ye? Ye'll step in and take the lead as is yer destiny. Ye'll save us all from Butler and those sons of Satan!"

Uriah's lips pulled back in a sneer. "Come, Quintana. I don't know who this woman is. The old hag's clearly lost her mind."

He kicked his mount and continued on toward the commandant's headquarters, but Quintana lagged behind. "Do you know him well, madam?"

The old woman had appeared crestfallen, but now she drew herself up and a haughtiness that was chillingly familiar came over her features. "I should say that I know him very well indeed. He's my only son! Ain't that so, Amos?"

The man addressed as Amos looked to Quintana, who gazed speculatively after Uriah. "You really Wolverine Wade's daughter?"

"I am," Quintana replied. "And who might you be, sir?"

Amos smirked. "They tell me I'm that imbecile's pappy, but I can't says I go 'round braggin' on 't." He spat again, and his dark eyes took on a look of grudging admiration. "I gotta give him credit, though. I never thought he'd manage to go so far on so danged little. I s'pose he'll get his colonelcy too, now's he's got your pappy's help."

Quintana frowned at Uriah's retreating back. That he'd lied about his parents' prosperity was blatantly obvious, yet she was soon to discover that it was not the extent of his deception.

The prosperous farm Uriah had spoken of so often was in reality a cabin not far from Fort Forty; the prestigious family consisted of his drunken lout of a father and his frail mother whose dreams for her only son far exceeded their modest means.

Therein lay the greatest irony of all, for Winston Wade, master manipulator, who had gone to such lengths to bring her to this perilous pass, had been hoodwinked by a man more cunning and deceptive and ambitious than he.

When Quintana confronted him with her suspicions later that same day, Uriah became defensive. "Surely you will not believe the insane rantings of that unscrupulous pair above the word of your betrothed!"

Quintana watched him through narrowed eyes. "No, not on their word alone. I heard Colonel Denison speak to the same woman you rebuffed, and he called her Mrs. Bell."

He turned on her then. "What would Denison know?" he demanded. "He's a second-rate commander of a second-rate post, not fit to polish my boots!"

"I want the truth, Uriah," Quintana warned.

He walked to where she stood, and slid a finger along the curve of her jaw. "You want truth? The truth, my dear, is that you are a fallen woman. Tainted goods. And if you had an ounce of sense you would be grateful that I would have you to wife after you gave yourself to that lowly cur in full view of the garrison."

Quintana remained very calm, very cold. "I would remind you that if not for that 'lowly cur,' as you call him, I would never have considered you as a husband, and I certainly would not have come all the way here."

"But you are here, aren't you? And since John Butler and his Seneca are between you and Winston, there is nothing for you to do but smile and accept me."

Quintana drew herself up, her silver eyes blazing. "If you think I will marry you now, you are mad!"

"You have no choice," Uriah said. "You will become my bride, if for no other reason than to save your lover from a court-martial and a hanging. Do not forget that I have witnesses to his attempt upon my life, and they will be happy to corroborate my version of what occurred that day."

Quintana smiled in the face of his threat. "The charges against Draper have been formally withdrawn, and they cannot be raised again without you looking the greatest of fools! And you, sir, have nothing with which to hold me here a moment longer."

The blood drained from Uriah's face. "You cannot back down from our agreement! You gave your word, your solemn oath!"

Quintana laughed, a brittle sound. "You lied to me and my father about your origins, your so-called prosperity. How dare you expect me to keep my end of the bargain, when your end was based on a blatant falsehood?"

Quintana went immediately to Colonel Denison, asking for an escort back to Fort Pitt, but he was distracted by his own difficulties. "I'm sorry, Miss Wade. I'd like to help you, but just now it is impossible. There are hostiles out there, and we have no idea how large a force we face. You understand."

Quintana did understand, yet she was not prepared to give up so easily. She could think of nothing but returning to the Monongahela Country, to Draper, and she did not want to remain in Wyoming a moment longer than was necessary. "I'm only asking that you release the six men who accompanied me here from Fort Pitt," she said. "We'll make our own way back."

Denison shook his head. "I can't do that, miss. We need every last man. I can't agree to anything that would weaken my defenses."

He hurried off toward the gate, where two scouts, newly arrived, awaited him. "What news?" Quintana heard him ask before she turned away.

What news?

It was the question asked a thousand times a day and more. Quintana was every bit as anxious as the residents of the valley. More so, perhaps, because she was more a prisoner here than most.

The news that trickled in was grim. There was still no estimate of the strength of Butler's forces, yet neither was there any doubt that the enemy was near.

Very early on the morning of July 2, a shaken twelve-year-old John Hadsall had stumbled into Fort Jenkins, a fortified blockhouse some miles upriver from Fort Forty.

Young Hadsall had been with the party of twelve men who had departed Jenkins the day before to work their cornfields, and he was one of five survivors of the Indian attack that took the lives of his father and older brother.

Shortly thereafter, Colonel Denison took two companies out to the site and returned with a trio of bodies. Quintana caught a fleeting glance of the pitiful remains, but quickly turned away, sending up a prayer of thanksgiving that Draper, at least, was far from this place.

The following morning three men arrived at the gate of Fort Forty, carrying a flag of truce. Quintana learned from Blanda Bell that the first man was Blue Throat, a Seneca of some prominence. The second man was one of Butler's Rangers, and the third an American, now quite obviously a prisoner of Indian Butler.

They'd come to offer terms for the surrender of the fort. Forts Wintermoot and Jenkins, both fortified blockhouses, had capitulated without a shot being fired. Fort Forty stood alone and defiant.

Colonel Denison listened to the terms offered by Butler's man, but he would not give in as easily as the smaller fortifications. He laid the matter before his officers and enlisted men, and by early afternoon, it was decided that the militia would carry the fight to the enemy instead of awaiting a long and painful siege.

Uriah Bell, in deference to his rank and experience in the turbulent West, was made second in command of the right flank.

He looked splendid in his uniform and brass-hilted dress sword when compared to his rag-tag companions, and there was that same air of arrogance and superiority about him that had served him so well where Winston was concerned.

Quintana wasn't fooled. That ingrained hauteur was nothing more than a grand facade designed to conceal a long list of character flaws in the man himself.

Blanda snuffled loudly beside Quintana as they watched the troops file by on their way out of the fort to do battle. "Keep safe, son!" she cried as he passed by.

Uriah did not deign to look his mother's way.

Blanda's thin shoulders, permanently hunched from too many years of hardship and deprivation, slumped even further at her son's heartless cut.

"Don't grieve for him yet, Mrs. Bell," Quintana said, taking pity on the older woman. "Uriah has a knack for self-preservation."

Blanda brightened. "He does have a way of comin' out on top, now don't he?"

Quintana smiled slightly and said nothing. Uriah was a coward, and cowards had a way of saving themselves in the most dire of circumstances.

The militiamen from Fort Forty had progressed a mile along the road to Fort Wintermoot when the column of smoke appeared in the sky.

Uriah kicked his mount forward, coming alongside Colonel Denison, who was conferring with the other officers. "Sir! Wintermoot's ablaze," Uriah said. "It's Butler's headquarters, and if they've fired it, it can mean only one thing: they've discovered we're on the march and are falling back. We need to press on now, before they've a chance to retreat."

Denison glanced at the smoke hanging low above the trees, hesitating. "We could be heading into trouble, Lieutenant. We still have no idea how large our enemy's numbers happen to be, despite the intelligence reports. It might be wise to turn back to the fort and wait till we know more—"

"Turn back!" Uriah said. "Where is your courage, Colonel? If you've got no stomach for giving Butler a resounding sendoff from our valley, then perhaps you should fall to the rear and let someone more fitting, more willing to fight, take command."

A chorus of sullen-sounding "ayes" followed Uriah's heated statement, and several arguments broke out among the ranks as men sided with one or the other.

The arrival of two scouts at that moment decided the matter. "Small force up ahead, Colonel."

Denison held up a hand to quiet the grumbling in the ranks. "How small?"

"A hundred Indians and two hundred odd Rangers, sir!"

The grumbling grew louder the longer Colonel Denison delayed. The militia was anxious to meet the enemy. Colonel Denison turned to Uriah. "Very well, Lieutenant. You shall have your wish. Form up! We'll show Major Butler precisely what we're made of!"

At Wintermoot's they did indeed meet and clash with the enemy. As the scouts had indicated, their number was small, but it was a decoy force Butler had purposely employed to draw the Americans into his carefully contrived trap. Their fire was sporadic and ineffectual; they easily gave way, firing and falling back, firing and falling back, to the fence row where the main body of Butler's twelve hundred Rangers and Indians lay in wait.

The Americans advanced upon the fence row. When they were at a distance of one hundred yards, Butler's Indian allies opened fire, followed by the Rangers.

The shot cut through the stunned ranks of the Americans like a giant scythe.

Uriah could not believe his eyes. The men he'd been leading a second ago lay like broken bloodied dolls upon the grass, barely visible through the sulphurous pall that overhung the field.

Piteous moans rose up in a collective force, seeming to issue from the earth itself, an eerie sound steadily growing in volume and rising in pitch until Uriah realized the cries came not from the wounded, but from the eight hundred Seneca and Cayuga streaming from the fence row to cut off the left and the right flanks.

In a moment they would be surrounded.

Panic coursed through Uriah. He flung himself from the horse's back, and jerking the sword from its scabbard, screamed for his men to fall back and regroup.

The private to Uriah's left threw down his weapon and took to his heels. More men followed. Soon there was general chaos among the ranks as those able to do so ran for their lives.

Uriah saw young Josh Milton, his boyhood friend and neighbor, crumple beneath a blow from a Seneca war club. Josh's blood streamed dark upon the trampled grass, filling Uriah's vision, blocking out all else, and then Uriah threw down his sword and was running, the beseeching cries of those he abandoned to Butler's bloodthirsty horde spurring him on toward the bright glimmer of the Susquehanna River.

Twilight fell, and those fortunate enough to have survived the afternoon's debacle began trickling into Fort Forty. Quintana stood just inside the gates, listening with rising dread to each new tale of terror.

The atrocities committed on the battlefield that afternoon shocked and sickened Quintana, and prompted Colonel Denison— who had survived the battle and remained in command of the fort—to take new measures to secure the safety of the women and children should Fort Forty fall into enemy hands.

"Quietly, quietly, to the boats and don't despair. Surely God will watch over us all in the face of this present danger." Chaplain Evers herded the wives and mothers, daughters and sweethearts and young sons of those slaughtered that day through the gates of Fort Forty and toward the waiting canoes. His voice had a soothing peaceful quality, but Quintana saw his hands quiver and wasn't fooled.

Chaplain Evers was frightened. No benevolent god was watching over them this day.

The thought turned Quintana cold as she took Blanda's arm and helped her into one of the great dugout canoes.

Fort Pittston was situated a few miles north of Fort Forty on the eastern bank of the Susquehanna River. It was smaller than Fort Forty, Quintana thought, and undermanned, but Colonel Denison had assured them all that Pittston was safer and presented less of a target than Fort Forty, which seemed destined to fall into enemy hands.

But Denison could not have been more wrong, for shortly after their arrival, and just before full darkness fell, Major Butler's Rangers and Indians surrounded Pittston, and the small fort was given into enemy hands, and once again the mass of women and children was turned out into the night.

Blanda Bell moved like a sleepwalker among the other women, plucking at the sleeve of each man she passed, most of whom were the enemy, seemingly unaware of the terror unfolding around her. "Have ye seen my son?" she asked in tremulous tones. "Is there news of my Uriah?"

Uriah was missing; he had not been among those who had returned to the fort. Quintana was skeptical as to Uriah's fate.

Poor Blanda was utterly distraught and disoriented, beyond simple consolation. She weaved her way through the midst of the milling throng, repeating again and again her querulous cry, "I can't find my son, sir. Is there news of Uriah? Can ye tell me aught of where I might find him?"

Screams drifted over the river, slicing through the thick acrid smoke that filled the air and seared the eyes and lungs. The cries were unceasing, inhuman-sounding, the vociferous wails of the unfortunate souls taken prisoner that day and now caught in the throes of unimaginable torment.

They wore upon Quintana's frazzled nerves, tore at her heart, until she longed to cover her ears, to block out the sound, to retreat from this nightmarish scene.

Blanda alone seemed oblivious to the haunting cries, but carried on with her plaintive inquisition. "Where is my son? Where is my Uriah? Have ye seen my Uriah?"

Across the river a series of sporadic shots rang out, followed by the sound of war cries, of hideous, heartless, mocking laughter echoing down the endless night . . .

The evacuees moved slowly through the

gates, past the commander of Fort Pittston, who stood grim-faced beside a man Quintana surmised was the notorious Major Butler, past the garishly painted Senecas who gathered close.

"Have ye seen my son? Have ye any news of my poor Uriah? I do so fear he's been hurt and has wandered away."

Edging her way closer, Quintana took Blanda by the arm. The older woman looked at her, but her eyes were vague. At first she didn't seem to know Quintana, then all at once she brightened. "Oh, 'tis ye, deary. I'm glad ye've come. Ye can help me look for Uriah."

Quintana felt a strong surge of sympathy for the older woman, who had pinned all her hopes, all her dreams, on a son who was as grasping and petty as he was false. "In a little while we'll look for Uriah," she said gently. "Just now we must find a safe place to rest."

Blanda seemed not to be listening. She was staring fixedly at a Seneca warrior who stood along the path. He was tall and not unhandsome, with a soldierly bearing and an officer's dress sword strapped to his side. He watched them without expression as they neared him, and something in that fathomless gaze caused a chill to snake up Quintana's spine.

"Come along," she said urgently, tightening her hold on Blanda's scrawny arm, but the older woman clawed at the restraining fingers and broke free, and ran toward the warrior with clawlike hands outstretched, screeching mindlessly.

Quintana watched in horror as Blanda flew at the man, raking his cheek with her broken nails, leaving behind bloody furrows. For an instant he looked startled, but as his attacker came at him again with claws raised, he struck her a vicious blow with his war club.

Blanda went down like a stone and lay still, blood leaking from her temple, but it didn't seem to satisfy the Seneca, who straddled her fallen form and, grasping her long iron-gray locks, plied his scalping knife.

Something snapped inside Quintana. She knelt beside the crumpled form, glaring up at the warrior with hate-filled eyes. "Damn you!" she cried. "She was just an old woman, addled with grief!"

The Seneca only laughed, showing strong white teeth, then took Quintana by the arm, and dragged her to her feet. "You come, One Fox," he said.

"Please, let me go," Quintana said. He tightened his hold against her struggles, and his fingers bit painfully into Quintana's soft flesh. "I can't—I can't leave her like this!"

One Fox kicked Blanda's fallen form and his lip curled disdainfully. "Goddamned witch dead," he said. Reaching out with a blood-stained hand, he fingered Quintana's sun-bright locks. "You stay, you die too."

Quintana stared at One Fox and longed for Draper's rifle. If only she had a weapon, something with which to defend herself. But she did not. And she was being given a choice: to stay and die beside Uriah's mother, or to go with this man and live.

One Fox must have seen her indecision, for he shook her ungently. "You come, One Fox, eh?"

Quintana's heart fluttered in her chest like a frightened bird, but she managed to raise her chin, the only gesture of defiance that she could afford at that moment. "Yes," she said. "I'll come."

Chapter 22

The devastation of the Wyoming Valley was complete. A thousand homes, mills, barns, and the forts lay in smoldering ruin. The acrid taint of smoke was everywhere.

"Bluddy bastards," Absolute said. "They didna leave a stick nor stone untouched . . ."

Draper, who stood beside the Scot on the eastern slope of Scovell Mountain, surveyed the damage and remained ominously quiet.

For six days he'd pushed himself to the limits of his endurance, then, knowing that Quintana waited at the end of the long hard trail, pushed himself again, but it appeared that his best efforts had not been good enough.

"We'll find her," Absolute said, seeming to read Draper's thoughts. "She'll be there still, ye'll see. Quintana has sense, for all tha' she's a Sassenach."

Draper told himself that the Scot was right, that he would find Quintana somewhere amid the rubble that constituted the Wyoming settlements, that she would be alive and unharmed, yet no matter how hard he sought to squelch them, the niggling doubts, the fears he felt, just would not go away.

They descended the mountainside, entering the valley near the site of Fort Jenkins. Not long ago, the structure had been a sturdy blockhouse, but now all that remained of the carefully constructed fortification was a pile of smoking rubble.

An elderly man knelt not far from the blackened ruins, placing the last few stones on a newly dug grave.

Draper paused before him and, folding his hands on the muzzle of his rifle, nodded a terse greeting.

"Mornin', son," the older man said, rising to his feet with a groan. He squinted at Draper through bleary eyes and wiped his hands along the legs of his ragged homespun breeches. "Can't recall seein' you 'round here before."

The note of suspicion in the older man's voice was not lost on Draper, but given the circumstances, the man had every right to be wary. "I'm Captain Draper Boone, of the Seventh Virginia, and this is Corporal Farquar. We're scouts, attached to the garrison at Fort Pitt."

"That so?" The old man's eyes brightened, and he gave a short wheezing laugh. "Well. You boys sure are a long way from home. What brings you here, if you don't mind my askin'? You part of a larger relief force, by any chance? 'Cause if you are, you've come too late."

Draper shook his head. "I'm looking for a young woman. Her name's Quintana Wade."

"Wolverine Wade's gal," the old man said.

"Aye," Draper replied. "Have you seen her?"

Again the wheezing laugh. Draper frowned. "Oh, I seen her, all right. Before the Seneca come and kilt the militia. Blasted red devils lured our boys into a trap and slaughtered 'em nigh to a man. Three hundred dead." The old man turned his head and spat. "After that they set to burnin' everything . . . and what they din't burn, the thievin' bastards carried off. Din't leave us with so much as a spade to bury our dead—" He broke off with a sigh, and for a moment seemed lost in some private reverie.

Draper, impatient for news of Quintana, felt a wild urge to shake him, but he fought it down. "What about Miss Wade?" he prompted.

"She was with my wife, Blanda, when they took the women and the young ones to Pittston Fort. That was last night, just before dark. Colonel Denison thought they'd be safer there than at Fort Forty where we was—but Butler took the fort anyway, and turned all them women and kids out into the night. My Blanda here was kilt . . ." He nudged the stones that covered the grave with the toe of his worn boot. "She was a fine companion, and a looker in her younger years, though you wouldn'ta knowed it to look at her in recent times. Like me, she'd seen better days."

"I'm very sorry, mister," began Draper. "Now I'd like to know—"

"The name's Amos. Amos Bell, and if you want to know about Wolverine's daughter, then you'd best ask him."

Amos nodded toward the charred ruins of the fort, where a solitary militiaman moved among the blackened beams.

Draper's face hardened as he turned to the Scot, and a muscle leaped convulsively in his cheek. "Hold on to this," he said, placing his long rifle into Absolute's keeping. "I might be tempted to use it." Then, pivoting, he crossed the scorched grass and seized the officer's arm, spinning him around to face him.

"See here!" Uriah said. Glancing abruptly up, he saw Draper, and beneath its layer of soot, his angular face went pale.

"Where is she?" Draper demanded harshly.

Uriah was clearly shaken, yet in the next instant he recovered, drawing himself up and straightening his uniform coat with a jerk of its tails. It was immaculate no longer, but tattered and torn and covered in places with soot; his hair was stuck through with burrs, the tangled tufts standing out from his head at strange angles. "Boone," he said, a note of disdain creeping into his voice, despite the absurdity of his situation. "What are you doing here?"

"Looking after my interests," Draper said flatly. "I asked you a question, and by God I'll have an answer. Where's Quintana?"

Uriah's mouth thinned to a sullen line. "She's gone, and I hope that it pleases you. After all, it's entirely your doing. If not for you, Quintana and I would be safe at Fort Pitt. If not for you putting your filthy hands on her, none of this would have happened!"

Draper snarled low in his throat and, seizing the smaller man's uniform coat in his fists, hauled him off his feet and shook him hard. "I've half a mind to kill you now and save Winston the trouble."

"I don't know where she is! I didn't come out of the woods until after they'd all gone. Since then I've . . . been trying to . . . find my sword. I've managed to lose the blasted thing, and a man cannot command without a proper sword!"

"Quintana's gone, and you're lookin' for your goddamned sword!" Draper shook him again and this time Uriah cried out, clearly frightened. The uniform coat was drawn tightly around the lieutenant's throat, and beads of sweat stood out on his brow and upper lip.

"I'd gae on an' kill 'im were I ye," Absolute said, his black eyes gleaming. "Such a worthless slug as he doesna deserve ta live." The Scot grinned evilly in his wild red beard. "Sae long as 'tis done Injun fashion, who's to know?"

The dark promise on Draper's lean visage and the mocking air of the Scot served to loosen Uriah's tongue. "All right! They took her north along the river."

"Who took her?" Draper demanded. "Is she with Butler?"

Uriah shook his head. "No—at least, I don't believe so! Th-there's a woman named Mrs. Stroud who found her way back this afternoon. She claimed to have seen an Injun man called One Fox leading away a young woman who fits

Quintana's description. It's all that I know—I swear it!"

Amos ambled over and stood eyeing Draper. "He ain't long on guts, son, an' you keep on shakin' 'im like that, he's liable to mess hisself."

Draper set Uriah abruptly on his feet, giving him a shove that sent him staggering in Absolute's direction. "See that he doesn't get lost again. I haven't finished with him yet." When he took his rifle from Absolute, his expression was grim.

"You know this here One Fox?" Amos asked.

"Aye," Draper said. "We crossed paths once, long ago. I drew a bead on him, but he got away. Now I wish to Christ I'd killed him."

"A determined man might overtake them pretty easy. Like the boy says, they're headed north along the river, and since they all but wiped us out, I don't expect they'll be in no particular hurry."

"When did Butler leave?" Draper asked.

Amos scratched his grizzled beard with a gnarled hand and squinted at the sun. "Three, maybe four hours."

"I'm obliged to you." Draper took up his rifle, looking to the Scot.

"Do ye want I should cum? Ye may have need of an extra musket."

Draper shook his head. "I can make better time alone. Can you meet me at Bentley's camp on Miller's Creek tomorrow? We'll circle back to the west and lay up there."

"Aye, ye know I will," Absolute replied.

Draper started off, but Absolute called him back. "Draper, lad?"

"Aye, what is it?"

"Be certain to watch yer back."

Six hours had passed since One Fox and his small band of Seneca had left the destruction of the Wyoming Valley behind them and begun the long trek to the Seneca towns.

Six hours, and in all that time Quintana had trudged along, expending energy she did not know she had, forcing her quaking muscles to execute just one more step . . . and one more step . . . until she moved in a sort of mindless state, a numbness that reached the soul and did not allow pain or fear to come creeping in.

On some deep level, Quintana welcomed the numbness. It was best not to feel, to think. Thinking would only bring back the horrors of the previous night, the fear and the feeling of impotence, the frustration and mindless black rage that had filled her being through the night of the massacre.

Thinking might very well send her careening wildly over the edge of the emotional precipice on which she now teetered, ultimately into madness.

Best not to think if you wish to live, Quintana thought, staring fixedly at the grisly trophy swinging from One Fox's belt.

And she did wish to live . . . for Draper . . . for all those helpless souls who had lost their lives to the British-allied Indians the previous night . . . for revenge, if indeed she could attain it.

And so she tore her gaze away from Blanda's iron-gray locks which were hanging from her companion's leather thong belt, and deliberately surveyed her surroundings.

The country through which they made their laborious way was densely wooded, rife with laurel and huge gray boulders, cluttered at times with deadfalls and debris that might possibly be used for concealment if an opportunity to escape arose.

The likelihood was remote, but Quintana still clung to it. She was being taken to the Seneca towns in the northwest Draper had talked about so long ago, and there was no one to know, no one to follow, no one to care . . .

The thought brought tears to her eyes, but Quintana fought them back. This was no time to succumb to a bout of self-pity. She thought of Rowena and straightened her spine.

Life had defeated her mother, but she would not allow it to defeat her. She was, after all, the daughter of Winston "Wolverine" Wade, and she was determined to survive.

She made a deliberate effort to survey her surroundings carefully, taking note of any landmarks that might help her find her way back to the Wyoming Valley, and eventually back to Fort Pitt.

Quintana's efforts, unfortunately, did not go unnoticed, for Red Deer, One Fox's cousin, nudged her in the ribs with his musket and motioned for her to keep her eyes on the path.

She reluctantly obeyed. The path wound back upon itself, climbing abruptly here, sloping there, but keeping always in sight of the river.

They made their way down a steep declivity, across a level plain, then started up again. Halfway up the slope, One Fox abruptly stepped off the path and slid behind a tree to check the priming of his musket.

Red Deer jerked the trailing end of the rawhide noose still looped about Quintana's neck, quickly bringing her to heel. She mouthed a silent curse and savored thoughts of her revenge while trying to peer around his shoulder at the cause of the alarm.

And then she saw him standing atop the low ridge, and her heart stood still.

He was tall and lethal-looking silhouetted against the scarlet and gold of the evening sky, a dark, featureless figure projecting an air of unearthliness and impending retribution.

His sudden appearance caused great unease among the Seneca; they exchanged frowning glances and murmured among themselves.

Quintana shared their sense of disquiet.

Somehow he'd managed to find her. Somehow, Draper had come to take her back.

Dear God, was he mad? There were five against one! She had to do something, warn him away, beg him to leave her; anything to keep him from being killed. But there was no time, for in the next instant he raised his rifle high and, tipping back his head, let loose with a blood-curdling cry.

The flesh prickled along Quintana's spine. It was a challenge that he issued, and One Fox answered with a loud whoop, firing at the ghostly figure on the ridge, while Quintana bowed her head and furiously prayed.

The shot went wild, kicking up dirt two yards to Draper's left. Red Deer eased his head and shoulders into the open and started to draw a bead on the enemy, but the frontiersman's rifle spoke first, a rich, full-throated boom that echoed off the hills, and Red Deer pitched backward, slamming into the trunk of a young pin oak, a neat black hole drilled between his brows.

The surviving Indians howled and sent a hail of balls to the top of the ridge.

Panic welled up inside Quintana. Draper's rifle was empty, yet instead of taking cover to reload, he came barreling down the slight incline toward the startled Seneca.

Draper saw Quintana from the corner of his eye as he raced past, whooping and laughing to draw out the Seneca, as if he'd lost his mind.

She was terrified; he could see it in her face. Yet Draper didn't slow his breakneck pace. The Seneca had fallen in behind him, and were busily trying to run him to ground. There would be ample time to comfort his lady once the danger was past.

He stretched out his legs and sprinted madly on, letting go with another whoop, and chuckling at the answering yells that floated out behind him. His heart was racing; the hair at his nape was standing on end. Death was hot upon his heels, yet every cell of his being screamed with life and the exhilarating thrill of the chase.

The Seneca pounded the earth behind him in their pursuit. He'd discharged his rifle, and because of it they considered him easy prey, but he'd never been easy, not even as a lad.

He sprinted around a sharp turn in the path and started to reload the long rifle.

Insert the ramrod to extinguish any lingering spark.

The procedure was second nature to him. He could do it in the dark, if need be, or on a dead run. It was a rare talent, and one that few men possessed.

Pour a measure of powder into the muzzle.

He could hear very clearly the sounds of pursuit as the Seneca strove to overtake him.

Wrap the greased patch around the ball and fit into the muzzle. Ram it home.

The first man was gaining on him. Draper picked up speed, just enough to put him a few more yards out in front.

Prime the frizzen pan, and slow your pace enough to turn—

The brave behind him gave a triumphant yell and raised his tomahawk to throw, just as Draper spun and hurriedly drew a bead on his breastbone.

The long rifle belched fire and sulphurous smoke, and the first man was lifted off his feet and flung backward into One Fox. The two went down in a tangle of limbs, while another remaining Seneca whooped and darted around them to continue the chase.

Draper picked up his pace to reload the long rifle. From behind came the boom of a musket. The ball whizzed past, plucking at Draper's sleeve. He spun and his rifle barked a reply; the third man wilted in his tracks.

Only one of the Seneca remained. Draper's lungs were on fire. He could no longer hear the sounds of pursuit; the thunder of his heart filled his ears.

Sweat coursed down his face, stinging his eyes, blurring his vision. *Shove the ball home, prime the frizzen, turn and—*

A chill crept along Draper's spine. The track was empty, the brush ominously still. Had One Fox fled? He started to turn when it seemed as if a huge invisible hand swatted him on the back and knocked him sprawling. He realized in that instant that he'd been shot.

Draper went down hard, his face connecting with the uneven path. "Goddamn..." He blinked and wheezed air into his burning lungs.

For a few seconds he lay on the path, stunned and feeling nothing. And then with a roar his body came back to life, and every muscle, every nerve bowed before the waves of white-hot agony surging over him.

He had to rise, find his enemy and dispatch him. Quintana was out there, damn it, and there was no one else upon whom she could depend...

Absolute's words rang in his ears, smote him in his misery. *Draper, lad? Be certain to watch yer back*. He tried to rise, tried to reach the long rifle that lay a few feet beyond his fingertips, but every time he moved, his body screamed in agony. He heard the rustle of the brush beside the path, saw the Seneca's moccasins and leather-clad ankles come into view, and then there was a blinding pain in his scalp as One Fox wrapped the long hair at Draper's crown around his fist . . .

Draper ground out a string of vile curses and clawed for the knife in his belt just as a flash of linsey-woolsey came into view behind One Fox. The Seneca's fingers closed over the hilt and he dragged the blade from its sheath, but Quintana was already raising the war club she gripped with both hands above her head.

Before Draper could react, Quintana brought the club down forcefully. One Fox pitched forward on the path, and Draper closed his eyes, breathing a sigh of relief.

"Is he—?" Her voice quivered.

"The hell with him," Draper grated, struggling to rise. "Quintana, you'll have to help me up. I can't seem to manage on my own, and we have to get out of here. The sound of the shots will have carried, and there's a damned good chance someone will come to investigate. I don't want you anywhere near here if that happens."

Quintana helped him rise. He leaned against the sturdy bole of a tree while she retrieved the rifle. "First, let me see to your wound. You're bleeding profusely."

"Later."

"You can't go far like this," she said. "You haven't the strength."

"I can make it as far as the river," Draper replied through clenched teeth. "There's a dugout canoe hidden in the willows. I happened upon it a few minutes before I found you. We can drift downriver as far as Bentley Bowes's hunting camp. It's on Miller's Creek, eight miles south of here. Absolute will meet us there."

They made it to the river and found the canoe. Draper waded into the shallows, dragging it out into the current. "Get in."

Quintana climbed over the gunwale and sat in the stern at Draper's direction, and then with his last ounce of strength he shoved the canoe off and tumbled over the gunwale into the bottom, where he lay panting. "Remember, lass. Miller's Creek. Eight miles south on the west bank . . ."

Something soft touched his cheek, brushed back the damp hair that had fallen forward into his eyes. "Rest now." Quintana's voice seemed to come from far away, a mere whisper of sound he sensed more than heard above the faint buzzing in his ears. "I'll see to your wound," she said, "and everything will be all right. We are together at last, and nothing can separate us ever again . . ."

"Uriah." He struggled hard to form the word.

"He lied," she whispered. "And because of it I refused to honor the agreement. Rest and get well. Nothing stands in our way."

With a ragged sigh Draper released his tenuous grip on consciousness, slipping effortlessly into the warm inviting darkness.

Quintana waited until he had drifted off before setting to work. His shirt was slick with blood and needed to be removed, yet Quintana didn't have the heart to disturb him. Instead, she took his scalping knife from the scabbard at his waist and carefully split the buckskin hunting shirt up the center back. Then, folding the tail of the shirt aside, she exposed the wound.

"Dear God." Closing her eyes, she fought hard to regain her composure.

This was no time for panic. There would be time to panic later, once the task was completed and Draper was out of danger, once they reached the camp on Miller's Creek . . .

Working methodically, Quintana cleansed the wound with cool water from the river. Using strips torn from her chemise, she staunched the flow of blood, but with every moment that passed, her worried frown grew more pronounced.

The wound was grievous. The ball had plowed a deep furrow through Draper's flesh and entered his body at an angle four inches below his left shoulder blade. There was no way to determine just how deep it lay, or how extensive was the damage it had done, and there was nothing Quintana could do but pick up the paddle and make a valiant effort to hasten their passage downstream, praying all the while that Absolute was indeed waiting.

Absolute would know what to do, she told herself steadfastly. Absolute would save him if anyone could.

Yet as day turned into evening, and evening changed to night, Quintana's worries became a slow creeping panic.

She felt it rise a little more each time they rounded a bend in the river and there was not the smallest indication of the entrance to Miller's Creek. She felt its sickening sense of dread plant its roots a little deeper into her vitals each time she glanced at Draper.

He lay on his side in the bottom of the canoe, his dark head pillowed in her lap. His skin was ashen, and he was terribly, frighteningly still, his rasping shallow breathing the only indication that he lived.

Quintana was heartsick. Draper was dying, leaving her to face life alone, after all they had been through.

And all she could do was sit helplessly by and wait for death to claim him, her only love, her life.

It wasn't fair, Quintana thought. He should not be leaving her, not now, not yet! It was too soon!

Her anger, her panic, her frustration and grief threatened to suffocate her, welling up in her throat in an anguished, heart-wrenching sob too great to contain. She found his hand and clung to it; it was cool and limp in her grasp, the pulse in his wrist was far too weak, far too slow . . . almost nonexistent.

Until this moment, Quintana hadn't cried. She'd determined to be strong, for Draper's sake, if not for the sake of her own sanity. Yet now her defenses were worn, her strength waning, and there was nothing to hold back the emotional torrent that burst free as the terrible certainty settled upon her.

He was going to leave her very soon, and there was nothing she could do to make him stay.

Holding tight to his arm, Quintana rocked back and forth upon her knees, and the sound that escaped her was the sound of her heart shattering into a thousand tiny pieces. "Why?" she said aloud, pressing his palm to her cheek. "Why did you have to follow me, Draper? Why couldn't you have just let me go? Fool! Bloody, arrogant, pigheaded fool!"

Draper's hand stirred weakly in her grasp, the fingers turning, entwining with hers.

"Aye," he said, so softly that she had to strain to hear. "I'm a fool . . . a stubborn, lonely . . . heartsick fool . . . who's lost . . . without you." His eyes were dark slits in his face, and his smile was slight, a mere ironic curve of bloodless lips. "I had to come . . . Quintana. I could . . . do nothing . . . else. I love you . . . sweetheart . . ."

"If you love me, then swear to me that you will stay," she said. "Please, Draper! Don't leave me here alone."

He squeezed her hand, gently, as his only reply, drifting off again while Quintana wept her heart out.

By the time the mouth of Miller's Creek came into view, her tears had ceased to flow, but her heart was just as heavy.

Absolute was waiting, just as Draper had said he would be. He waded out into the shallows and grasped the bow of the dugout canoe, pulling it up on shore where Bentley Bowes and Jules Fitch were waiting. "Ye'd best cum gie me a hand," he said to his two companions.

Quintana watched anxiously as they lifted Draper from the canoe and carried him up the bank and laid him in the shelter of the lean-to that served as a hunting camp.

Absolute peeled back the ruined shirt and grunted at the bloodstained bandage as Bowes and Fitch stood back, watching. "He's lost a fair amount of blood, but there's naught to be done aboot that noo."

"Absolute, do you think you can cut the ball out? If it should mortify—" She could not bring herself to finish the thought. It was too horrible to contemplate.

Absolute grimaced. "The slug's too deep, an' if I dig to find it, I may do more hurt than good. We'll hafta leave it be an' hope for the best." He looked sharply up at Quintana. "What of ye? Ye look a mite worn."

"I am," Quintana said. "I was afraid we wouldn't make it—" She broke off, unable to say more, glancing at Draper.

Absolute produced a flask and put it in Quintana's hands. " 'Twill help to fortify ye. Just tip it up, this ain't no time for niceties."

Quintana brought the flask to her lips. The whiskey was raw. It blazed a path down her throat, singeing her belly. The burning sensation was temporary, however, and soon settled into a soothing warmth. She sipped again, then returned the flask to Absolute and went to sit by Draper, whose wound had been cleaned and bandaged by Absolute.

The morning mist was heavy in the air when Draper opened his eyes and looked slowly around, his gaze at last coming to rest on Quintana. "We made it," he murmured. "Good lass."

Quintana stroked his hair and smiled softly down at him. "Yes, we made it. How do you feel?"

That infinitesimal smile curved his lips. "Like bloody hell. Where's the Scot?"

"Right here, lad."

"You ready . . . to move, Corporal?"

"Ye oughta wait a bit, daen't ye think?"

"Wasn't thinkin' of me," Draper said. His eyes drifted to Quintana's small white face. "See her safely into Winston's hands and . . . don't . . . delay . . . for anything."

Quintana was shaking her head, and in her eyes was a look of dawning horror. "No! I won't leave you! Not like this."

Draper caught at her hand, drawing her gently down until she lay against him, enfolded in his embrace. He closed his eyes and kissed her sun-bright locks. "Aye," he rasped. "You will. Because I ask you to. I will not rest until you're safely away from here."

"You ask too much," she said. "If I leave you now—"

Draper put a finger to her lips. "Don't say it, Quintana. I swear to you . . . if it is within my power . . . I will come back to you."

He held her until his slight store of strength ebbed away, until her tears had ceased to flow, until he thought that he could bear no more without breaking down himself and begging her to stay. Then he met Absolute's steady gaze, and he gave a single nod, watching as the Scot took his lady's arm and helped her to her feet. Quintana leaned heavily against Absolute, and Draper watched the pair slowly walk away.

Chapter 23

Fort Pitt
The Monongahela Country
August 31, 1778

The hot and humid days of July had drifted into sweltering August, and there had been scant news from the hunting camp on Miller's Creek. When at last word did come, it was not the welcome news for which Quintana had been hoping.

The party of scouts dispatched by Winston to bring Draper home had returned without the young frontiersman. The tale they told was grim. The hunting camp lay in ruins, the lean-to had been reduced to ashes a week before the arrival of the party, and there was no sign of the young frontiersman.

With the scouts' return, Quintana's hopes flickered and died. Draper was not coming back.

She knew that now, knew that his body had been lain to rest in a lonely wilderness grave. It pained Quintana greatly to think of it, and so she determinedly turned her thoughts to the future.

350

Tomorrow was the first day of September, a new month, a new beginning. The time had come to leave Fort Pitt and all its bittersweet memories behind her. The time had come to go home.

The knock that sounded at her door did not surprise her. She had been expected downstairs twenty minutes ago. The guests at the gala Winston had arranged in her honor were waiting, and Winston "Wolverine" Wade was not a man known for his patience. Quintana smiled at the man standing in the doorway. He was tall and straight and raffishly handsome, despite his middle years, and Quintana thought that she really should have a word with him about his own future before her departure. He was too young and vital yet to be all alone.

"Tilly said you were changing for the reception. Our guests are waiting, and growing impatient."

"I hope you will convey my regrets. I've had a change of heart. I'm not feeling up to this evening's festivities."

"Would that you would suffer another change of heart, and consent to stay," Winston said.

"Father, please, we have been through this already," Quintana said. "I see no point in going into it yet again."

"Yes, we have been through it many times, but I remain unconvinced that yours is a wise decision. England is so far away, Quintana. That much distance makes it deuced difficult for a man to get to know his offspring—or for that man to make amends for past mistakes."

Quintana smiled at that. Draper's death had touched them all, and Winston had not been left unaffected by her own overwhelming loss. To his credit, he had done everything in his power to ease her grief, yet he couldn't erase it completely.

No one could.

Winston drew himself up. "Let no man say that Winston Wade does not learn from his mistakes. And I have learned not to argue with you when your mind is set on something."

"Why, Father," Quintana said. "If I didn't know better, I should think that you were showing signs of softening."

"All good things mellow with age. Or so they tell me. However, if I am to let you go on the morrow, then I must insist upon this night. You will attend the gathering that I have arranged in your honor. Ah, ah!" he warned when she made to protest. "Must I remind you that I am your father, commander of this post, and the source of your own inherent stubbornness? I will not take no for an answer."

Quintana sighed. "Very well, then. I will change and be down in a few minutes."

True to her word, Quintana emerged from her chamber a short while later, garbed in the saffron silk she'd packed for the voyage to America so long ago in London.

When she descended the final stair, Winston offered his arm. "Would that Captain Boone could see you now," he murmured.

His mention of Draper brought tears to

Quintana's eyes, but they didn't linger. The night was lovely, the air soft and faintly redolent of autumn, the dark night sky full of stars.

Arm in arm, they strolled across the parade ground to where the guests were gathered. Absolute was first to greet them. He cleared his throat twice before holding out a strange bundle wrapped in oilskin. "The lad had no kin, and so I thought ye might like these here things as a sort o' keepsake."

Quintana accepted the bundle with a quizzical look. Beneath the oilcloth and knotted string was the tawny hide of the catamount that she had confronted and Draper had killed, and inside that, Draper's powder horn. Quintana smiled sadly down at her own likeness etched on the horn. "Thank you for thinking of me, Absolute. I shall cherish them always." Stepping close, she hugged him tightly for a moment, then kissed his bearded cheek. "I shan't forget you, ever."

He blushed as red as his hair and, mumbling something unintelligible, went to join Tilly.

A long line of well-wishers followed, each with some small token of remembrance and a wish that she would reconsider and stay.

The time passed quickly, and it was growing quite late when Winston again took her arm, leading her onto the open parade ground. "Fiddler," he said, "if you please, play something lilting and sweet. I should like to dance with my daughter."

It seemed very strange to Quintana to be

handed through the movements of the minuet by a man she had once detested. But she had matured since leaving London; she'd grown up and perhaps gained some wisdom; she had found love and she had lost it . . .

The past seven months had been for her an odyssey, and she had one man's memory to credit for it.

Winston turned her, a curious smile on his hard unyielding mouth, and then with a small courtly bow he stepped back so that her new partner could take his place.

The notes of the violin trembled on the air, poignant, high, and hauntingly sweet as he came to stand before her. "Would you dance with me, m'lady?" Draper questioned softly. "Would you sway in my arms until we can slip away unnoticed?"

Quintana stood very still. Her throat was tight, but it didn't matter. She was afraid to speak, afraid to breathe, afraid of breaking the spell that her father had cast and discovering that it had been nothing more than a dream.

Reaching out, he took her hand in his, leading her through the final movements of the dance, and when she felt the life and the warmth, the undeniable promise of tomorrow that was in his touch, she flew into his arms, burying her face in the flowing white shirt he wore . . . Winston's shirt.

Quintana's eyes were streaming as she looked over at her father. "You knew, yet you didn't tell me."

Winston was nonplussed by her tone of accusation. Indeed, he seemed inordinately pleased with himself. "Yes, I knew. He came in a few hours ago, looking like the very devil and demanding to discuss your future."

"But you could have informed me—"

"He wanted to tell you himself, immediately. The delay was entirely my doing. I thought it only fitting that the captain clean himself up before proposing marriage to his commander's only daughter."

Quintana looked from Winston to Draper. He was thinner than he had been, but his pallor was gone, and he seemed fit. "Marriage?" she whispered.

"You know that I've little to offer, Quintana," Draper said.

"There is precious little I require," Quintana replied.

"We'd be starting from scratch, but my back is strong, and I know of a piece of land in the Valley of Virginia that's mine for the asking."

"The Daughter of the Stars," Quintana murmured. "It will please me greatly to see it again."

Still looking on, Winston sighed. "For heaven's sake, Captain. Will you get on with it?" he said.

Draper took a deep breath. "Quintana Wade, will you consent to be my bride? Will you share in all of my tomorrows beginning with the dawn?"

Quintana smiled up into his dark handsome

face. "Yes, Draper. Yes, to all of that and much, much more!"

He pulled her in against him then and kissed her passionately, oblivious to those who cheered around them.

Avon Romances—
the best in exceptional authors and unforgettable novels!

FOREVER HIS Shelly Thacker
77035-0/$4.50 US/$5.50 Can

TOUCH ME WITH FIRE Nicole Jordan
77279-5/$4.50 US/$5.50 Can

OUTLAW HEART Samantha James
76936-0/$4.50 US/$5.50 Can

FLAME OF FURY Sharon Green
76827-5/$4.50 US/$5.50 Can

DARK CHAMPION Jo Beverley
76786-4/$4.50 US/$5.50 Can

BELOVED PRETENDER Joan Van Nuys
77207-8/$4.50 US/$5.50 Can

PASSIONATE SURRENDER Sheryl Sage
76684-1/$4.50 US/$5.50 Can

MASTER OF MY DREAMS Danelle Harmon
77227-2/$4.50 US/$5.50 Can

LORD OF THE NIGHT Cara Miles
76453-9/$4.50 US/$5.50 Can

WIND ACROSS TEXAS Donna Stephens
77273-6/$4.50 US/$5.50 Can

Avon Romantic Treasures

*Unforgettable, enthralling love stories,
sparkling with passion and adventure
from Romance's bestselling authors*

COMANCHE WIND *by Genell Dellin*
> 76717-1/$4.50 US/$5.50 Can

THEN CAME YOU *by Lisa Kleypas*
> 77013-X/$4.50 US/$5.50 Can

VIRGIN STAR *by Jennifer Horsman*
> 76702-3/$4.50 US/$5.50 Can

MASTER OF MOONSPELL *by Deborah Camp*
> 76736-8/$4.50 US/$5.50 Can

SHADOW DANCE *by Anne Stuart*
> 76741-4/$4.50 US/$5.50 Can

FORTUNE'S FLAME *by Judith E. French*
> 76865-8/$4.50 US/$5.50 Can

FASCINATION *by Stella Cameron*
> 77074-1/$4.50 US/$5.50 Can

ANGEL EYES *by Suzannah Davis*
> 76822-4/$4.50 US/$5.50 Can

If you enjoyed this book, take advantage of this special offer. Subscribe now and get a

FREE
Historical Romance

No Obligation (a $4.50 value)

Each month the editors of True Value select the four *very best* novels from America's leading publishers of romantic fiction. Preview them in your home *Free* for 10 days. With the first four books you receive, we'll send you a FREE book as our introductory gift. No Obligation!

If for any reason you decide not to keep them, just return them and owe nothing. If you like them as much as we think you will, you'll pay just $4.00 each and save at *least* $.50 each off the cover price. (Your savings are *guaranteed* to be at least $2.00 each month.) There is NO postage and handling – or other hidden charges. There are no minimum number of books to buy and you may cancel at any time.

Send in the Coupon Below

To get your FREE historical romance fill out the coupon below and mail it today. As soon as we receive it we'll send you your FREE Book along with your first month's selections.